Eunoia

THE EUNOIA SERIES
BOOK ONE

HANNAH BREE CAMPBELL

*Dear Azalea, you are in every way the
person I am and hope to become.*

Chapter 1

IF EVERY MORNING STARTED THE SAME

THE START OF EACH DAY is always different, but its warmth and kindness can always be found by a like-minded individual. How can a world as corrupt and polarized as ours always be so hopeful each morning? I contemplate this as a beautiful autumn breeze sweeps through my soul. The sun's rays peek over the Rocky Mountains out in the distance like a slow smile lifting rosy cheeks, a pearly, white-toothed grin greeting everyone she meets. I lift my right hand above my head, and my fingertips are kissed with the orange light. I let my arm fall to my lap as the rest of the world around me awakes. Birds chirp their sweet tune as they soar overhead. Clouds whiz past before fading away in a state of oblivion. My feet dangle freely from the confining grasp of such things as shoes. The beauty of this world astounds me each morning! The soft and continuous breeze sweeps through my braids, but try as it might, it cannot free all my hair. I tuck the loose strands behind my ear as my lungs fill with the scent of grass and wildflowers. We all hold a place in our heart that is dear to us; this is my place to observe, imagine, and speak freely. To any other this escape may seem like the ridgepole of our roof at the front of the house, but to me it is the highest tower of my castle.

I wish all humans could restart every day like the sun could, not holding onto past events, imperfections, or mistakes. A new chance for everyone. I close my eyes and wait for the light to reach me. Once it does, the warmth of the sunshine fills every inch of my face, making me smile bigger than ever before. I would give anything to stay right here, right now, forever. Never having to live up to expectations. Just right here, right now. Forever.

"What are you doing?" I open my eyelids. Looking up at me is my older sister, Florence. She holds the empty milking pail in her dominant hand while using her right hand to shield the sun from her eyes.

"Taking in the scenery. Aren't the views just ravishing?" I gesture to the country around us.

"I suppose. You best run along and finish your chores. That is, if you have even begun them." She turns and jaunts down the beaten pathway to the barn where our milking cows are. Florence speaks to me as if I am a child, but I'm only four years shy of her age! I am not opposed to an argument, but this is one I could not win, for I know if the chores are not finished before breakfast, then there will be consequences.

With a nod of agreement, I throw my leg over the side of our pointed roof and slide to the bottom. I cling to the shingles, digging my nails into them as my body dangles a short distance above the ground. Gravity pulls me down to the soil with its forceful grasp. My bare feet hit the Earth with a thud of triumph; I did not get hurt this time! My shoes lie right where I left them on the ground. I tug the boots onto my feet and tie the shoelaces haphazardly.

The barn is a short walk from the house but seems like a mile-long trek. The heavy wooden door creaks open, and my presence is announced to all, much like Cinderella arriving at the ball. My cows, dubbed Sense and Sensibility, moo by way of greeting. I give Sense a scratch behind the ears and hand Sensibility some hay. Florence, who is sitting on the stool next to Sensibility, gives me a look as if to say, "Go collect the eggs from the chickens." So I obey. Our chickens run around squawking and clucking in their pen, which is tucked in the back corner.

Grabbing a handful of chicken feed, I litter it on the dirt inside the large pen. Picking up the wire egg basket that I had left here by accident yesterday morning, I carefully step toward the shelves built into the walls.

"What an abundant harvest today!" I remark quietly as each egg is placed in the basket. There are two shelves, both lingering inches above the ground. The eggs lie perfectly inside the nests that sit on top of the shelves. "I will be back tomorrow, ladies," I chirp as the hens pick at the feed scattered on the dirt floor. The basket swings on my arm as I step over the pen and make my way back to the barn door.

My deepest desire is to have a pony, but Pa has expressly explained to me that the barn is too small. With the chicken pen in the back-left corner, the hayloft ladder in the back right, tools hanging along the left wall, and the cows' stalls along the right wall and right corner, there is no more room for a pony to stay.

A cold breeze creeps into my bones. My arms become prickled with goosebumps as I push on the heavy door to the house. I stomp my boots on the faded blue rug, hang my second-hand coat on the nails that were halfway nailed in the wooden walls, and set the egg basket on the table. Marching to the sink, I pump the water onto my hands. Once the soap washes off, I dry my hands on the cotton white apron worn over my spruce brown dress. I barely notice my sister come in with the milk pails, then disappear.

"Dear heavens! Child, you look like a savage!" a shrill voice exclaims behind me a few moments later.

I spin around to see Mother sitting in the wooden rocking chair as light leaks in from the glass windowpanes. She remains frozen, her sewing forgotten, her expression one of disbelief. My hand flies to my hair, where the wind undid my braids. I can feel the knots intertwined all throughout my head. It would take at least a half hour to brush it back to normal.

Mother corrals me up the stairs and sits me down in a chair as she carefully brushes through the array. I twiddle my fingers anxiously, waiting for the stern talking-to I am bound to receive. Yet, I sit here in silence, no sounds except for the bristles swooshing through the tangled mess woven on my head. I sit right in front of my vanity mirror and it reflects Mother's expressions as clear as day.

"Azalea, what were you thinking?" she says scornfully whilst smoothing my light chestnut locks back to their normal straightness. I open my mouth to respond but realize it was a rhetorical question. "Florence told me you woke before dawn just to sit on the roof. Child, you could have fallen to your death! And you clearly disobeyed me. I told you last time: there will be no more of this undomesticated attitude." Mother looks up my reflection constantly, only half-focused on brushing my hair.

Even though it is bound to get me deeper in trouble, I cannot sit here and be deceived! I must speak my mind. "What does Florence even know? She hasn't a speck of adventure nor a morsel of imagination." Once I begin, there is nothing holding me back. My mind screams, internally saying *stop*, for I am surely digging myself a deeper grave, but my mouth won't listen for one second. "Contrary to what she said, I did no such thing! I watched the sunrise from a different perspective, just a simple excursion. I do not see any problem with that! The roof is merely a few feet off the ground. It is not likely for me to lose footing and fall. It is not as if I was late to get my task finished. There is a basket of eggs downstairs that proves my innocence in that respect." My face grows red as I declare my innocence in the matter. I finish, flushed and out of breath.

I would never claim these words if they left my mouth, but my older sister is the sole source of my jealousy. When we were younger, when our bond consisted of me looking to her for guidance and as my closest friend, I felt differently. But many years and quarrels have turned my emotions in the other direction. Though nobody else might notice or care, I hate constantly living in her shadow and being told that she's what I must become: a lady.

Mother's devout attention goes into making us "suitable brides." I know that deep inside, she thinks that I am a lost cause when it comes to marriage, for my knowledge does not consist of playing the piano, speaking fluently in some foreign language, or baking delectable treats. I don't resent my sister or Mother for feeling this way one bit. I'm sure Pa would have preferred a boy and Mother another sensible daughter that would obey without questioning authority. Nonetheless, they were given me: a child who is often called whimsical and has only progressive thoughts for the future, for the unknown.

Mother stops and slams the brush onto my vanity. I snap around, fearful of the trouble I have just gotten myself into. "I forbid it! I refuse to hear another word of your tomfoolery about why you needed to climb on top a roof!" She huffs, looking at me dead in the eyes. Her disappointment is clearly painted in her manner. A lump of guilt forms in my throat, and try as I might, it will not vanish. It's not like I wanted to be sinful and disobey my parents, I just wanted an adventure! "I have no time for this. Go finish your chores. Right now!" Mother whips around forcefully, her footsteps receding down the staircase and echoing out of earshot.

Chapter 2

A LESSON IN DISOBEDIENCE

THE WATER IN THE TIN PAIL reflects my misery. I scrub every inch of the floor with the soapy water. The brush is grueling to work with for hours on the wooden surface. Thankfully the floors upstairs were cleaned yesterday, or else I would have to spend the last daylight hours doing nothing but scrubbing. Once finished, I carry the pail outside and pour it on the ground.

I shield my eyes from the sunlight with my hand. Pa stands in the field to the side of the house with the cows, most likely letting them graze on picket lines. Pa has never been like Mother in the sense of lacking imagination. Though it could be wrong to think, I have never understood how they even ended up being the great match they are. Mother is strict and Pa can be at times, but he maintains a much gentler attitude. Just like Florence is like Mother, I am like Pa. I think on this as I trudge over to him. Once he sees me coming, he grins and waves for me to hurry. I break into a run and meet him, watching the cows grazing.

"Hey, Bluebird!" he gladly exclaims. Ever since I found an injured bluebird last spring, Pa has called me that. I miss that bluebird so much now!

I remember it like it was yesterday... *I went out to the barn to get the eggs, and flowers were starting to pop up all over the ground as the breeze carried their sweet pollen scent. As I walked through the barn, I noticed there was no hay for Sense and Sensibility. Even though I knew climbing up into the hayloft was dangerous, it was only a few ladder steps away from the ground. So with a thrill I held my skirts in one hand and climbed up the wooden rungs with the other.*

To be honest, balancing on the rectangle-cut steps, holding up my skirts, and hanging on to the step at my eye level was rather hard to do. A look of triumph was on my face as I made it to the last step. I snatched a few handfuls of hay, lifted the corners of my apron, and put the hay there. I began to make my way back down the ladder when a sudden noise came from the back corner of the loft.

I climbed up the step and crept cautiously to the back. My eyes scanned over the big piles of hay, but there was nothing there. The chirp sounded again, louder this time. My hand swept over the spot I thought the chirp came from. Sure enough, there was a young bluebird snuggled up in a nest built of dirt, feathers, and hay.

My eyes softened at the sight of this young bird. This was, after all, the closest I'd ever been to a bird before! Its bright yellow beak was so small, and its feathers were not yet fully developed, but its colors were magnificent! I held my finger out gently, stroking its tiny head as the bird looked at me with its big black eyes. How in the world had this bird gotten up here? There was no sign of a mama bird or any other babies around. I swept more of the hay away and discovered a crack in the wall. It was just big enough for my hand to fit through and went directly outside.

"Did your mama leave you here? What about your siblings? Hm, well, I think Mother will understand that I mustn't abandon you here!" I cooed softly to the bird in order not to startle it.

So I scooped up the baby bird, put it on my apron with the hay, and carefully made my way back down the ladder. I can still recall the sound of my footsteps thumping on the ground as I walked closer to the house, my eyes fixated on the little bird. When I walked through the door, I saw Mother at the wood-burning stove over by the sink in the corner of the room. She flipped a pancake and turned around to face me. I could only imagine what I looked like based on the shocked expression on her face.

"I found a baby bird in the hayloft! Look at it. Isn't it just the cutest thing you have ever seen? I was thinking it must be cold! We just need to set up a place for the bird to stay. Oh, maybe Florence can lend me some of her fabric scraps so I can make it a nest! Oh dear." I looked down as some hay fell onto the floor. "Sorry. Do we have a basket I could use for it? If I create a warm nest in a basket, then that might feel like an actual nest. We ought to name it! Something nature-y would work nicely. For example, Sparrow, Birch, or Sky!" I exclaimed widely. A million different names popped into my head within a moment.

Mother's eyes were wide, she held her hand to her forehead as if feeling for a fever. The only words she could muster were, "My goodness."

Now that I think about it, that's her response to many things. I wonder why.

At that moment, Pa walked through the door carrying some freshly cut wood. He stood looking from me to Mother to the bluebird in my apron, until he finally set the wood down on the floor and scratched his head questioningly. Mother turned back to the stove and scraped the now-burnt pancake off the iron skillet. For once, she was at a loss for words!

"I am making breakfast. Can you please handle this," she simply declared while gesturing at me with the spatula in her hand.

Pa nodded and came over to look at the bird. "What do we have here? That is a baby bluebird! No more than a few weeks old I would guess!" I smiled at his response. Pa would not scold me for this as Mother most likely would if she was not cooking now. I explained to him how I had found the bird and that we need to build a nest so that the mama bird would come back for it.

"I don't know about that. A mama bird will not come back if she knows her baby has been near us. It isn't in their nature to accept a baby that smells

like a human! The only option is to take care of it until it can fly. But that is a big responsibility. Will you be able to take care of it?" I looked from Pa to the bird. He was right. I would have to do chores, help cook, and take care of the bird! I bit my lip as I thought it over. My arms grew weak from holding up my apron for so long.

"I do not have a choice, Pa. I shall not leave this bluebird to die!"

The next week was quite the struggle! I had to wake up early each day to finish my chores. Then I would mix some mashed-up fruits with a few drops of water to feed to the bird, who I had named Vireo because its sweet song-like chirps sounded so similar to those of the vireo songbird. Vireo's feathers were bursting with color; what a sight to see!

Mother has always been quite the artist, even though her talent is rarely used. She once told me after I badgered her with questions that she was taught by her mother. After my constant begging, Mother drew a sketch of the bluebird on a paper for me. There was a twitch of a smile in her lips upon my reaction to the drawing.

I still have that sketch pinned on my wall to this day, and sometimes I try to mimic the strokes of the feathers or lifelike eyes, but my ability in artwork is limited.

One day, Pa said that Vireo was probably two or three weeks old. I understood his meaning: if Vireo could not learn how to fly soon, then he might never be able to. So every day I took my beautiful bluebird outside. We started off with me sitting down and having the bird step from my hands to the ground, which was only inches away. Then we progressed to a little higher up and added more height each day.

On the sixth day, we had progressed to the height of my shoulders. I gave Vireo a little toss into the air, expecting the same little flutter of his wings until he reached the ground. But a miracle happened. The sun parted ways with the clouds, and sunshine rolled over the grasses as Vireo spread his wings out. But this time, instead of free-falling, he took flight! He gave several song-like chirps, swooping down to the ground and then back up to the air. A smile exploded across my face, for my little bird was flying for the first time! I was so proud of my protégé that I had not realized how far Vireo had gone.

"Vireo! Come back! Where are you going?" His blue feathers gleamed at me, revealing the truth: that he was never coming back. He was leaving to live a life of freedom where he rightfully belonged. Even so, I still wanted my bluebird to stay with me. Because without him, I was alone again. "Goodbye, my Vireo. May God bless you," I whispered as a tear streaked down my cheek. His final goodbye to me was a joyous chirp.

I wish to always remember that chirp because, for a moment, it sounded like an angel singing. I shall forever value the time I had with my bluebird. But reality pulled my attention away from that sweet memory and back to this moment of Pa and I watching the cows.

"Hey, Pa. Mother is being so unreasonable! With no spark of adventure or imagination!" I exclaim, tossing my hands into the air. "Won't you please take me with you to town? I cannot spend one more moment in this dreary house, Pa! Honestly, if I must clean, scrub, or sweep one more thing, I will go mad! If we go into town, I will behave. I promise. I can even mail off a letter if we need a reason to go! Please, Pa, won't you say yes?" I beg profusely. I know for a fact that a breath of air away from the stuffy indoors will do me a world of good.

The cows moo as they rip mouthfuls of grass from the earth. Pa considered the idea, but I have always been able to read his thoughts through his facial expressions. He strokes his chin playfully, knowing his decision is clear to me.

A smile erupts on my face as he laughs. "Thank you, Pa! I shall go get ready!" I run the short way home. My shoes stomp up the steps as I dash to my room to fetch a paper and pen. Sitting down at my vanity, I pull out my fountain pen, a piece of paper, and an envelope. The ink flows onto the page as I write.

My cousin, Nora, who I have known almost all my life, lives a few days' trip away from us. Nearly every fall after harvest season ended, her family traveled here and stay a few days. Oh, what fun we always have! Nora is like to me in so many ways that even the thought of her causes my heart to yearn for her presence. There cannot be two people more kindred than we are in all of Wyoming! I suddenly revisit a memory from two years ago—which is when we last saw each other.

Mother and her sister—my Aunt Nancy—were cooking all day in the kitchen with Florence. Nora and I sat at the table listening to the stories Aunt Nancy told us, including the one about how Florence's name came from Grandma Flora. When Mother was younger, she had promised to name her children after flowers in honor of Grandma Flora. Until I had heard the reasoning behind my name that day, I had not liked it one bit. Although I still think Florence is a much better name than Azalea.

"What about my name, Mama? Why didn't you name me after flowers? I want a pretty name!" Nora whined, crossing her arms with a pout. But her profuse pouting would not change the name she had been christened with.

Aunt Nancy blew out a sigh. She bent down to our eye level and looked at us through her big blue eyes. "How does an adventure sound instead? You girls should all go play outside until dinner is ready." Our faces gleamed at the possibility of her words.

We ran to the nails that held our jackets. Mother helped us into our coats and handed us the mittens in our pockets. "Florence, do you want to go outside? The weather will turn colder in a matter of weeks. You should enjoy the fresh air while you can," Mother asked as Florence sat by the fireplace with her knitting set.

Florence's face showed her dislike for the cold that lay outside the front door. "Mother, I'd rather not." She continued knitting a hat as she spoke. I shrugged, as did Nora. Then we sprinted out the door.

My laugh echoed into the great sky that held not a single cloud on that day. The tall grasses whipped at our bare legs as we spread our arms out to fly. I stopped suddenly as Nora caught up to me, collapsing on the ground. Out of breath, we both lay there for a moment of silence.

Nora raised her hand to the sky as if she could touch the heavens. I laughed joyously and followed her movements.

"Nora?" I whispered secretively.

"Yes, Azalea? What is it?" We did not look away from the sky as we spoke, for this moment was too precious. Lying on the ground while tucked into the tall grass, she stared above with a carefree attitude.

Even though it had always been my personal rule that adventures should not be ruined by serious talk or expressions, a life-alerting question crossed my mind. "Do you want to get married when you grow up? I heard Aunt Nancy talking with Mother of Florence's future. I wondered if you would also like to be married…one day." I spoke simply of my thoughts. Together we needn't correct our grammar like we had to around other people. Our thoughts flowed into words without hesitating; hesitation always spoils an idea.

Her silence meant she was considering the question. She played with her dark blonde locks before responding to my question. I continued to play with the idea myself.

I was only twelve at the time, and you've got to be at least eighteen to marry or else it's considered improper. Nora is only a year older than me, so it's not like either one of us would grow up that fast—or so it seemed at the time.

Smoothing out her bright blue dress that was caked with dirt, she finally gave an answer. "No, I think I'll be a child all my life. This woman in my town has remained unmarried for the past few years. Now she'll be twenty-five this spring! Even though everyone despises the idea, I think unmarried life suits her. I shall only pray that it does me! Bearing children does not seem a part of my life."

I nodded my head in agreement. "Me too. We mustn't be like Florence! She has already talked about the names she will give her children. Besides, how will we travel west together if we're married with children? I feel that being a child is much better than being an adult! Don't you agree? We shall promise to never be married for as long as we coexist in harmony!" I exclaimed, leaping to my feet. I searched the grasses quickly, looking for the object on my mind.

After plucking it, I held up a dandelion, ready to make my declaration. Nora beamed with excitement and leapt to her feet as well. We both stood in the middle of the field holding the dandelion whilst the breeze swept our loose hair into unruly knots. I quickly considered my words and spoke them aloud.

"I, Azalea Stanton, promise to never get married for as long as Nora and I coexist in harmony. I also promise to travel with my dear Nora to the western skies when we are grown up! We shall race horses along the prairie by day and sleep under the stars by night. Not bound to rules written by others but instead only the ones of our own freewill. For the rest of our lives." I smiled sweetly at my unofficial twin.

Our plans filled the future with so much hope. I had endless dreams over countless slumbers that consisted of our hypothetical rendezvous in the west.

"I, Nora Lee, promise to never get married for as long as we coexist in harmony. And we shall never give in to the confining boundaries of marriage. We will travel the country in our wagons and visit the great wonders of Earth's natural beauties! For the rest of our lives," she finished strongly.

On the count of three, I nodded. With one big breath, we blew out the dandelion.

I am snapped back to reality in an instant. I hold the fountain pen in my hand as I scribble more words down. I remind Nora of our vow, though I am sure she still knows the words by heart just as I do. I am almost one hundred percent positive that Nora and I got our wild spirits from Aunt Nancy, for she shares some of our discontents with the rules of society and the world that goes with it.

The red wax drips from being engulfed by the flame's heat. Drops of hot wax fall onto the envelope that will soon bear my personal seal with my initials. I was gifted three wax sticks along with a brass seal stamper last Christmas. I only ever used them for my letters to Nora. The thought of the very letter in my hands traveling to her is exhilarating! Pa yells my name from outside as I blow out the candle's flame with one breath. I snatch my coat and blue bonnet from the nail on the wall.

My boots stomp the grass below me as I dash to where Pa waits for me on the road. Town is not too far of a walk, and besides, we have no horses to get us there.

"We have about a mile until we arrive, and we must be quick to get home before twilight," he says while tucking his short, left-parted hair under his black cap that sits loose on his head.

I tie my bonnet in a bow under my chin as he speaks. Even though trees line the dirt road almost all the way to town, I still don't want my face getting sunburned.

The walk is rather quiet. Neither of us speak except for an occasional hello to someone passing by us. Normally, I would be exploding with questions or remarks, but the memory of Nora is still fresh in my mind. Pa is more of a quiet man around others, but he greets friends with a whole-heartedly yell of a hello. Not once does he ask a penny for my thoughts; instead, he realizes my aversion to speaking right now, for I am still lost somewhere in my head. We reach the town of Lorretta a little past midday. I am sure that he told Mother we were going to town and will not be home for dinner at twelve o'clock like usual.

Lorretta is a rather petite town. Although I am unaware of the exact population, it's less than one hundred fifty souls. The necessary shops line the dirt street: the blacksmith's, Rodefer's General Store, Mrs. Hattie Schneider's dress shop that is just one big room built on the side of her house, and the postal office at the end of the road.

Our quaint little town is not as fast-growing as Mother thought it would be when we first moved here. There's no train or railroad that comes through, but there is a stagecoach sign at the end of the road. The stagecoach runs from here to Brockschmidt, a large city when compared to Lorretta. My family has only ever gone to Brockschmidt once or twice, but from what I remember, it has a much bigger population. A few weeks ago, Mother had brought up the idea of a trip to Brockschmidt in the spring because, in her words, "Florence needs to be acquainted with the young men of the city." Pa said nothing at the time, so I am sure that by springtime Mother will get her way.

We finally make it to the postal office at the end of the road next to the stagecoach.

"Can I help you?" the clerk asks with a kind smile. The buttons on his navy-blue coat gleam as he scratches his long black beard.

I stand behind Pa shyly. We don't come into town too often, and speaking to strangers makes me quite uncomfortable. Nonetheless, Pa turns to me and urges me forward without saying a word to me or the man.

My palms grow sweaty as I quickly line up the words in my mind. I look back at Pa with a pleading sparkle in my eyes, but he has already walked over to the news board. I shall have to do this myself. "I have mail to send. Here's the letter," I say, placing it on the counter.

The man reaches underneath the iron bar window that stands between us, sliding my letter through the little slot between the bottom of the bars and the counter. He places my letter into the bag marked "Mail." I nod my head in confirmation as Pa comes over and pays the mail fee. We walk out of the postal office and start our journey back home. Once we are back on the road, I am in a flurry of questions.

"How does the mail travel so fast, Pa? I suppose my letter will reach Nora in a week, does that sound like enough time? Oh, my goodness looks there is a rabbit by that tree! How do animals know winter is coming? Maybe they sense the coldness in the temperatures as we do. If you could be any animal which, would you choose?" I blabber. My thoughts never wait—they just come out of my mouth. This has gotten me into trouble, but it's a force of habit.

The leaves swirl through the wind as the sun shines through the trees above our heads. The dirt road seems to be an endless stretch of walking. I study Pa's features that are similar as he thinks of his answer. His hair is a darker brown than mine, which is almost dirty blonde. Pa has dark green eyes while Mother has brown, and thank goodness I have inherited the green eyes, although they seem to be lightening to a handsome emerald. I do believe our noses are the same. Both Florence and I have Mother's diamond-shaped face and visible jawline. I have always thought that my looks are derived from Pa, but now I not quite sure which parent I resemble more.

He clears his throat to chase away the thoughts that cloud his mind and begins speaking. "Well, if I must choose any animal in the world to be…it would be a hawk. It's mind-boggling how they see the mice in the field from such a distance! I don't know what to make of it."

I nod to show I am listening. Mother always says to nod at least once when someone is speaking in a conversation, even when you may not be in it. "Yes, a hawk would fit you nicely. I shall choose a deer! Never mind, they're hunted every autumn. I would love to be a bird! Maybe a bluebird or a hummingbird. Flying above everything seems like such a thrill! Though I must admit being a human is far better than being a bird!" I exclaim with a laugh. Pa laughs along with me and says he agrees; being a human is far better than being some sort of creature. But despite his engaged presence in our conversation, I sense something is distracting him.

Chapter 3

ONCE UPON A MIDNIGHT FORESIGHT

THE TRIP TO TOWN is rather lengthy, so we do not reach home until just before supper is on the table. We hang up our coats and wash up before finally taking our seats. Mother sits to my right, Pa to my left, and Florence across from me. After saying grace, we start filling our plates with carrots, pork, mashed potatoes, and slices of the bread that I helped make yesterday. Florence speaks of the book she is reading, which seems boring from the way she describes it. I have long since stopped trying to convince my sister to read a Jane Austen novel or '*Wuthering Heights*', books that are so brilliant that they could change one's perspective of life. In my opinion, that is what a good book should do. Mother pauses us to correct our words as we talk. Pa remains silent, which is very unusual. He normally talks about his day as the rest of us do.

He breaks his silence with a simple sentence: "Margaret, what would you think of moving out west?"

We all stop moving as if frozen in place. He called Mother by her first name, which only ever happens during something serious. A buttered slice of bread is held inches from my mouth as I hesitate to move. I inspect Mother's expression carefully; if she does not like the idea, then it is best not to add my opinion on the subject. At first shock, then consideration, seems to cross her face. She places her fork, which holds a tiny piece of pork, down on her plate.

"Albert!" she half-laughs, using his name. Like Pa, Mother only ever uses her spouse's name when she is deadly serious—or angry. "What brought on this sudden notion? We have only lived here for a few years! Do you propose we just pick up everything and leave?" The worrisome look on her face is rather infectious; Florence appears to have it too.

Pa pauses his eating to speak. "When we were in the postal office, I read a news article saying that more gold was found in a mine over by the coast. Gold! Can you imagine if we tried our hand at striking it rich? I've heard of men that find nuggets of gold the size of their fist!" he exclaims, holding up his balled-up hand for each of us to see. My eyes grow big and round at the possibilities. We really could move out west! Maybe Pa could even convince Aunt Nancy and Uncle Edward to come with us! If that happens, then Nora and I would be years ahead of our promise to travel there.

"Albert, the Gold Rush ended decades ago! There is no need to stir up those foolish dreams of finding gold." She puts an end to the conversation with that.

Nobody speaks one more word for the rest of the night. I scrub each dish clean, and Florence wipes them dry while Mother sits by the fire reading. Pa is still deep in thought in his seat at the table. Once finished, we wish our parents goodnight and head up to our rooms. Before I open the door to my room, Florence gives me a hesitant look while strolling past me. I notice her worried expression as she contemplates the idea of moving west. We moved to Lorretta four years ago, and three years ago Wyoming officially became a state. Before that we only ever lived in Colorado. It feels impossible to imagine us anywhere else but right here.

A cold breeze sweeps through the cracks in the floorboards, chilling me to the bone. I peer out my bedroom window, and sure enough, there are big, thick snowflakes floating down from the sky. Clear as day, the first snowfall of the season has started sticking to the ground. Even if by God's miracle Mother agrees, we will not leave this house until spring. I untie my apron, unbutton my dark brown dress that almost reached my ankles, pull off my white stockings, and throw my shoes on my vanity chair. The dress will most likely be wrinkled beyond belief tomorrow. Even so, the tiredness of the evening lures me to bed. I crawl into bed wearing my cotton nightgown.

"Our Father, who art in heaven, hallowed be Thy name," my voice whispers into the darkness of night. "I ask you to please forgive the sins I have committed since my last prayer. Will you please keep me and my family, safe, happy, and in good health? If it is not too much to ask, will you sway Mother's mind and allow us to move west? Amen." After saying my prayers, I drifted off to sleep as the moon rose in the sky.

〜

The prairie grasses laugh as I frolic among them, running my fingers over their wispy bodies. Looking over my shoulder, I can see Pa, Mother, and Florence in the wagon being pulled by two unfamiliar oxen. As I turn back around, I halt dead in my tracks, for off in the distance is a man on a roan and white horse. His skin is a dark brown face is serious as he gallops toward me. I am frozen in place and cannot move. My struggle seems to quicken his pace. His horse comes closer and closer until it suddenly stops in front of me, eyes ablaze with fury and nostrils flaring wildly. I reach my hand out to touch the horse, but suddenly I stop myself. Everything starts fading away, and I am falling backwards. I scream, lungs aching, but no sound comes from my mouth.

I awake with a startling shake. The sunshine creeps along the floor and to my face as if to comfort me. Despite the flash of angry equine eyes that is seared into my brain, I smile to greet the new day. The conversation between Mother and Pa last night slowly seeps into my head.

Surely, they have decided by now. After dressing, I make my bed and brush the tangled knots out of my hair. Mother's voice echoes up the stairs as I braid my hair.

"Girls, it is time for chores!" she yells.

I hear the front door closing downstairs with a slam. I quickly tie my hair ribbon at the end of my braid and then run down the stairs. As I whisk past the kitchen, my hands reach out to grab my coat and the basket. The clock on the mantle chimes, reminding me that I am late for the morning and demanding me to hurry along. Mother enters the barn as I quickly catch up to her; the snow is only a few inches deep, so it is not too much work to walk through. The animals greet us both with moos and clucks. The climate in here is a drastic—and welcome—change from outside.

This would be the perfect time to ask about their decision and if we are to truly move! Excitement mixed with fear beats in my chest. I collect the eggs as she sits down on the stool and begins to milk one of the cows. Sometimes she has Florence start breakfast preparations as she collects the milk instead.

Breathing out the last of the air held anxiously in my lungs, the words come from my lips quietly. "Mother. If I may?" I hesitate, waiting for her permission to continue. I'm guessing she already knows what I shall ask. It's no secret that my deepest desire—apart from having a pony, of course—is to travel to the western grasslands. She gives me a quick nod, and I continue speaking. "Have you and Pa…reached a verdict of moving us west?"

She clears her throat—not in an annoyed manner but rather in the way of bringing bad news. "Verdict on." She corrects my grammar softly. "Azalea, we are not going. Florence has not spent enough time in town or Brockschmidt to become acquainted with the young men there. We must not move until she has been married off." My heart falters at her words. Florence is the only thing keeping us here? Are we all just supposed to keep biding our time until she finally gets married? It could be another two years until that happens! But I cannot express my grief, for it is a new day and I'd rather not start an argument this morning. I will just have to hold my thoughts, anger, and disappointment internally. I briefly nod and carry on with my work.

The silence in the house is deafening once we come back from the barn. Pa sits at the table reading the latest newspaper without looking up at us. Florence stands at the table kneading bread dough for our breakfast. Mother strains the milk and takes the eggs out of the basket that I didn't realize had left my grasp.

After quick contemplation, I reluctantly pick up the broom and begin sweeping the floor. The wind blows in small snowflakes through a crack under the door, creating small puddles on the wood. Once I sweep all the dirt into the corner, I start preparing a bucket of soapy water for the washing. My eyes watch Florence as she kneads the dough, puts it into the oven, and begins to clean the dishes. She does everything with such ladylike perfection. Jealousy sneaks into my mind, and for a second, I wish I could have been raised to be as perfect as she is or that God would have graced me with her blonde hair that turns golden in the sunlight. I then remember who I am. My name is Azalea Stanton, I do not need to be anyone but myself! I will not let the devil get into my mind and turn it into pure jealousy! I scrub away at the floor for the next hour until every mark or spot vanishes from sight. The rest of the day is nothing but eating, cleaning, sewing, and reading—all of which require no talking.

⌒

The next few days pass by slowly. The only thing to look forward to is Nora's response to my letter! It strikes me as rather odd that so much time has gone by without getting a letter back. I start worrying until finally, of all people, Aunt Nancy writes to me. She does not write about Nora's quietness but instead says the family is all healthy and will come visit us once the snow lets up. I share the letter with everyone at the dinner table that night. Mother is ecstatic to see her sister again after so long, and Pa is excited to have guests come visit us since we can't even get to town because of the snow. As for my sister, she comments about working on her embroidery with Aunt Nancy.

The beginning of December passes by in a flurry of snowflakes. We spend countless mornings hiking in the four-foot-deep snow to get to the barn, only to walk back before the snow can even melt off our shoes. We endure the same food rationing we have to bear every year.

One year in particular, after we had just moved here, a snowstorm blew in unexpectedly. The fire was impossible to light, and we had to divide the leftover food so it could last for the coming days. Once the storm passed that evening, leaving six feet of packed-down snow on the ground, there was no hope for Pa to journey to town and buy supplies. The windows were shielded by the snow, and nobody dared to even open the front door, for a pile would collapse onto the floor. Every last crumb had been eaten when the snow finally melted two days later. I was too young to understand how close we all were to death in those three days before Pa could finally get to town in the snow. In some ways, I am grateful to have been that ignorant. Fear did not grasp my heart as it would if we were in the same situation now.

We awake to gloomy gray clouds that shake out thick snowflakes for the fifth day in a row. Our energy levels have reached an all-time low as the biscuit batter is kneaded, the stove is lit, and the egg yolks are placed in a pan on the stovetop. My fork stabs another piece of bacon on my plate. I have grown tired of reading my book while waiting for the hours to pass by. For once in my life, the only entertainment in my day is helping

Mother with the cooking. After Pa read today's verses—most of which are from Proverbs—he bundles up and goes to feed the cows.

I finally break my silence after becoming frustrated with the handkerchief I am sewing. "Uhh! I cannot seem to focus long enough to keep sewing. Look at this edge! Practically messed up beyond repair. Mother, can we please have Sunday Schooling? I need something to do before I go mad! The sound of the wind against the house and the endless days of torment are driving me to insanity!" My voice seems whiny, but these troubles are clearly felt by us all. Mother takes one look at her daughters' dull eyes, the spark that was once in them drained out.

"If you feel that way, then of course. Florence, please fetch the board, rag, and a piece of chalk out of my trunk upstairs," she says, wiping her hands on the apron around her waist.

Since she was a little girl, Mother has always owned a small handheld chalkboard. Every Sunday when we were younger, she would teach us something from her own knowledge, whether it be vocabulary, basic arithmetic, or history. Now that our knowledge has long since outgrown the need for Sunday Schooling, it's quite unnecessary. Nonetheless, today's gloominess might just dissolve if we have Sunday Schooling. Our lesson is filled with US history from Mother's knowledge. By the end of the day, our moods are lifted back to normal!

The snow finally lightened up after so many days spent inside. I still wonder about the reasoning behind Nora's silence in response to my letter; Aunt Nancy said they were all in perfect health, so she can't possibly be sick. Perhaps she wishes to save some exciting news and wait to tell me when they visit! This is yet another reason for me to get through the days; every night that passes is another one closer to seeing my cousin!

Sunday is a day of rest and relaxation from the constant cycle of chores. We stay inside, as always, and Pa reads a few verses from our Bible. It gives me great comfort to listen to God's words in the scriptures, particularly Hebrews 11:6, for I feel as though Him and Jesus are here with us listening to Pa's soft deep voice read aloud.

" 'But without faith it is impossible to please him: for he that cometh to God must believe that he is, and that he is a rewarder of them that diligently seek him.' "

Chapter 4

IF JOYFUL DAYS COULD LAST FOREVER

IN THE WEEKS LEADING UP to Christmas, we all stay tucked in our bedrooms whenever there is a spare minute. I work endlessly on my family's Christmas present. For Mother, I sew a handkerchief—made with fabric from the scrap basket. I embroider flowers on Florence's favorite apron, which I borrowed without telling her. Finally, I work tirelessly alongside Mother and Florence to help make Pa a new blue cotton shirt out of the leftover fabric from a skirt that Mother made a year ago.

It is Christmas Eve when I place the presents, individually wrapped with brown parchment paper, under the tree that Pa cut down and brought inside yesterday. I hold the string as my sister strings popcorn onto it. Once we are done with the decorations and finish cleaning up after supper, we say our goodnights and return upstairs. Joyfulness beats in my heart as I am whisked off to sleep. A smile is still on my face as my dreams overwhelm my subconscious.

⸻

"Azalea! Wake up sleepy head. It's Christmas!" a voice joyfully yells at me. I am rudely yanked out of my dream. I open my eyelids with a grumble and see Florence standing over me wearing her white nightgown with a smile. "Hurry up! There is even snow outside!" she says as she sprints out of my room and down the stairwell. I leap out of bed, bolting to the window. Clear as day, a white Christmas morning lies before me! Little symmetrical snowflakes stick to the cold glass window. Hearing Pa's voice downstairs, I quickly put on my slippers and rush down in order not to miss anything. Pa holds a lit candle in his right hand, with its wax dish catching the drops that fall from it. He points to a messily wrapped gift that is from me. I hand the present to him, and it's passed to Florence as I settle on the floor. Mother stops working on the sizzling pork sausages to sit on the floor and watch us open the gifts. Florence tears back the paper and pulls out the apron I embroidered.

She gasps as her hands fly to her mouth. "Azalea, did you make this? It's so beautiful!" she exclaims in awe.

I shrug modestly and respond, "I know I am not half as good at sewing as you are. I must comment it turned out better than I expected it would!" Her smile warms my heart, and for a quick moment it feels like we are as close as we once were. That is truly the best gift of all!

"My gosh! Thank you so much!" Pa yells in joy before giving a hearty laugh. He holds up the blue cotton shirt up against him. Mother, Florence, and I smirk slyly because we only had one of his older work shirts to use for measurements.

A heavy gift from Mother is handed to me, as she anxiously waits for me to open it. Sitting in my lap is the most exquisite fabric I have ever seen! The milk-white cloth is blanketed with a myriad of delicate blooms. I spot roses, tulips, and daffodils of all sizes sprouting from green stems. I run my fingertips along the material, marveling at its softness.

"Thank you so much! It is just so beautiful! Where in the world did you get it?" I speak my thoughts aloud but do not take my eyes off the fabric.

Mother smiles and explains, "I bought it back in the summer and kept it tucked away for Christmas! Honestly, I was not sure what to do with it. You can choose what you want made from it. There's enough there for an apron or even a dress!" I pass the fabric around so both Pa and Florence can see it.

"A dress would be perfect! Would y'all help me make it?" Nobody notices my improper English; instead, everyone nods cheerfully.

Mother unwraps the handkerchief and declares that it is the best one she's ever possessed! We each open one more present, but none of them amount to the special gifts like the apron or the fabric.

Once we finish listening to Pa reading Isaiah 9:6-7; "For unto us a child is born, unto us a son is given: and the government shall be upon his shoulder: and his name shall be called Wonderful, Counsellor, The mighty God, The everlasting Father, The Prince of Peace. Of the increase of his government and peace there shall be no end, upon the throne of David, and upon his kingdom, to order it, and to establish it with judgment and with justice from henceforth even for ever. The zeal of the Lord of hosts will perform this."

Afterwards, Mother gets up from the floor and finishes breakfast. When Florence and I try to help cook, Mother dismisses us and says, "Go play outside! Today is Christmas, and we must enjoy it while it lasts. It will, after all, be another three hundred sixty-five days until Christmas comes again!"

Looking at it that way makes today even more special, so we both get changed into our dresses and wool stockings, put on our shoes, and button our coats.

Pushing through the front door, I am delightfully met with winter's icy breath. Everything outside on this very morning is full of everlasting peace. Birds are cozied up in their nests and do not utter a peep. It appears as though the entire world is covered in a blanket of powdery white snow. In some way, it is comforting. I pull my hat out of my pocket and put it on my head.

Something hits the back of my head and breaks apart; a cold shock slices through my body as the snow starts melting and sliding down my neck. I spin around as Florence scoops up another ball of snow with her bare hands. For a moment I am shocked by the sudden change in her personality. It reminds me so much of how she used to be before being consumed with what is respectable and proper. The observation vanishes as I too bend over, gathering a handful of snow and molding it into a ball. She screams and bolts as the snowball flies through the air, missing her by an inch.

I go after her happily, refusing to give up. The cycle of movement is repeated over and over: we each bend over for a second, gather as much snow as possible, then attempt to throw it at each other. I look back at the house, which is only a short distance away. I stand still for a moment, taking it all in as Florence runs further away. Spreading out my arms, I fall back to the earth. A hard blow to the ground is now cushioned as I land with a dull thump. The sky is such a wide and brilliant blue due to the absence of clouds! I hear the rhythmic crunch of approaching footsteps. Florence collapses beside me. Remaining silent, we both look up at the sky.

Observation—in my opinion—is a great necessity. Without it, how could humans have any opinions? What we observe about others and ourselves is what helps us change in a good way. I wish that every day of my life could be like this: simple in a way that makes me feel complete! I wonder why that is. Tomorrow, life shall return to normal, but today Florence is closer than a sister, almost a confidant! Jealousy shall not cloud one centimeter of my heart today. I wonder if anyone else has ever wanted to stay in a moment as much as I do right now.

Once it becomes too cold to stay outside any longer, we shuffle back home. Before I enter the house, I gaze back at the spot where we lay staring up at the sky. I wonder how many times this memory will replay itself many times in my head over the next few years?

Two weeks have passed since Christmas, and my dress is coming along rather nicely! Mother and Florence helped me take measurements and hem the bottom of the skirt. I cannot help but wonder how a piece of lace would look at the ends of the sleeves or at the bottom of the skirt where it touches my ankles. However, even if a few pieces of lace would make this dress better, we don't have any lace, and spending money for it would be ridiculous. I will have to go without it.

Aunt Nancy, Uncle Edward, and Nora shall arrive here next Saturday. We have four days to prepare the house for their arrival. There shall be no rest until we finish the ironing, folding, dusting, sweeping, and the rest of the chores, which will help steady my excitement for their visit!

Every night after saying my prayer, I go to dreamland and fantasize of the fun Nora and I will have! I have already drafted many different stories we could play out. My favorite is playing princesses out in the field. A deceitful witch will come along, putting a spell on one of us—most likely me because Nora always loved the hero role when we played pretend during her last visit. Princess Nora, determined to save me, will embark on a perilous journey to find the witch and demand to reverse the curse placed upon me. The witch will strike a deal, agreeing to Nora's demand only if Nora releases her birthright to the throne. Will she give up her throne to save me or refuse and instead search for another cure to wake me from the curse?

Chapter 5

THE GHOSTS OF OUR PAST SELVES

EVER SINCE I AWOKE this morning, there has only been one thought on my mind: this is the day that Nora arrives! In the past two hours I have paced around the kitchen, stared out the window, and attempted to entertain myself with books. Now I sit at the kitchen table, reading my Jane Austen novel for the fourth time. Florence sits across from me, also reading. Just as I release out an anxiety-filled breath, Florence's voice pipes up.

"Azalea, I have a question for you. Why in the world do you read the same books so often? Do they not get repetitive?" she asks, setting her book down to look me in the eyes.

I put my book down as well and consider the question, thankful for the distraction. "No, I cannot say that they do. I find that I realize something new every time I reread a book, even though I am just reading the same words as before. There seems to be a different meaning each time. Wouldn't you agree?"

Suddenly, we hear the whinny of a horse and muffled voices just outside the door. My heart skips a beat as I stand. Mother quickly travels down the stairs and smooths out her hair.

"Girls, they are here. Come greet our guests!" she whispers, and we graciously take our place behind her. She swings open the door, and three pairs of eyes stare back at us. I dart in front of Mother in a very unladylike manner, but I cannot care less! Uncle Edward offers his hand to Nora, who sits on top of the wagon. She takes it, climbing down slowly. Her face has gotten thinner, her hair longer, and her stature is taller than mine by an inch. And is it just me, or does her expression look rather bland for the occasion at hand? I stand with my arms stretched out, waiting to receive a hug. When I lean forward to embrace her, she instead holds out a hand. Surprised, I step backwards. With a perplexed look, I shake her hand as if we are adults meeting for the first time.

I laugh, thinking it is a joke. "What are you doing? Do you want to see Sense and Sensibility? Oh, how they have grown! You ought to see my new dress that's being made! Did you get my letter? I figured you wanted to wait and talk about it all once you got here." I blabber out ecstatically. She holds a look of confusion mixed with disgust on her face. Did I say something wrong?

"My gracious, cousin, you really must slow down. Your words are very messy," she says softly. I become frozen in utter confusion. What is wrong with her? At first, I figured she was just joking around, but I see now that she has changed since the last time we were together, physical appearance aside. Even her voice is not as low as it once was.

"I don't understand?" I mutter. Florence clears her throat behind me. I turn and step aside, perplexed. Why would she want to say hello to Nora? She always ignored her when we were younger. I recall one time when Nora and I had our rag dolls and asked Florence to come play with us, but she completely dismissed the idea because she wanted nothing to do with either of us. Of course, we were only children then, but it's not like Nora or I have too much in common with my sister now.

"Dear Florence!" Nora exclaims, giving a quick curtsy that Florence returns. "How have you been? Sorry I did not return your last letter! It came three months ago, but for the life of me I was so busy! Our sewing circle back at my school has been meeting every Wednesday and Friday.

Speaking of school, my studies are very overwhelming. Did that sewing pattern work well for you?" My mind is instantly flooded with questions. In the less than sixty seconds we've been in each other's presence, Nora has spoken a whole paragraph to Florence but only two sentences to me. When did Florence send a letter? Did I offend Nora somehow?

As they walk arm-in-arm inside, I realize that my worst fear has come true. My cousin has become the spitting image of Florence! And even worse…she has become a lady. I frown and go to help Aunt Nancy with the things they packed. My arms strain under the heavy trunk that we lift down, and once everything is out of the wagon the men carry it inside the house.

I hear Aunt Nancy mention that their visit will have to be rather short, two weeks at most. I have a fortnight to fix Nora before she goes back home, so that is what I shall do.

Nora sits in the rocking chair by the fire as Florence sits to her right in one of the chairs from the table. I stay standing and study them from afar. My mind comes up with ways to get my cousin back to normal, my heart beats with jealousy, and I cross my arms in anger. Every laugh or word they exchange is another one I am not a part of! Did my sister ever feel this way when Nora was my best friend?

Nora covers her mouth as she whispers something in Florence's ear. They both glance at me and break into a fit of giggles.

"I must show you the embroidery that I've completed!" my sister exclaims loud enough for me to hear. "I will go get it. Shall I bring my yarn so you can show me the knitting for those mittens?"

"Yes! Did you want some help with the double loop? If I may be so bold, I do believe I have mastered it," she proclaims proudly.

As Florence opens her mouth, I shout that I'll help fetch the yarn. All I need to do is set the record straight with Florence. I take her arm and drag her upstairs with a fake smile. Once we are in her room, I slam the door behind us.

She acts confused as I stand with my back against her door, refusing to let her leave until I speak my mind.

"What in the world are you doing?" Heat fills my cheeks as I glare at her intensely.

"What ever do you mean? I am coming to get the yarn for Nora." She grins and pulls out the basket of yarn that lies underneath the bed.

"You know what you are doing! She is *my* best friend. You didn't care about her before, and suddenly during this visit you're pretending to be friends! You take everything from me; I will not let you steal one bit of my happiness," I exclaim with such force that I have to take a step back. My heart broke when I said the words, but even so, that does not make them any less true. My face is hot with the fury that has existed in me for so long. All those moments that Mother focused her attention on Florence, whenever she was put on a pedestal above me, when she was presented and spoken highly of by our parents…it has all become bottled up inside of me. That's just what happens when you spend your whole life being compared to someone else. Is it so wrong to pray for the day when she falters and I can take her place as the beloved daughter? I could finally be the perfect child.

Florence's expression turns from a sly grin to fury in an instant. Her face grows red as she steps closer to me. She towers a few inches above my face, but I refuse to shrink down to her.

"I do not care about your feelings. Because you don't know how it felt to see you two have fun without me! Laughing at jokes that I was not a part of. Well, now it is your turn to see how it feels!" She points her finger accusingly at me as she speaks. I dig my nails into the palms of my hands to keep myself from slapping her across the face.

"You had every opportunity to hang out with us! But no, you must pretend you're the perfect daughter! You know, I'm glad we did not have you play with us as children. You would have ruined the fun." I try to stop the words from coming out of my mouth, but it is too late. Every regretful, jealous word I say chip away at what little bond we might have had. "I am sorry you live in this miserable hole that you dug yourself into!" It would be an understatement to say that she is baffled by the sudden outrage that had long since waited to come out of the confines of my heart.

Florence picks up her basket, shoves me aside, and wipes the tears away as she walks down the hallway. She does not fight back because she knows there is truth in my words.

Once I am alone in my room, the tears start. I cannot hold them back no matter how much I want to. The guilt of my words weighs down my conscience. I crawl into my bed while still in my dirty dress and shoes, but I don't care.

Thoughts flood my mind. Why would Nora do this? Whatever happened to being best friends or kindred spirits? We promised to not become like Florence; does this mean all our promises mean nothing now? I am not even sure if Nora wants to go west anymore. I have no one to talk to, and if I did, they would never understand the way she used to. Maybe I am being overdramatic, but how could anything hurt more than watching your best friend—the person who understood me the most—become a stranger right before your eyes? Just the thought of Florence and Nora downstairs right now, laughing and making jokes that I am not a part of, hurts me down to my core.

I guess the saying is right: people don't change. They just become more of themselves. Maybe that is why I feel like I have never really known her. The part that confuses me the most is why her sudden change in personality means we cannot be as close as we once were. Sure, Nora now has way more in common with my sister, but who knows, maybe we still have things in common. We need to become acquainted again. And so I will do just that!

I get out of my bed and sit at my vanity. I take my messy braids out and begin brushing through my light chestnut hair. I fan my face with my hands to dry my tear-stained cheeks. I leave my hair down so it can return to its normal straightness. My thoughts are so loud they could shake the Earth to its core. But that is all they are: just thoughts, things I will never say aloud to anyone for fear of them thinking me a horrible person. Vain, selfish in the sense of wanting my best friend to myself, and jealous even though it's a sin.

Sunlight flows through my glass window as I swallow my pride and prepare to extend the olive branch. I make my way back down the stairs and spot Florence and Nora still sitting by the fireplace. *Here goes nothing.* I cross my fingers behind my back.

"Would you like to come outside to the barn? You haven't seen the cows in a couple of years." I hold my breath effortlessly.

"No, thank you," she responds, returning to her knitting.

I have to think of something that Florence would like to do. If my sister were to engage in an activity, then Nora would follow. Not to be plain or rude, but Nora has practically taken on my sister's personality. I scan the room to find something.

"Okay, what about baking something?"

Nora glances up, annoyed. "Not really," she begins to say, but Florence cuts her off.

"That sounds like a great idea!" She smiles. I look back to Nora, who is suddenly nodding in agreement.

Florence puts on the apron that I gave her on Christmas. I am proud of how well I did with embroidering it, for my sewing skills are horrible beyond belief! Hopefully Nora will notice and admire it. It could show her that we still have something in common.

We thumb through the recipes, debating on which one to use. The three of us turn out to be a very indecisive group. My cousin does not want to make cookies, I refuse to make another loaf of bread, and Florence wants to make everything.

We finally settle on making a vanilla cake from the recipe that Grandma Flora created long ago. Nora runs to the cupboard and collects the ingredients as I read them off the recipe card. Florence hunts for the round cake pans and the big wooden mixing bowl. The pots clang together as she searches through the cabinets. Once we have everything we could possibly need, we lay it all out on the dinner table. Nora reads the instructions as my sister adds everything to the bowl.

For a second, I stand back to take in this moment. I am sure I will never forget such a happy time as this. This may be the first time all three of us are working together! I step in, reaching for the sugar tin, but I am stopped just as it is in my grasp. Pale white hands snatch the tin off the table.

I look up, perplexed, to see that Nora has it cradled in her arms. I try to grab it from her, but she pulls back with a snarl. My smile quickly fades as I realize she is serious.

"Can I have the sugar tin? We have to whisk it in with the eggs and butter!" I say with a forced laugh to break the tension in the room. I looked to Florence, but she, too, is severe. Have I missed something?

"*Florence and I* have to whisk the eggs and butter. Why do you even want to make a cake? How about you go play outside?" It feels like someone has taken my heart out from its place in my chest. Nora is never going to be the same again, is she? It is not as if she changed overnight; it's been two years since we last saw each other. I wonder for a moment which would be worse, changing overnight or over the course of two years? It doesn't matter because this is the real Nora now. No olive branch can piece a friendship back together when one side is not willing.

How foolish I have been to think we could reconcile! I want to scream at her with all the words inside of me. *I have done nothing to deserve this coldness.* Tears well up in my eyes even though I try to blink them away. I will not make myself look even more like a child by crying at a few words, even if those words sting particularly deep.

"May I speak to you outside?" The question is more of a rhetorical one. I grab Nora's hand, guiding her out the door. I strengthen my hold on her wrist as we walk farther away, past the barn where Pa and Uncle Edward are. I keep going until we are at the very place where we promised long ago to remain our truest selves and to follow our dreams.

"I must speak my mind," I begin calmly. She crosses her arms once I let go of her hand. She squints her eyes at me, waiting for me to continue, then rolls her eyes as if bored. This one small action makes me furious. "What is wrong with you!" I scream in her face, losing all sense of propriety I had previously gathered for a civil conversation.

"What is wrong with *me*?" she echoes back. "What is wrong with *you*?" Nora says, pointing her finger in my face accusingly.

"You're the one that changed! I don't even know who you are anymore! You're just like Florence. We were friends, kindred spirits! Do our promises mean anything to you now? Do you not remember our plans for the future?" The tears come back to my eyes, and this time blinking them away would not work. I don't care because I want to be weak and broken. I want my kindred spirit back because, without her, I am lost in the darkness. "Why can't we reconcile our friendship? Why did you change in the first place? You have left me alone when you promised to always be here! Why did you choose Florence over me? You may never understand the pain you've put me through! Because you were the only person that ever truly knew me! And now…you've become a stranger. Why did you leave me?"

My vision becomes blurry from the constant tears. I want to crumble into a ball on the ground and cry my emotions away. My body aches from the cold; when I began dragging Nora out here, I didn't take a coat with me.

Nora's emotions are easily visible on her face. Shock, anger, sadness. Her voice booms into the sky. "We may have been friends or kindred spirits at one point, but not anymore! Are you honestly that stupid and gullible? We were kids, for crying out loud! Promises mean nothing anymore. Azalea, just be realistic! The only reason we were friends is because we're related! The two of us are not, under any circumstances, going west. Those were childish dreams. And in case you have not noticed, I am an adult now. But clearly, you are—and always will be—just a *child*." Her voice changes from a yell to a poisonous whisper as the final words escape her lips. Nora's newfound height is more evident now than ever, with her towering above me and calling me a child.

Before I realize what I am about to do, my hand raises up into the air. For a second it seems like the world moves slower. My palm whips through the air and slaps Nora across her face. She is knocked over to the ground. She looks up at me with wide eyes, her mouth open and her hand soothing the mark forming from my palm. My hands fly to my mouth out of pure shock—but not regret.

"That is what you deserve," I remark, breaking into a run with my sights set on the house. Nora is bound to come inside and tell Aunt Nancy and Mother that I laid a hand on her. If I get there first and deny every word she says, then I may make it out of this predicament alive.

Upon entering the house, I grab *Persuasion* and sit comfortably in the rocking chair by the fireplace, thumbing through the pages until I reach the last scene I recall reading. Florence continues to stir the cake batter and glances at the front door. The minutes keep going by as my worries grow, my shoulders tense up as I wait for Nora to come barreling through the door. The clock reveals that it is nearly evening, and she has still not come inside.

I get up from my chair and go to find Mother upstairs. My room is the first on the left, then Florence's, Pa and Mother's, and finally the small guest bedroom that we mainly use to store things. There was a time when Florence's room and mine were joined as one, but Pa built a wall to separate the two.

As I walk through the doorway to the guest room, Mother and Aunt Nancy are placing square pieces of spare fabric on the floor. The room is rather simple: a bed pressed up against one corner, a table in the other, and no windows. Instead, candleholders hang on the walls. On top of the table sits an enormous basket overflowing with ribbon and a variety of fabrics. My unfinished dress is draped across a chair that is pushed to the side of the table. Mother stands, cutting different fabrics that she pulls out of the basket into identical squares. She hands the square pieces to Aunt Nancy, who sits on the floor arranging them less than an inch apart. She mumbles to herself, then switches a cream-white square with a bright pink one.

"What are you making?" I ask. The floor is covered in these fabric squares, but unless they are sewn together it will not make any dress or apron.

"Oh, hello, dear! Come here." Aunt Nancy waves me over from my spot in the doorframe to where she sits on the floor. "It might not look like much, but once we are finished, it will be a quilt! You could help us with the project! What is your opinion on this arrangement?" Nancy asks, gesturing to the squares.

I am not shocked that my aunt would want to include me in the sewing. The only problem is my abilities. I am not fond of sitting for hours lacing a needle and thread through cloth. This generally results in awful stitches that take twice as long to fix as they did to create.

If only we owned a sewing machine! I saw a picture of a sewing machine once in town, but Mother exclaimed rather forcefully that it was foolish to spend hard-earned money on something we did not need since "we possess the ability to sew." I frowned and flipped through the catalog to a different page.

I shake the thought out of my mind. I must stay focused on the task I have been given. Disregarding my horrid abilities, I pick up a soft navy-blue square that tickles my fingers, a rough denim textile from a pair of Pa's old pants, and a home-woven wool square. After a moment of consideration, I place the denim where the wool was, the navy blue in place of the denim, and the wool where the blue once was. I look at the quilt from a new perspective; these are not just disembodied scraps but important pieces of a soon-to-be-quilt, of a larger whole.

Aunt Nancy claps in approval with an adoring smile. For a quick flicker of my heart, I question what it would be like if she were my mother. I love my family, but wishing some things would change is natural. For example, I often wish that my hair was like Florence's or that I acquired Mother's confidence since nothing seems to rattle her.

I feel instantly guilty about wondering how the future would change if my sister had a different personality or if my aunt took the place of my mother. The thought haunts my mind the whole time I help sew the patches together.

Nearly four hours later, the quilt is only half-finished. So far, it is as tall as Pa and wide enough to wrap around me. I grin half-heartedly at the cozy blanket, but my smile soon fades as the front door opens. The undeniable voices of Pa, Uncle Edward, and Nora travel through the air to my ears.

"You ought to start the cooking, Mother!" I anxiously twist my hair rapidly around my finger. Mother nods in agreement. Her and Aunt Nancy fold up the blanket and start making their way downstairs.

I rush to my room, closing the door. Pressing my ear up to the door, I cannot make out what their voices are saying. Fortunately, creaking it open the tiniest sliver works wonders. Nora apologizes to my sister for taking so long in the barn with Pa and her father. Uncle Edward rambles on about something random, as always. Aunt Nancy once told me that he could talk at the speed of a train and with the abruptness of lightning. From what I can make out now, he is saying how cold it is outside. Then he begins to talk about the scenery, and this somehow ends in him going on about wheat prices. To be honest, I do my best to stay away from Uncle Edward on account of his talkative personality. I never can come up with a good excuse to leave his long, drawn-out conversations, so they often continue until he is needed by somebody else.

I assume that Florence is frosting her cake and Mother is flipping through dinner recipes. Out of all that I have heard so far, there is no mention of me striking Nora. Not wanting to risk it, I stay in my room, avoiding the lion's den downstairs until supper is ready.

Even after we all finished eating, Nora does not speak one word of our fight! It is rather odd. I avoid her for the rest of their stay.

⌒

The coldness nips at my bare hands as I hug my relatives goodbye. The late January weather is relentless. Spring cannot come soon enough! I wander solemnly to my cousin struggles to lift her trunk into the back of the wooden wagon. Trying to be helpful, I take the right side as she takes the left, and we slide it into its place between the wrapped-up quilt and a bag.

"It was nice that you came for a visit," I say. Even though she did not want to come and visit me, I am still glad to have seen my cousin. "I will miss you." There is some truth in that; I will miss who she used to be, but not who she is now.

For a moment Nora appears sincere, as if she's realized how much has changed between us. The look on her face makes me think how different everything could be if we went back in time to when we were younger.

"I will miss you too," she says, reluctantly reaching for a hug. After enduring the mutually awkward embrace, I give her a quick nod before retreating to my family. I do not know if the ache of her betrayal will ever truly leave me.

Nora climbs into the back of the wagon as Aunt Nancy gives each of us a tearful goodbye. Uncle Edward mumbles about the roads as he climbs onto the front seat. Pa offers Aunt Nancy a hand up, and she happily takes it and steps up to sit next to her husband. With a cluck, the horses start trotting away. I turn to see Mother waving her handkerchief. Florence has a tearful look in her eyes but also a glimmer of happiness, perhaps thinking of their next visit. Pa offers a thoughtful wave of his hand with a tip of his hat.

As the wagon rolls away with our relatives, I feel as if it is carrying away any chance that Nora and I have at reconciliation. We will never be the same; our lives shall progress without communication or each other's involvement. I bend forward to look at the place where our promise was made so long ago. Almost as if they are ghosts of my memories, I envision our two young souls standing in the field blowing out the dandelion. It brings a smile to my face. But then those same bodies stand yelling inaudibly. I relive the exact moment when I struck my cousin across the face, seeing the anger glimmer in her eyes.

Before I can think on that moment, the wind sweeps us away and I am still standing beside my family waving goodbye. Nora's blonde hair blows wildly in the wind. I choose to believe that her glare is a sad look, imagining that she too envisions our young souls in that spot. Maybe she did, but I will never know the answer to that.

The cold winter air stings my lungs as we all watch the wagon turn a corner and disappear, hidden by trees. A tiny glimmer of my heart chooses to believe that she may come to realize just how wrong she was to abandon our dreams, but only the future will tell what becomes of us.

I choose to stand outside for another minute while the rest of my family moved to the warm comfort of our home. My heart hurts from the regret, the pain, the memories. Memories hurt the most, whether they are happy or sad. They are just constant reminders of moments you cannot get back. But they can also be a reminder of time well-spent.

Chapter 6

REPENT FOR MY WICKEDNESS

IT'S A SHAME THAT Aunt Nancy, Uncle Edward, and Nora could not stay for my birthday, but nonetheless they rode off less than a week ago to return home. Lingering tension from my fight with Florence hangs in the air, making it unbearably awkward whenever we are along together. When she milks the cows each morning, I do my best to delay gathering the chicken's eggs for as long as possible. Once she carries the milk pails inside the house, I rush out to the barn and practically throw the eggs into my basket.

My feet thump on the ground as I quicken my pace, yet again rushing inside the house. Mother will likely scold me for my tardiness or question what took so long, but I do not care too much. The front door opens and out steps Florence. Distracted, I collide into her, sending myself and the basket to the ground. The eggshells give one pathetic crack before oozing their shaken-up yolks on to the ground.

"Florence!" I groan, rubbing the front of my forehead, where a bruise will surely form. My attention is soon taken away from my sister's vexed expression to the basket on the ground. "No! That was all of today's eggs. I will not be the one to tell Mother that half of our breakfast is lying in a heap of broken shells and orange yolks on the dirt!" Scooping up two eggs that had miraculously remained intact, I place them cautiously into the basket, which is also undamaged. That thing could go through a tornado before being bent.

"Azalea Stanton, you fully know that was due to your lack of focus! You cannot blame me for every problem that you think of." She gives me an accusing look as she spits out the words, then storms off past me. The barn door slams behind her as the front door shouted out in unison. My face remains hot as I stomp my boots on the floor, place the eggs on the table, set the basket back in its rightful place, and rip off my jacket. The fire is low on wood, and the last ember goes out as soon as I notice this.

I am almost positive that I was cursed as a baby, for I seem to always find myself in the worst predicaments at the exact right time for a scolding! This pattern repeats itself as Mother thuds down the stairs, her watchful eye missing nothing. She shivers and gives me a wicked look when she sees the cold fireplace, then the broken eggs.

"What are you standing around for? Grab some wood from the pile before we all catch our death! Honestly, have I taught you no sense as to not let the fire go out in the dead of morning?" She massages her forehead as she speaks. I run off to obey, and in my haste, I forget my jacket.

I shiver as snow starts falling from the gray sky yet again. Florence smugly walks in front of me as I head to the house, struggling under the weight of the wood in my bare arms. She lets the door slam in my face.

◞

My birthday is the only one in our family to fall in the first half of the year. Florence's is the first of August, Mother's the fourth of September, and Pa's the twenty-sixth of November. From the moment I come downstairs on the morning of my fourteenth birthday, I notice a small vanilla cake with frosting on it and my family sitting at the kitchen table.

"Happy Birthday!" they say in unison, making my grin grow wider.

"Thank you!" I exclaim as I hug each person, hesitating for a moment before hugging my sister. "May I speak with you for a moment?" I ask, pulling her away from the kitchen and over to the fireplace. I must be the first to make amends, for it is my fault that we argued. "I'm sorry, Florence. For yelling at you and…Can we just agree to a truce and put it in the past?"

Florence looks at me with skeptical eyes. "Fine. A truce for now." A tense nod is exchanged between us. As I begin to walk away, she lightly touches my shoulder. "Happy birthday, Azalea."

"Thank you." I expected a warm response and did not receive anything remotely cordial. But after all, neither one of us will soon forget our argument. The two of us sit down at the table as Pa slices into the cake, giving me the biggest piece. Even though it's all said-and-done, it still stings that the memory of my hateful words will not be easily erased with an "I'm sorry." For now, I will attempt to be cordial to my sister until the next fight inevitably happens.

Chapter 7

TRIUMPH OF NEW HOPE OVER DESPAIR

IT IS A BEAUTIFUL APRIL MORNING when Mother wakes with a mission. I hear the click of her shoes as she walks down the stairs.

The scissors in my hand cut through a flower's stem forcefully. I place the freshly cut rose, its red petals still young as they poke out of the sepal, in a vase filled with water. A funnel lily gazes at me adoringly as I run my fingertips along its little white petals. I must say that the multi-colored bouquet I've created looks breathtaking. Red roses, funnel lilies, broadleaf arnicas, and chicory flowers complement each other in the vase that I set on the table. I pick up a chicory flower that fell and hold it up to be admired. The small blue petals will be pressed in between the pages of one of my books later today.

"Azalea!" Mother hisses. I snap out of my daze. "Where is your Pa?" she questions.

Before I could answer, Pa barges through the front door. His eyes flicker between my tense stance and Mother's exasperated face.

"Albert. I have come to the conclusion that it is time to go to Brockschmidt! Florence must meet the young men before they are all swept up by summer! Lizzie Roast said just last week that there is an upcoming soirée in the city. All the eligible young men will be there," she expressed convincingly.

My laugh is covered by a grin before it ever escapes my mouth. I figured that Mother would find an excuse to make the trip to Brockschmidt at some point this spring. Her speech leaves even me convinced, even though I'm not included in the conversation. The main question: is Pa convinced? This is not the first or last time Mother would mention a trip to the city for Florence's benefit.

I realize that in a few years, I too will have to search for a husband. The idea of marriage does not please me; spending the rest of your life shackled to someone seems like the cruelest of tortures. That is my opinion, an opinion that both Mother and Florence disagree with. It is rather inconceivable to think of my sister walking down the aisle in the timespan of less than a year! Wedding planning will not take long once she is engaged.

Pa paces around the room. He is deep in thought, enraptured by the sight of the floor. His gaze does not waiver from it. I cannot imagine how hard he is taking this! His first-born child going off to spend weeks—or even months—in a bustling city, courting a stranger, then quite possibly being engaged and married in less than a year! This house will feel so empty with just the three of us—Mother, Pa, and me. A sad feeling creeps into my bones as I watch Pa.

He suddenly stops, ready to put forth his answer. It almost looks like Mother is holding her breath!

"I shall leave it for Florence to decide," he declares, nodding toward the stairs. Mother and I follow his gaze and see Florence standing at the bottom of the stairs, shocked. She must have heard the conversation between us and crept down the stairs, silent as a mouse. For a moment, her bewildered expression causes me to think that she will refuse, but I know my sister all too well.

She closes her mouth, regaining her composure. "It is a wonderful idea, Mother. We will work out the details at supper tonight." It is a proper response, one that only a true lady would say. Maybe she is ready to leave home and travel down the path of marriage after all.

Mother's grin is undeniably wicked. After countless years of preparation, her first daughter is ready for the task of finding a husband. Though Mother knows that we will have to come up with a dowry for Florence's future husband, this is nothing compared to the connections in the city that I know she is dreaming of. The future groom will get paid a sum of money for Florence's hand in marriage. It is yet another reason I do not wish to be married; in my mind, a dowry is as good as being sold into marriage!

"Let us help you pack! Come along, Azalea," Mother said, rejoicing. The pair of us nudge my sister up the stairs and parade into her room.

At the foot of her bed is a decent-sized mahogany trunk that we bought from a traveling salesman last summer. The man had pulled up to the house with a run-down old wagon with ever so many things in the back. We all came out of the house to look through the items for sale, and Florence loved the trunk from the moment she laid eyes on it. Pa bargained with the man for the trunk, and it was bought for Florence.

I skim my fingers along the engraved vines along the top of the trunk. It is astonishing to think someone spent hours chipping away at the dark smooth wood to create these details! With Mother's help we pick up the trunk and place it in the middle of the room. Florence starts taking all of her dresses, coats, stockings, and shoes out of her small wardrobe.

"Pack only your best dresses! No, not that one. How about the blue one with the vertical-striped skirt and that cream shirt? Do not forgo your hair ribbons!" Mother cries as she points to each piece of clothing in turn. I hurry around the room, trying to take the dresses, blouses, and skirts from my sister, then find the ones Mother is talking about. Even though the chest is a decent size, not everything will fit, so only the best can go with her.

"How about the green dress? Florence will look beautiful in it!" My suggestion does not seem to register in either my sister or Mother's minds.

Mother picks up a blouse only to set it back down and grab a skirt to go with it.

Unable to help anymore—whether that be with my unheard suggestions or folding things only to put them back into the trunk—I decide to find something to entertain myself. I stroll around the house but cannot locate Pa anywhere. The only other place he could be is the barn, so I make my way there.

The warm air engulfs me as soon as the front door opens. After such a cold winter, it is refreshing to hear those glorious chirps from birds and the swish of the tall grasses, along with the occasional trot of hooves from the path. With warmer weather comes the arrival of travelers in Lorretta. Although I'm not fond of strangers, it is a relief to see new faces when we visit town every so often. I imagine we shall have to go to town before Florence leaves for Brockschmidt.

"Pa? Are you in here?" My voice echoes through the barn as I push open the door. My eyes quickly adjust to the dim lighting in here. Pa stands with his hands resting on the gate to the cow pen. The cows walk around freely in their stalls, occasionally poking their heads out of the Dutch doors that open outwards into the world. I wonder what the world looks like from their perspective. To humans, being a cow—standing around all day in a barn, eating, looking outside, and being milked each morning—seems extremely boring, but it appears that Sense and Sensibility enjoy it!

"Hey, Bluebird! Come watch." Pa waves me over to stand next to him. "I have noticed how Sense likes to look outside and Sensibility always stands near the gate, ready for us to pet her."

I too have noticed this about my cows. How I love taking care of them! "Yes, she does seem to do that!" I pause for a moment to watch Pa's reaction to the words about to escape my lips. "Pa, are you sad that Florence is leaving? You seem distraught every time Mother mentions Brockschmidt. Though I shall miss her once she is married, we shall still be able to see her often, assuming she decides to live here in Lorretta."

Pa nods in agreement, but the sadness in his face is undeniable. He is not a man who speaks what's on his mind without filtering the words through his head first. I, however, differ very much; saying things that come directly from my head has gotten me into trouble on more than one occasion.

"Please speak your mind, Pa."

He sighs. "If I'm being frank, the idea of you and Florence leaving pains me very much. I can't put it in enough words to describe the loss I feel knowing she will leave. Handing one's daughter over to another man is a happy yet sickening feeling." His words are poetry when spoken aloud.

I contemplate his perspective. Whilst I do not wish to bear children, I can imagine the pain he is feeling. I wonder if Mother is upset, her excitement a mask for the emptiness we will feel once Florence really is married.

Sensibility walks over to me with a smile. I reach over the gate, scratching behind her ears as she offers a moo of thanks. I open my mouth to respond to Pa's words, but Mother's voice pierces through the air.

"Azalea. Albert! Come in for dinner!"

The thought on all our minds is the coming engagement season in Brockschmidt. Every step closer to home is another toward the inevitable future of letting go. I do not know how long she must stay in the city, but it will probably feel like a century, and Mother will have to go with her.

We walk inside, stomp the dirt off our boots at the doorstep, and sit at the table, tensely awaiting the upcoming conversation.

Florence sets the plates onto the table delicately, her face scrunched with what I assume is worry. I have a hard time finding the meaning behind Mother or Florence's facial expressions, as opposed to Pa, who is an open book.

Florence twiddles her fingers anxiously. "Everyone must be thinking about the trip to the city. My final decision is to attend the soirée, so we need to decide the details." She speaks nervously.

Mother clears her throat, bringing everyone's attention to herself. She gestures to the empty chairs, and both her and my sister join us at the dinner table. "The stagecoach is a bit expensive. Unless we hire a wagon driver—but that could a hassle to find a driver to take us there and back— the stagecoach is the only available option. You have five perfectly good dresses packed and ready, so there is no real need to go buy more fabric for another. You may borrow my tan velvet hat with the feathers on it, and Azalea has that small hat box you can use for it, pending her approval…" She turns to me as if it is a request. I am a bit shocked that she didn't demand my sister have the hat box.

"Of course Florence may use it! Might I be able to try on the hat? Please! Just for a minute!" I plead. Ever since Mother bought that hat several years ago, I have wanted to wear it.

Mother frowns at my remark and waves it away with the flick of her hand. "I will help you finish packing everything, my dear! What a wonderful bride you shall make! Tomorrow you must try walking in heeled shoes. I have a pair you can use. I heard a rumor that they are becoming a common custom in the city! Azalea will have to pack quickly if we want to leave on time, though."

Half of a bread roll is stuffed in my mouth when my family turns to look at me. I chew the last of it and swallow quickly. "I fear I have misheard you. Am I to come with you?" Hope makes its way through my words. Although I have no intention of living in the city, I have dreamed of visiting again. It strikes me as odd that Mother would invite me along, for nobody knows of my wish to revisit Brockschmidt!

"Yes, you must come with us." She speaks as if bored by my utter confusion. "Azalea, I expect your best behavior, even when no one is watching! You will be attending soirées in a few short years. This is splendid indeed! This will be a perfect time to increase popularity along with our list of contacts! You and I will spend our time with the mothers of the young men. Who knows, they might have a boy your age! An arranged marriage would be most beneficial!" Mother is in seventh heaven. Though she looks me in the eyes as she speaks, I can tell that her words are spoken more to herself than to me. I, however, have a few words of my own on the topic.

"An arranged marriage!?" My voice is one level away from a shout. My eyes plead to Pa, hoping he has the power to undo this. *I didn't ask for this!* my inner self-proclaimed.

"Azalea, you are not getting an arranged marriage," Pa says, patting my hand. Mother frowns, but Pa keeps speaking. "There will be further discussion on that. For now, Florence is our top priority."

Even though his words are meant to be soothing, they are not. It is common knowledge that once Mother gets an idea into her head, she will have it in her grasp in no time. Just look at how she is getting her way by taking my sister to the city! *"Florence is our top priority."* All my previously buried envy rises back to the surface. She is their top priority time after time, while I shall always remain the disappointment.

I sit silently with my head down as my family continues speaking. None of their words concern me, so there is no reason to talk. I excuse myself from the table without taking another bite of food.

⌒

"This one?" I repeat, holding up yet another pair of shoes.

"How about I pick the outfits?" Florence asks.

I sigh and gesture to the clothes that hang in my wardrobe. Then I slump into my vanity chair and watch my sister rummage through my attire. Florence pulls out my Sunday dress and smooths it out on my bed. I reach into my vanity drawer, which holds my hair ribbons and a brush. Considering my Sunday best dress is a violet purple with white vertical stripes on the skirt, I figure my dark purple hair ribbon will pair nicely with it so I tuck it in the bag.

I watch as Florence internally argues whether or not to pack my plain brown dress. Ultimately, she places it back inside the wardrobe and pulls out another dress. My dresses have always been inferior to my sister's. That is to be expected; after all, the older sister gets the most exquisite clothes, and the younger is left with hand-me-downs that are too big. My Sunday best is the only dress that stood out from my others. Other than that, I have the plain brown dress, a pale pink one with no ruffles or even puff sleeves, a hideous white one, Florence's light blue dress that doesn't fit her anymore—and that I might add is very worn down, to the point where the fabric has lost all its softness—and finally, the dress made from the fabric I was gifted at Christmas, which I am wearing this very minute.

"Florence, if I may?" I ask quietly, in case Mother happens to walk past my room and hear my upcoming questions. Florence, sensing my secretive tone, stops her task of choosing my dresses and sits on my bed, looking me dead in the eyes. I focus on her sky-blue orbs, which hold just a hint of green at the pupils, as I speak. "Is this what you really want? To attend the city's season, meet random men, and possibly be engaged at the first proposal? It's practically being sold into marriage." Her eyes flicker down at her hands that lie in her lap.

She clears her throat sternly. "I know your feelings about marriage are not exactly…welcoming, nor accepting. Nonetheless, this is what I want. What I *need*. A marriage to a man from a reputable family will give our family connections and opportunities that will help the three of you well beyond my wedding day. This is for my family, honor, and legacy. Every young lady must marry because that is what's proper! One day you will have to turn against your better judgement and marry for the good of our family. Imagine if I marry rich! We would never have to worry about money again!" she exclaims quietly.

Her words echo forcefully in my head. *This is what I want. What I need.* Her emphasis on the word tells me that my worst fear has come true. She has convinced herself that she wants to be married, but her real reason for doing so is that our family can reap the benefits of the union.

"So, you would still say 'I do' even if you had no feelings for him? What about love?" My questions must have dug deep, for Florence opens her mouth more than once but for her own sake couldn't find an answer. I nod silently and let her continue packing my outfits.

I do not believe it's in my fate to walk down an aisle wearing white, but nobody should have to do that out of pride and not love! This quick conversation gives me an insight into my sister's heart. I just wish she did not feel like she must do this for us. For me.

Chapter 8

A JOURNEY WITH MORE THAN ONE END

"WILL YOU BE OKAY WITHOUT US? I will miss you dearly, Pa!" I do not wait for his answer to my rather rhetorical question. He embraces me as a few people step out of the stagecoach. I close my eyes to remember this moment, for we may not return to Lorretta for another month or two!

Pa said that Uncle Edward agreed to travel to our home and help him with the chores while the three of us are away. Aunt Nancy approved of his going and wrote a letter saying her and Nora will get on fine. Uncle Edward will be arriving within the week, most likely full of things to talk Pa's ear off about.

"Bluebird. I will be fine!" He kneels down to be closer to me. "Now, promise me that you will not bother your mother too much, help Florence whenever she needs it, and most importantly: have fun! Who knows when you will get this chance again?" he whispers to me with a warm-hearted smile.

I beam happily at his words because there is so much truth in them. But it was not clear what he meant by me not getting this chance again. Does he mean visiting the city? Or spending time with Florence?

Mother stands alongside Florence next to the stagecoach door as people bustle past us. Quite a few new families have settled in Lorretta recently. Florence's trunk, my bag, and Mother's bag are all tied to the back of the ruby-red stagecoach.

"Here, take this ten-cent piece. Buy something in the city you really want. You can tell me all about it when you get back." Pa places the shiny coin in my hand. I gaze at him, astonished by the gift bestowed upon me.

"Thank you, Pa! Oh, I will get the most awe-inspiring thing." My emotions suddenly change once again as I realize that he will not be there to help me pick out my item.

"I love you, Bluebird. Very much. I will miss you all!" he says as a temporary goodbye.

I give a melancholy nod and climb into the coach with Mother and Florence. I tuck the ten-cent piece into Mother's handheld clutch. The seats are so plush and the ceiling so short that if we happen to go over a rock, I fear we shall all hit our heads on the top! There was one long seat on each side of the cabin. Mother sits facing Florence and me. She reaches her hand out the window, waving goodbye. I poke my head out the window on my side and call out to Pa as the driver clucks and the horses start trotting off.

"Take care of the cows, Pa! Make sure Sensibility doesn't become lonely without me!" I yell as he waves goodbye. I can only hope that he heard my request.

As the coach keeps going, Lorretta gets smaller and smaller until we can't see the town anymore. I clutch the edge of the window as we are jumbled around in the coach. Mother sits steadfast, and Florence mimics her every movement. One would never have been able to tell this was their first time traveling in a stagecoach by their calm expressions! I, too, tried to mimic them, but I was still tossed around every time we hit a rock hiding on the dirt road.

For as long as I can remember, we have never traveled too far outside of Lorretta. I marvel at the unfamiliar landscape while spending most of the time looking outside. Trees slowly go past, the grasses wave in the breeze, birds fly proudly in the sky, and rivers occasionally splash against the coach when we go through them. The driver constantly clucks and yells at the four horses hitched to the coach.

Mother explains to us that this was a celerity wagon, the driver is called a Charlie, and the Whip is the whacking sound that we hear every so often. It's all so foreign to me! I try my best to remember every word Mother says. Celerity wagon, Charlie, Whip. I must tell Pa all about those odd words once we get home. Perchance I can write a letter to him once we reach the city!

"My goodness! Look!" I exclaim, pointing out the window. Mother leans forward, and Florence cranes her neck to look around me. We all watch as the beautiful landscape unfolds before our very eyes.

The mountains stretch far into the sky, their white caps of snow seeming to touch the clouds. An enormous field of grass goes on for miles. A herd of wild horses stands close to the dirt road as we rattle past in the coach. Startled by the noise, a black and white paint horse holds its head up, giving a whinny. The other horses are instantly aware of our presence, letting out whinnies of their own. The paint rears on its hind legs and falls back to the earth. It seems to stare straight into my soul with those eyes, reminding me of a certain equine I have seen only in my dreams. The sight is exquisite! If I were as good of an artist as Mother is, I would paint that very image on canvas for all to see.

The horses gallop away in the direction the mountains, their thundering hooves echoing their departure. A foal follows a brown horse with a midnight black mane. I wonder what it feels like to be so wild…so free? Once the horses completely disappear, my sister and Mother lose interest, but I still watch the place they once stood.

My mind creates the image of me riding that very horse. My imagination takes over my eyesight, and suddenly I am sitting on the back of the horse. As I hang on to its mane, the horse rears once more. Adrenaline fills my heart. Its hooves thunder as we gallop across the endless field of prairie grasses. I look down to see the ground rushing by in a blur. A smile spreads across my face as confidence grows inside of me. I spread my arms out as if flying. The other horses from the herd gallop beside my paint.

The wagon rattles again, tossing me into the wall of the coach. I rub my head as I sit back down on my seat. I smile, remembering my almost dream-like vision. If only it were real.

"Azalea. Azalea, please wake up!" a voice whispers in my ear. I open my eyes slowly. When did I fall asleep? Florence is kneeling on the floor of the coach with Mother next to her. I am laid out across the long seat. Florence looks positively mortified.

"What is wrong?" I ask. The coach is no longer moving. We sit still with terrified expressions plastered on our faces. "What has happened, Mother?" I whisper, sensing the tension in their behaviors.

"Shhh. The stagecoach is being robbed." My mind does not recognize the words. *Robbed?*

A man's deep voice comes from outside. The driver pleads with inaudible words as I cover my mouth with my hands. Mother pulls me off the seat to sit huddled with them on the floor. We are trapped. The only way to escape the coach is through one of the two doors on opposite sides of the coach. With no clue as to what lies beyond the doors of the stagecoach, we have no chance of escaping. My blood turns cold inside of my veins, and goosebumps prickle my arms. *Are we going to die?*

Tears come quietly from my eyes. Pa will not know what has become of us for weeks. Our bodies will lay on the road for days before someone rides by and finds us. Our last embrace replays in my mind, making the sobs shake my body violently. I choke on my unspoken words. I squeeze my eyes shut and feel my family next to me. Florence's hand wraps around mine, both of our stomachs pressed to the floor. I peek at her, thinking she will be the picture of calm, but her blue eyes convey that same thought I've been dreading: *We are going to die.* How many robbers would spare a woman and two children on the road? We would be witnesses to his crime, he will surely eliminate witnesses.

A gunshot rings out. I jump and sniffle again. My body is shaking uncontrollably in fear. Footsteps pound on the ground, coming to the door. I pray with all my heart that the driver has shot the robber and is coming to the door to release us from the coach.

I look up as the door swings open. An unfamiliar face stares dangerously into my eyes. He wears a light brown cowboy hat over short black curls of hair. A bandana covers everything below his dark brown eyes, which are two pits of darkness. They twinkle menacingly at my terrified gasp.

"Step out of the coach, miss," he says, holding the door open as if he is a gentleman. Mother crawls out of the wagon first. My sister and I follow close behind, trembling. I cannot peel my eyes off the man and I trip out of the stagecoach. He inhales when I pass by him, and my stomach heaves at the disgusting display. The three of us stand side by side, watching him close the coach's door. The man strolls toward me as his eyes laugh. His worn-out cotton shirt is covered in dirt, and so is the tan finger that he runs down my face. I battle the urge to cry again, but a tear escapes my eyes and runs down my cheek. Like a concerned father, the man wipes it away. As he turns his attention to Florence, my breath catches inside my chest. My heart pounds rapidly, begging me to breathe, but I cannot.

As if my eyes deceive me, the body of the driver lies on the other side of the road, his face pointed at the wide sky above us. The sight of blood is unmistakable. The horses are nowhere in sight, but the tracks prove they were here at some point. The robber must have released them.

"Stay still, darlin'. This won't hurt you," his voice rasps. My hands are being tied behind my back, as are Mother's and Florence's.

"Now then." He scoffs. The rope scratches against my skin as he saunters in front of us. We stand stiffly while awaiting his next instructions—and our unknown fate. "Turn around. All y'all. Start walking until you reach that ditch. Lay down with yer faces on the dirt."

He pulls a pistol from the gun belt worn at his hip. His pants reach his boots that are caked in dry mud. I nod solemnly and shuffle in stride with my family. Every step is one more closer to death's cold grasp. The ditch is less than six feet away, but it feels like miles. We step down into the murky water. I sniffle one last time as my face touches the grass on the side of the ditch. My ears hear Florence's sobs to the right along with Mother's breathing to my left.

God, our Lord and Savior, please send your angel to save us! We have so much left to do in this life. Do not let us end like this! Please, dear Lord, let Pa recover from our deaths, my mind screams.

I listen as the hammer of the man's pistol cranks back, ready to release the bullet that is surely aimed at one of our heads. *Who will die first?* I wonder. *Would I rather go first to spare myself the pain of seeing my family die? Or would it be better for Mother to go first so as to not see the deaths of her children?* My morbid thoughts are interrupted by a gunshot. My eardrums are pierced by the sound! For a moment it seems as though I have lost all hearing, until the sound of my labored breathing comes back. My blood becomes warm. *Am I bleeding out?* I hoped for a quick and painless death but instead am forced to hemorrhage. I shift but feel no pain. I expected to feel pain when shot by a bullet. If not me, then who has been shot? I struggle to get off the ground with my hands tied behind me. I roll onto my back and look to the sky. Fluffy white clouds whiz by, and I am reminded of the time I watched the clouds from the roof of the barn. If only we were there now.

"Florence? Mother?" I ask. Florence shifts next to me. I bend my neck into a painful position to look at her. She is breathing! I glimpse over at Mother. She's fine! Doing my best to sit up, I peek around for the robber.

The man is twisted on the ground in the middle of the road. My eyes follow the road to my left. A boy not much older than me is sitting on top of an Appaloosa horse. He tucks his gun back into the holster on the horse's leather saddle. My mouth falls open with a pop.

The boy jumps off his horse, running over to us. Kneeling on the ground in front of me, he pulls a knife out of a leather holder on his hip. He flashes a bleak smile at my bewildered expression and dashes behind me to cut the ropes. My hands feel instant relief when they are no longer bound together. The boy releases Mother and Florence. He offers his hand to Florence; she is practically astounded but takes it anyway.

"Are y'all alright?" The boy's voice is soothing somehow, and he has a hint of an accent. I quickly thank God for saving us from ultimate death.

"Yes. Thank you, sir," Florence squeaks out. I struggle to find my footing and stand up. Jealousy sparks in my heart, and my face grows red at the sight of them together. He shyly takes his hand away from hers.

If I did not know better, I would guess he has been sent by God. His face is angelic with perfection. His eyes are a breathtaking lapis, skin a golden tan, and hair a midnight black. I blush deeply at the sight of him. I notice the shine of what looks like a silver chain around his neck. The chain is tucked into his shirt.

"Thank you for saving us…What is your name?" I ask. I try to brush the dirt off my dress, but it is no use. My dress is wet from my knees to my ankles and smeared with mud and grass stains. I yank pieces of grass out of my messy hair.

"Russell St. Claire," Russell says with a tip of his hat.

Russell St. Claire. The name ripples through my mind. I would never say these words out loud, but I can feel them on the tips of my rosy lips: *Azalea St. Claire.* It has a much nicer ring to it than Florence St. Claire. Russell seems only one or two years younger than my sister, so our ages are probably closer than I estimated.

Florence nods in admiration. Russell awkwardly looks away, taking off his hat and running his fingers through his hair. My gaze flickers between him and my sister. I purse my lips and clear my throat, bringing their attention to me.

"We are heading to Brockschmidt for my sister, Florence's, fiancé. Could you please point us in the direction?"

Florence whips her head around to me angrily. A smile starts to bubble up in me, but I force it to stay hidden. Russell won't even think about courting Florence if he thinks she is already engaged!

"Well now, I cannot let y'all walk to Brockschmidt alone! It would be my honor to accompany you." Russell grins at the sight of me, or so it seems like he does. I smile, forgetting for a moment the predicament we are in.

"Thank you, Mister St. Claire," Mother says. Her presence had completely slipped my mind in the minute that has ticked past. She seems jittery and nervous. We were all a second away from death, after all!

Russell's Appaloosa is breathtaking even up close. I gasp as we walk in the direction of the animal. It has the strangest eyes, one eye the lightest blue I have ever seen and the other as brown as the dirt in the ground! How peculiar it is to see horse with two different eye colors! I never knew that was possible!

Russell notices me staring at the animal and strides to me. He takes my right hand in his, bringing it to the middle of the horse's face. Its hair is a brilliant white speckled with hundreds of black dots ranging in size.

"Her name is Phantom. She's the calmest horse I've ever ridden! Don't worry, she isn't going to hurt you," Russell announces with a comforting smile. He stands across from me as I continue to pet Phantom. "I'm sorry what is your name?" He laughs, embarrassed to not have asked sooner.

I grin slightly, happy that he has finally asked. "Azalea Bree Stanton. Pleasure to make your acquaintance, sir," I joke, adding a playful curtsy even though the aftermath of our near-death pulses through me.

He senses my playfulness and joins in on the joke, bowing in return. For a moment it feels like we've met under normal circumstances. "Azalea."

My given name runs across his lips. I wonder if he too is imagining his last name after mine.

Mother stands a few feet away talking to Florence. We all start taking small steps away from the stagecoach and where the bodies lie. I am sure those moments before Russell saved us will haunt me for the rest of my life. If only Pa was here right now! We should have never left Lorretta.

Mother clears her throat, meeting us where we stand next to Phantom. "I have been thinking…We could wait here until another coach or wagon comes along, then ask for a ride to the nearest town?" She crosses her arms. This day has taken its toll on all of us, but especially her. But she should not blame herself for wanting to take us to the city; no one could have known that this was going to happen.

"We cannot just stay here and wait! I say we start walking; a wagon might possibly come along and can take us to the city but what are the odds of that happening soon? How far is the next coach station?" I ask Russell. Mother isn't herself right now, and we must get to the city sooner rather than later. Pa's not here right now, so I must take charge of the situation.

"You are from Lorretta?" he inquires, pointing at us. Florence nods silently, confirming the information. "It's a forty-five-mile journey from Lorretta to Brockschmidt. Do you know when you departed?" He draws a map in the dirt as we all stand around him watching.

I peek at Florence, then at Mother. We search our minds for any indication of when we left our hometown.

"Ten in the morning! The driver checked his pocket watch before we left, and it was ten o'clock!" Florence shouts out. Being able to help us figure out where we are seems to bring a bit of happiness back into her.

"That settles it, then…we need to get the pocket watch." I mumble.

My eyes dart behind my shoulder to the dead bodies lying on the ground, and an eerie sensation pokes at me. The robber is still twisted on the ground, the driver looking lifelessly up at the heavens. I turn away, unable to bear the sight any longer. It sends chills down my spine. How will I ever recover from this trauma? How will any of us? The moments seem to replay over and over in my mind: the ear-shattering gunshots, the robber's eyes laughing at the fear painted on my face, his breath so close to me, the ropes binding my hands. I massage my wrists, which are still red. Will I ever be the same, or will this haunt me for the rest of my days?

Russell understands my thoughts even though I never said them aloud. I wrap myself in my arms as Mother holds onto Florence. Russell walks back to the horseless stagecoach. My sister covers her eyes, and soon I wish I had too, but I cannot seem to look away in this moment.

Russell walks over to the driver and searches his pockets. A flash of light lets me know that he's found the watch. The sun hit the silver lid and chain, sending a ray of light our way.

As he hikes back, the unquestionable glimmer of blood is on Russell's hands. He appears to be tired however I knew it is the scaring fact he has someone else's blood on his hands. I take the watch out of his hand giving a knowing look. For a second, there is a nonverbal conversation between us. *Everything is going to be okay* his eyes seemed to say. *I hope you are right.* Underneath the fresh blood that covers it, the pocket watch is rather beautiful. It's such a shame. I quickly wipe the blood off the silver lid before anyone else notices. The watch shines in the sunlight as I click the button and it flips open. A small clock stares back at me.

"Four o'clock. Three more hours of daylight left." My voice squeaks out.

"I have taken the coach to Brockschmidt before. The station should be eleven miles away?" Mother says as she takes a step forward.

"After the station there are another fourteen or so miles until the outskirts of the city." Russell nods, looking down at his hand-drawn map.

My voice breaks the silence. "Even if we start walking now, we won't make it to the station until after nightfall. We'll have to set up camp for the night."

He shrugs, running the numbers through his head and double-checking the calculations. Looking down at the blood on his hands, he wipes them on the black pants he wears. His shirt, perhaps once a pearly white, is now dirty and stained.

"We had better start walking, then," Florence adds, glancing around one last time as if a wagon will suddenly appear.

He gestures to his horse, offering me a leg up. I nod and am lifted into Phantom's saddle. In the past, I've seen women ride horses on the road by our house; they all sat side-saddle, so I assume it is easy enough. I throw both of my legs over the right side of the saddle, but I keep slipping and almost falling off. Hanging onto the saddle horn with all my might, I realize this will not work for the next eleven miles. Shifting around, I toss my left leg over the horse's neck.

Mother once said how improper it was for a man to see a woman's legs, but in this moment nobody bothered. I feel so free! Looking at our circumstances, everything seemed funny for a moment. In one day, I have left the one place on earth that holds any familiarity to me, ridden in a stagecoach, seen wild horses, witnessed the beauty of Wyoming, been held at gunpoint, looked death in the face, and tried to ride side-saddle! Humor is a strange thing indeed.

I reach my arm down, giving my sister something to grab on to as Russell lifts her up. She takes my arm while nervously looking at Phantom. To be honest, I half-expected the horse to rear and gallop away, but Phantom remains as obedient as Russell said she is! Seeing the way I'm sitting, Florence follows suit and lifts her leg over to one side, letting her knees show. Russell gives a cluck, and Phantom starts taking slow steps forward. One more cluck and Phantom raises her head up, alert. Her hooves clop softly on the ground as we go into a steady trot. Russell walks beside Mother, talking quietly. I grip the braided leather reins, digging my nails into my palms. Florence wraps her arms around my waist. I can feel her shake with fear every couple of seconds.

"It will be okay. Do not worry, she isn't going to hurt us," I whisper Russell's words of encouragement loudly enough for my sister to hear. She nods her head but remains quiet.

We ride for what seems like days but in reality is only two hours. When Mother gets tired of walking, I get off the horse and let her take my spot. When I get tired of walking, Florence offers her spot. I try to force my feet to continue walking for as long as possible, but I fail miserably. Russell walks whole time. Seeing Florence walking next to him bothers me more than I would like to admit. She laughs politely when he says something to her. With the loud sound of Phantom's trot, I am unable to follow along with their conversation. As soon as Florence tires of walking, I insist she take my spot. My sister relents—even though she says she is "fine"—and sits in the saddle.

"So where are you from?" I shout to Russell over the sound of Phantom's hooves. *Did he just look at Florence?* My cheeks flush red, but I push away my jealousy.

"My brothers and I live on a cattle farm not far where your stagecoach was robbed at," he says the last words quietly as if remembering the image. "I was out riding Phantom looking for one of the calves when the gunshot…I'm not going to be able to unsee that. The man aiming the pistol. The bodies on the ground…I've never killed anyone before," he whispers, not looking me in the eyes. I slide my hand into his. He seems surprised at first, then seems to find comfort in my touch. Words fill my head, but nothing can fix the thought of taking a life away, even if that life was not an innocent one. We keep walking, remaining quiet. He never lets go of my hand, so I don't let go of his.

A BROKEN MIND VERSUS A BROKEN HEART

ONCE THE SUN'S LIGHT starts to fade, we stop near a patch of trees just off the side of the road. We have no blanket to create a tent, so the ground will have to work. I begin gathering fallen branches for the fire as Mother instructed. Her and Florence are out looking for any non-poisonous berries we can eat.

I drop the wood on the ground and start clearing a place for our fire. Russell's words run through my head again. If only I could convince him that he is not a murderer, but what would I say? I watch as he takes off Phantom's saddle and smooths her coat. Placing some rocks in a circle on the ground, I start to fill the makeshift firepit with broken twigs and branches.

"Need any help?" I look up to see Russell standing over me.

"Yes, I have never built a fire before. My Pa once said to place the rocks in a circle and put the wood in the middle. But it just doesn't look right!" I admit, embarrassed at the pile of wood lying before me. If only I paid more attention when Pa was trying to teach me; then I might be able to help more!

The sun starts to dip below the horizon. The orange rays warm my face. I turn back to Russell, and for a moment it seems like he is astonished by me. He shakes it away and goes back to putting the fire together.

"Can you get some more wood?" he asks.

I nod, running off to grab more. The fading light makes it all the more difficult to see in the shade of the trees. I bend down to pick up a broken tree limb and add it to the cluster in my arms. I awkwardly carry the arm full of wood back to our little camp. I wonder if Mother and Florence have found any food yet. My stomach growls, announcing that it is empty. I squint and try to remember the way back to camp. To the right of the road is the patch of trees, then a big boulder lies straight ahead. To the left is the tree that looks as if was struck by lightning long ago, and the camp should be ten yards past that. I wander around like a blind mouse for what feels like twenty minutes. The sun has completely gone down, the stars hang in the sky, and the moon is concealed by mischievous clouds.

"Ahh!" I scream as the wood falls out of my arms and cuts my right palm. The pain starts to throb as blood rises to the cut. Gripping my dress in my hand, I pick up the wood and hold it awkwardly in my left arm. I bite down on my lip, hobbling back in the direction of the camp.

After wandering even further away, I finally hear voices and see the orange glow of firelight. Throwing the wood on the ground, I sit by the fire feeling defeated. I wince as I peel back the dirty fabric of my dress from the oozing cut. My breathing is ragged as pain travels to my hand.

"Azalea? What happened?" Russell asked worriedly, looking from my face to my hand.

"It is nothing. Just a small cut," I whisper through a wave of stinging pain.

He rushes over to sit next to me. Grabbing my hand rather forcefully, he extends my arm closer to the light of the fire.

"These kinds of cuts can get infected easily out here. I should know!" he says with a laugh. I smile, unsure of what exactly he means. Considering he lives out in the middle of nowhere, I guess he must not talk to very many people. "It isn't too bad! You got rather lucky. If we bandage it soon, you should be okay."

Before I can speak, he pulls down his suspenders and untucks his shirt. He yanks it off and takes the knife out of the leather holder at his hip. A small golden ring gleams at the end of the chain around his neck. The knife easily rips through the fabric of his shirt. In the firelight I can see his bare chest and muscles; he must be incredibly strong. I try to not gaze at his eyes, considering the enchantment of them engulfs me in a surprising way. Noticing me staring at him, he grins with a faint laugh at his lips.

Once he has cut a strip of cloth from the sleeves, he lays the now-sleeveless shirt on the ground. Taking my hand, Russell starts wrapping the strip of cloth around the cut. I take a quick peek at his face, and he smiles, looking up at me every so often as he bandages my hand.

I clear my throat quietly, unsure of how close Mother and Florence are. "You're not a killer." I spoke just above a whisper.

He pauses, gazing up at me questioningly. I know he heard me. I can tell by the way his lapis eyes glance around, contemplating my words.

"How do you know? Azalea, I murdered that man! Didn't even think twice about it." Russell gestures with his right hand as he wrapped my hand slowly with his left and spoke worriedly.

I lift my free hand to his face. He suddenly stops without saying anything else. I am taken aback by his ambience. Staring deeply into someone's eyes can tell you so much about how they see the world. It is as if he sees it not as a complicated place but as a place that he can change for the better.

"Russell St. Claire," I say, using his full name. "I repeat: you are not a killer and shall never be! You saved us. Look in my eyes. I would be dead if you had not saved us from that man!" Taking my hand away from his cheek, I nod for him to resume bandaging my palm.

For a moment it seems as if he will say something, but he remains quiet, thinking over my words.

"All finished," his voice whispers. The feeling of his soft fingers touching my skin sends shivers through me. I blush deeply as he speaks.

"Do you really mean that?" He suddenly asks, searching my face for any indication that I was lying.

"Yes," I respond. I lie down on the ground, looking up at the sky. Clouds conceal the light of the moon, but the stars twinkle every moment that they are not covered by darkness. I glance over at Russell to see that he too is lying with his back to the ground and staring at the sky.

He speaks quietly so as to not disrupt the fragile moment that hangs between us. "I have never met anyone like you, Azalea Stanton."

My smile is unconcealable. "And I have never met anyone like you, Russell St. Claire." It seems as though every time I use his name his face lights up with happiness.

Our hands are centimeters away, but we remain silent, looking up at the sky. I hold my breath as our fingers touch. We hold hands without saying another word. At some point, tiredness engulfs me, and I drift off to sleep.

⤬

Sunlight fights its way under my eyelids. I blink away the sting of the light, sitting up. The fire's embers have long since gone cold, and Mother and Florence are still sleeping close by. I look around but cannot locate Russell anywhere. The only place he could possibly be is with Phantom.

My dirty, worn-out shoes thud loudly on the uneven ground. Gopher holes tried as they might to trip me, but I walk carefully around them. The makeshift bandage is still messily wrapped around my palm. I unbraid the rest of my hair as I walk toward the lightning-struck tree, to which Phantom is tied to by her reins. Her hair tickles my fingers as I run my hand down her speckled coat.

"Good morning," a voice says behind me. I turn around to see Russell standing with the saddle in his hands. He wears the white shirt off of which he had cut the sleeves for my bandage.

"Good morning," I repeat. He strolls over to Phantom, tosses the saddle on her back, tightens the girth, and steps up into the saddle. "Where are you going?"

"I found a creek this morning. Want to come?" Russell asks, giving me a playful grin. Already aware of my answer, he holds his arm out. I take it gladly, stepping in the stirrup and throwing my leg over the side. He gathers the reins and directs Phantom toward the rising sun.

The sound of rushing water is exhilarating. It is tucked in the patch of trees, and it boggles my mind that I did not see the creek when I was gathering wood last night. The sound gets louder with every foot we travel. As soon as it comes into view, I leap off Phantom and run to see the creek, it is only a few hundred yards from the edge of the trees. Little waterfalls not much taller than me carry the water down the creek. My laugh rings out as birds fly between the canopies. A twig snaps as Russell walks to me with Phantom.

"It's beautiful! Everything I could have ever imagined," I exclaim, reaching down to touch the cool liquid.

The creek is only a foot deep and no more than six feet wide. After tying Phantom to a tree, Russell comes to feel the water too. I shriek as he playfully flings it at me, and I return the gesture. He chuckles in return, running to the other bank. We laugh and splash water on each other until both of us are soaking wet. I turn to run to the other bank where he stands but slip. For a joyously wild and improper moment, I feel like a child again, even after the events of yesterday.

"My dear, you seem to be completely wet!" Russell declares, offering his hand to me.

I give him a mischievous look, taking his hand and pulling him into the creek. "You seem to be all wet too!" Russell laughs, running his hands through his short hair. I notice him staring at me oddly. Before I can ask what he is looking at, his lips are on mine. I break away with an astonished look on my face. Neither I nor Florence have ever been kissed before!

With us doing school at home and rarely ever going into town, we have never had any romantic involvement with boys. When I was little, back when we visited town more often, I played with the other children, but besides right now I have never been alone with a boy before.

Russell looks absolutely mortified at my expression.

"I'm sorry! I thought that you…" he says, scrambling to his feet.

I too jump to my feet. We stand for a moment in the middle of the creek as the current pulls at our legs. Without a second thought, I put my hand on his cheek, and our lips meet again. Every sound is blocked out of my mind in this moment, every bird chirping or woodpecker knocking at a tree. For a second it feels as though we aren't even standing in the middle of the forest.

We break away, standing only an inch apart. His lapis eyes search mine as a smile spreads across my lips. Warmth fills my cheeks as we walk over to where Phantom is tied up. I shake out the water weighs down my skirt. Taking his hand once more, I step into the stirrup and throw my leg over the side. No words are exchanged between us until we get back to camp. The short ride back is spent immersed in our own thoughts.

⌇

As we ride into our makeshift camp, I run my fingers through my wet hair. Knots are wound all throughout it. The memory of Mother scolding me for climbing on the roof to watch the sunrise pops into my head. What a cherished memory that is now!

"Dear child, what happened to your hand?" Mother yells, dashing to my bandaged hand. She peeks under the cloth wrapped around my palm.

"Mother, it is just a cut. I am fine!" Sometimes it surprises me when she becomes so worried over nothing! Maybe that is something all mothers do.

"The stagecoach station should only be another few miles. We might be able to get to the city by tonight!" Florence declares to me. She seems so happy to finally have our travels come to an end. If only that did not mean leaving Russell behind…but I have no choice.

We start walking on the dirt road, past the thicket where the creek runs. The small pond where the creek lets out is right next to the road. My heart aches to leave our camp behind. The city just means more people, more change, and more challenges yet to come. But I have no choice. As much as I wish to stay out here in the wilderness forever, we have to keep moving on and leave the memories behind. I sit on Phantom as Russell leads her by the reins. Russell, Florence, and Mother walk side by side.

⌒

The stagecoach station sits at crossroads. I can clearly tell that Florence's heart leaps to see it after all that has happened, and Mother is ecstatic as well. The four of us continue with our sights set on the brown-painted building. Every step seems to take a century.

Russell comes around to the side of Phantom, putting his hands on my waist and lifting me down from the horse carefully as I place my hands on his shoulders. For a second it seems like the world stops spinning and we're the only two people on it. Staring into his eyes, I can envision us as star-crossed lovers. God's will brought us together. How odd that before this trip the idea of marriage seemed so different than it does now.

A man stands behind iron bars like the ones at the postal office in Lorretta. Mother marches up to it as our unspoken leader. "Excuse me, sir? Yesterday, my family was on a stagecoach from Lorretta to Brockschmidt when it was robbed. We have to get to the city *today!*" she explains, gesturing with her hands to emphasize our predicament. The man glances worriedly from Mother, to me, to Florence, then to Russell. I guess however disheveled we look convinces him enough.

"I will fetch the Station Keeper!" the man yells before opening a door inside and disappearing. He then returns with an older gentleman who has a gray beard and a bald head. He wears a black vest over his cream shirt. The words "Station Keeper" gleam across the pin attached to his vest. The old man peers over at us through the iron bars.

"Mr. Finch," the station keeper says, addressing the other man, "please do get these travelers some johnny cakes." The station keeper waves his hand. Mr. Finch opens a door for us to come inside, then scurries off. Russell leaves Phantom tied to a hitching post outside.

The inside of the station is beautiful! Eccentric tiles adorn the floors, and dark wooden benches sit against pink-flowered walls. The station keeper gestures for us all to sit down on the benches, so we do. My cheeks flush red as Russell sits next to me. Mr. Finch comes running to us with a dish full of what I assume are johnny cakes.

The station keeper stands in front of us. He clears his throat and speaks in a hoarse voice. "All our travelers are served johnny cakes at each station." This addresses my unspoken question. The cakes were almost like cornbread. My mouth waters as I bite into the crumbly treat. Despite being incredibly dry, they are not half bad! "The road agents have become relentless these days! There is a relay of horses here that the hostlers can hitch up to the next stagecoach that comes through. According to my schedule, that should be within the next half hour. Were your bags or trunks were left behind where you were robbed?" he asks, looking at each one of us for confirmation.

"Yes, they were left behind. We were robbed approximately eleven miles down that road," Mother says, pointing the way we came. "The driver and robber were…killed."

The man nods grimly. "I will have Mr. Finch send a rider to retrieve your things. Your bags will be sent to your hotel in Brockschmidt, pending your approval." Mr. Finch rushes to the man at the sound of his name. The station keeper whispers something in his ear, then Mr. Finch disappears yet again. Florence, Russell, and I sit quietly as Mother and the station keeper make the arrangements for what will be our last stage of travel to Brockschmidt. Once their conversation ceases, I kindly ask the old man if I could borrow a piece of paper and a pen.

The station keeper fetches the items for me then shakes each one of our hands, before disappearing behind a door. I anxiously tap the heel of my shoe on the floor. Tension builds as I avoid Russell's gaze. I do not know what to say to him or what to do. Once the coach comes, we're going our separate ways! A clock hangs on the opposite wall, the hands on it slowly ticking by.

An hour later, we hear a whinny from a horse and the rumble of wagon wheels coming from outside. The man jaunts outside to talk to the driver. I lean forward to see out the window. The driver has a confused expression on his face as the station keeper talks. He glances through the window at us. Embarrassed, I lean back in my spot on the bench.

Russell looks at me for a second, but I still refuse to look back at him. *Can't you see you are making this harder than it needs to be?* I want to scream at him. All these glances at each other, the brush of our fingers, and my mind replaying our kiss is tearing my subconscious apart! How will I be able to say goodbye to him? My feelings have turned into something more…does he have my heart now?

I huff in relief to see the station keeper wave to us to come outside. The four of us make our way through the door and are formally introduced to the driver.

"Hello again! This will be your driver. You all are safe in her hands," the station keeper says, gesturing to the driver.

Her? I stare at the driver's face. What appeared as a man's short hair is really locks of red tucked under a cowboy hat. A woman stagecoach driver! Who ever heard of such a thing? Based on her clothes, which obviously once belonged to a man, and her hair, which is tucked under her hat, I guess that other people must not be as welcoming of her chosen profession.

Mother's face clearly expresses her thoughts on the topic. Her wide eyes hold a hint of disgust. She scoffs under her breath, climbing into the back of the stagecoach. Florence has the same wide-eyed-doe look as she takes one last glance at the woman and climbs into the coach as well.

The woman shakes the station keeper's hand, then takes her place on the box seat at the front of the wagon as the horses are switched out. I too am about to climb into the coach, but before I can, I hear a voice speak out from behind me.

"Azalea," Russell says, looking at me with a hint of red in his cheeks.

"I guess this is goodbye," I whisper under my breath. A second passes by in awkward silence.

He gives a melancholy nod. The sunlight gleams across his chain as he untucks it from his shirt. He suddenly slips the necklace over his head. "I want you to have this," Russell declares, taking my hand and putting the jewelry in it.

I open my mouth to refuse the costly gift, but he speaks first. "My mother gave it to me years ago when I moved out here to work the cattle ranch. I promised to give it to…somebody special to me. I want you to keep it." My green eyes stare at him with a certain question. *Someone special?* As in his future wife? I half expect him to get down on one knee and propose to me this very minute like men do in books, but no such thing happens.

I nod. "I will forever cherish it! I promise," I whisper, well aware that my family is within earshot of our conversation. I slip the chain over my head, observing the intricate carvings in the ring. "Here is our address. I asked the station keeper for a piece of paper to write it down earlier. We can write letters to each other," I say, handing Russell a small piece of paper. He takes it gladly, putting the paper in his pocket.

"Goodbye, Miss Azalea Stanton," he whispers with a bow.

"Goodbye, Mister Russell St. Claire," I whisper back with a curtsy.

I step into the stagecoach, sitting on the seat opposite of Mother and Florence. With a cluck from the woman driver, we lurch forward and are off to complete our journey. The necklace shines around my neck as I turn to meet Russell's eyes one last time. He nods, then mounts Phantom, turning in the opposite direction. Here we are, two kindred spirits ripped apart by time. If only we met under different circumstances, then perhaps we could have been together. Still, I am glad to have met Russell at all, despite the circumstances.

The coach turns right at the crossroads, and I see Russell St. Claire for the last time. I imagine his brothers probably miss him and want to hear about the adventures that have taken place over the last two days. I wonder if he will tell his family about me.

⸏

The three of us stiffly sit on the seats for the entire ride to the city. There are so many things to talk about, but I remain silent in contemplation. The dirt roads are soon crowded with wagons carrying fruits, horses tied to iron hitching posts, and people out walking. A woman much older than me wears a pink dress with puffed sleeves and a lace collar. She waves at us as we go by! Soon, the clopping of hooves on cobblestone roads is everywhere. The buildings stand side by side, towering over each other. My gosh, some buildings reach four stories high!

There are so many things to see in every direction. A sign hangs above a door with hand-painted scissors next to the words *Barber Shop*. Susan's Dress Shop has extravagant gowns in the windows for passersby to see. Down an alley are several people selling things. A butcher shouts out today's prices. Piano music spills out in the streets from a place called Public Pub, outside of which are a few men taking swigs from their dark bottles and laughing hysterically. Women wearing fancy dresses carry parasols over their shoulders and walk by with their noses in the air.

"Did you see that?" I yell over the noise to Mother and Florence. Florence's eyes are wide with enthusiasm. Mother seems energized by the bustle of strangers as if she is used to this chaos. "If I possessed a dress of that caliber, I would never leave the house out of fear of it getting dirty! Costs a pretty penny, no doubt about that!" I sing out in amazement. In Lorretta, no lady wears gowns of this nature! There, an everyday dress is suitable and common, but that would surely stand out horribly here!

The deeper into the city we get, the calmer it becomes. We pass by fancy houses that almost resemble the palaces I've imagined in books. Iron gates stand firmly in front of them, connected to short brick walls painted white.

Shifting in my seat as we trotted past a wonderfully vast park, I can spot an old man fishing in a shining pond, a married couple walking along a dirt path, and a little girl chasing a boy around the benches. The ambience is so unfamiliar and astonishing to me! We finally reach a two-story building on a corner. The stagecoach squeaks to a stop in front of a sign that reads Grand Brockschmidt Hotel. The cream-white building gleams delicately.

I jump out of the coach, running to the two French doors that welcome me inside. Mother thanks the woman driver and follows closely behind me, equally amazed. Florence looks intimidated by the buildings and the girls that walked by. She profusely smooths her hair, but it is no use. It still sticks out in odd directions. I pay no attention to the odd stares we receive.

Pushing open the doors reveals a new world to me. Polished tiles gleam below my dusty shoes. Far out in front of me is a big wooden counter with a young woman behind it. I ignore her questioning stare and rush to the second pair of French doors to the right. Sheer white curtains flow with the breeze as I step through them. Down a short brick path stands a glorious greenhouse! I open the glass door, finding that familiar smell of nature. The walls and ceiling are all made of glass! The ceiling spirals up into a dome, allowing light to flood the greenhouse. Butterflies flap their beautiful, delicate wings at me. Reaching out, I dare to touch a monarch butterfly. She steps onto my finger, sticking her tongue out at my skin. I giggle at the sight! The butterfly grows tired of my lack of flower-ness and flies away to find food.

If I did not know any better, I would think this is the Garden of Eden in all its heavenly glory! A fountain stands in the middle of the floor, splashing water droplets into the air. Ever so many plants line the walls in flowerpots. Vines travel up stone pillars that hold up an archway. Every color known to mankind could be witnessed in this greenhouse. A flower that doesn't seem native flourishes in a flowerbed on the ground. A set of table and chairs stands near the fountain; I wonder if anyone ever comes to talk or have tea here?

Sensing that my presence is needed elsewhere, I wave goodbye to the greenhouse and run back inside the hotel. Opening my arms, I step through the curtain wall once more, the soft fabric flowing around me before revealing me to the lobby. Mother is talking to the lady at the counter. Florence, ever the lady, stands tall with her hands tucked together in front of her.

"Mrs. Stanton? Yes, I see your reservation. Here is the key to your room, 2B. Up the stairs, to the right, second door," the lady directs, handing Mother a metal key with a tag labeled 2B connected to it. "I have received a notice that your bags will be arriving this evening! We will have them brought to your room."

Mother nods, walking to the grand staircase that spirals up to the second floor. The marble stairs have red velvet carpet draped over them. I follow closely behind Mother as we travel up the shining stairs. The cream-colored walls wear paintings on them. One canvas reveals a beautiful portrait of a young woman wearing a blue dress, her hair wrapped up with curls framing her porcelain face. Although it is vain, the wish in my mind is clear: *If only I were that beautiful.*

We walk past grand, mahogany doors that read 2A, 2B, and 2C in brass letters. With every step we have taken from the first floor to this door, I have imagined the most gorgeous room. My eyes can barely contain my enthusiasm as the door swings open.

Mother, Florence, and I peer into the room without taking so much as a step inside. Finally, my feet force me forward as I was silenced from being stupefied. The walls are covered in the whitest of cotton wallpaper with little hand-painted flowers scattered along it. The polished marble tiles are sullied under our dusty shoes and a purple velvet couch sits next to a grand fireplace. Oddly shaped candleholders sit atop the side table next to the soft velvet couch, and the same transparent curtains shade the glassy windows.

There is a door to my right leading into the biggest bedroom I have ever seen! A bed big enough for three people stands in the middle against a wall, and the same odd candleholders from the living room are perched atop side tables. There is also a fireplace in this room, but it seems to be more for decoration than for heat.

A little room, branching off from the bedroom, has an odd water pump and a strange object that looks like it belongs in the outhouse. I turn the knob on the water pump and water start flowing without stopping. Running water! I have never seen running water before. Mother once talked about how the city she lived in—before she ever met Pa— had running water and electricity. That is what those odd candleholders must be!

I dash to the candleholder, looking around it. A stiff piece of fabric in a cone shape sits on top of the holder, and I look under it to find a lightbulb! I click the button on the side, and light explodes from inside the bulb. My eyes burn from staring at the lightbulb, but I cannot turn away! Nobody in all of Lorretta owns a lightbulb; electricity can only be found in cities or big towns, so there is no need for lightbulbs when we cannot use them.

Rushing to tell Florence of the magic bulb, I see a flicker out of the corner of my eye. A mirror hangs over a small dresser and reflects my image. I take in my appearance: my hair is frizzy from being wet earlier, my dress disastrous, my skin tanned and sunburnt on my neck, my lips bleeding from my awful habit of biting them, my fingernails almost black from the dirt underneath them. I look nothing like the elegant woman in the portrait. No wonder the woman downstairs looked at me with disgust.

I search through the dresser and side table drawers until locating a hairbrush. A bowl with a pitcher lies on top of the dresser, and there are towels folded up in the bathroom. I pour cold water into the bowl and splash it onto my face. Using the towel to dry off, I gaze into the mirror once more.

The person staring back at me cannot compare to the other young ladies that walk the cobblestone streets outside. Their waists are so small from the corsets they wear, and their dresses are in an array of different styles and colors that I shall never own. Everything is so fancy here; I have never felt so out of place!

The brush tugs at my messy hair. I grimace through the pain until my hair is smooth. The bandage on my hand becomes unraveled, revealing my wound. Dried blood sticks to my palm around the large cut. I wash my hands with soap in the bowl of water until my skin turns red from being scrubbed. My eyelids begin to droop. Exhausted from the journey and the anticipation of tomorrow's events, I quickly fall asleep on the enormous bed.

⌒

"Azalea! Hurry up. I need your help getting ready for the soiree!" Florence's voice echoes in my mind. I open my eyes, forgetting where I am for a moment. For the past four years of my life, I've always awoken to the familiar sight of my quaint room and the same kind of yell from my mother telling me to collect the eggs.

I murmur a yes and hear angry footsteps stomping away from me. The morning sunlight shines into the room from a nearby window. Pulling myself out of sleep, I walk into the other room, where Florence sits on her bed whilst Mother pins up her hair. Next to Florence's room is Mother's. All our rooms have the same look of elegance.

Our bags lie open by Florence's bed, their contents everywhere. I rummage through my bag, searching for my Sunday best: the violet dress with a dark purple hair ribbon. My hands smooth out the wrinkles in the fabric from the journey. I also dig through Florence's trunk, holding up her outfit options for the day. Her face scrunches with worry as she gives each dress a "no" or "maybe".

"How about this one? It is pretty!" I comment, holding up a blue-striped skirt paired with a white blouse. Mother picked this particular outfit and packed it back when she presented the idea of visiting Brockschmidt.

Florence, unable to make a decision, looks to Mother for guidance. Mother analyzes every last detail of the outfit that I hold in my hands.

"Yes, that will do nicely," she says sternly.

I collapse onto the bed, watching Mother pin up my sister's hair. My sister is by far the most beautiful girl in Lorretta. I am positive that she will have many interested suitors from the moment she walks through the door at the soirée! Even though our bond isn't nearly as strong as it ought to be, I am still happy for her because this is what she has been wanting.

"Can I have my hair done up?" I interject, unable to help it. "Oh, imagine braids twisted into a bun and little wisps of hair framing my face like Florence's! How regal it would look, with white lace gloves on my hands paired with a beautiful ocean-blue dress with lace at the collar and end of the long sleeves. The skirt would reach my ankles, with white embroidered flowers at the hem and a white ribbon tied around my waist with the bow in the back! It would only be fitting to match it with a blue velvet hat with a feather plume on it. Now, if I were to walk down these very cobblestone streets wearing that, I would not be one bit surprised if a whole heap of suitors collapsed at my feet begging for my hand in marriage! In conclusion, Mother, may I please put up my hair like Florence's?" Describing the dress I picture so clearly in my imagination, I twirl around the room, holding Florence's outfit up to me. I collapse onto the soft feather bed. My sister's jawline is so nicely accentuated with her hair spun up in a bun. I have never noticed before that she styles her hair down far more often than up.

"No, Azalea. It is out of the question! How silly would it look if you both were to walk into the soirée with the same hairstyle? Not to mention you are not old enough for your hair to be up. It would be improper to do so." With those words, my dream of the ocean-blue dress, the regal hairdo, and the velvet hat are practically crushed beneath her heel. In simpler words, Florence is meant to be the star. I ought to have brought my plain brown dress just so that my sister could shine even brighter when standing next to me. I heave a sigh, grabbing my purple dress and walking back to my room to change.

After I've changed, I anxiously pace around the hotel room, searching for my purple ribbon to tie my hair. Mother calls my name as she opens the door to the room, stepping out into the hallway. I quickly locate the ribbon and tie my hair back, grabbing the ten-cent piece Pa gave me on my way out. I put it in my dress pocket, hoping to find something special to spend it on. My skirt barely misses being shut in the doorframe as I close in it a hurry. Mother locks the room with the key and starts off, both of us trailing behind her like ducklings.

I wave a quick goodbye to the portrait as we stampede down the red-carpeted stairs and stroll through the vacant hotel. The streets here are much louder, with noise coming from every direction. I gaze longingly at images of astonishing beauty as women and young ladies walk past us with their expensive and extravagant apparel. My country bumkin braid seems dull in comparison. My hair starts to frizz at the top of my head no matter how much I flatten it down. It shall be obvious to everyone else that I am no city girl.

I am never too excited to be amid strangers, but today is an exception. If I act like I am just another random person, then maybe, I will go completely unnoticed today! I watch the men, women, and children walk by with their own itineraries and destinations planned out in their minds. Sometimes it's so easy to forget that the person walking next to you has their own life. It sounds silly, but it's the truth!

I stare at a tall, dark-skinned, long-bearded man wearing a crisp new suit as he walks past us on the sidewalk. Does he have a family? Maybe a little boy and girl waiting at home for him? Did his wife dust off his suit as she kissed him goodbye for the day? Maybe he works in a busy office located in the middle of the city.

What really strikes me as odd is that everyone possesses all these different memories and life experiences! A little girl with a pretty white-toothed smile walks hand and hand with her mother. She has her whole life already laid out in God's eyes, but nobody could ever predict it. Sometimes it's difficult to look outside your own life and see everyone else's. Sometimes we all just have to be reminded that the world does not revolve around ourselves.

The sidewalk is hard concrete, with iron hitching posts cemented on the side of the road. To our left are the iron fences and gates that shield part of our view of the fancy houses. Mother touches her pretty hat, making sure it is firmly pinned to her head while going over the rules of being, "obedient, well-rounded, perfectly behaved young women."

"Do not raise your voice above a simple whisper. Keep your hands clasped neatly in front of you. Curtsy to the owner of the house into which you are being invited. Address every older woman by her husband's last name with a simple 'Mrs.' in front of it." Her words go in one of my ears and out the other.

Mother walks alongside Florence, and I follow closely behind. They step around two children lying against a stone wall. I hesitate, peering down at them as we walk. The youngest boy grabs the end of my skirts, causing me to come to a complete halt.

"Food, please? Have not eaten in couple of days," he pleads in broken English. A hint of what I assume is an Italian accent comes through in his voice.

My heart shatters to watch this young boy, who cannot be more than seven years old, begging on the streets with another boy next to him. My eyes flicker between their dirty, grime-covered faces. Just yesterday I was in almost the same physical state: hungry with no money and a disastrous appearance. Holes are pierced throughout their clothes. These poor little boys have been left alone in this world with perhaps no parents to provide for them. Too young to do any manual labor, and with no source of money, there is no other fate for them besides living in an orphanage, which is most likely no better than sleeping outside.

I reach inside my dress pocket and pull out the ten-cent piece Pa gave me. I intended to spend it on one of the delicious caramels or peppermint candies that I saw in some of the storefronts. But Pa will surely understand why I feel compelled give this gift away.

Bending down, I offer the shiny coin to the young boy. The boy's eyes brighten. I have no doubt that he is thinking of the food he can buy with the coin. Although the coin will only fetch a pound or two of apples, it will surely be enough for a few weeks.

"Thank you, miss. God rewards kind," the youngest boy says politely, bowing his head in thanks. "I get food. Domizio will be back soon," his voice squeaks out. He gets up and limps across the street to the market. I stand up, watching him hand over the coin to an aproned man and pointing at some red apples in a basket. The man nods, handing him a bagful of apples. Domizio looks as if God himself sent an angel to bless him with that food.

"'Sell that ye have, and give alms; provide yourselves bags which wax not old, a treasure in the heavens that faileth not, where no thief approacheth, neither moth corrupteth. For where your treasure is, there will your heart be also. '" I whisper to myself, quoting the verse from the Bible.

Mother and Florence have halted, and they watch me as I walk to rejoin them. Nobody says anything until we reached the house where the soirée is being held. Mother holds out a paper with the address scribbled on it. Surely, she acquired the address and other information regarding this soirée from Mrs. Lizzie Roast, the lady that had alerted Mother of the coming engagement season in this city.

I take a deep breath as we prepare to step into the lion's den.

Chapter 10

FOREVER-UNCHANGING FRIENDSHIP?

THE HOUSE IS SO ENORMOUS that you would naturally assume anywhere from ten to fifteen people live here. The iron gates part, revealing a small pathway leading to a few steps that arrive at a large door. Roman columns hold up the triangle-shaped overhanging roof. The house is painted a bright yellow, and countless windows line the front of it. Connected to the iron gates is a short stone wall that stretches along the street. The neighbors' houses are equal in elegance.

I am tempted to reach out and pluck one of the flowers that droop into the pathway. But just as I lift my hand, I notice that a short woman with dirty blonde hair and pale skin stands at the door. I hadn't seen her because her dress almost exactly matches the yellow house. And oh my, what an extraordinary dress it is! It has flowing lace at the collarbone, short sleeves that are covered in the same lace, and a hoopskirt that makes the dress even more majestic.

The woman, who is a few inches shorter than Mother, asks for evidence of our invitation. Mother searches through her clutch and pulls out a stiff paper with fancy handwriting on it. The short woman snatches the paper in her gloved hands and scans the words as if suspicious of how we came to possess the invitation. Her eyes look each of us up and down, pausing for a moment on my frizzy braids. I focus on the detail and exterior of the house as she reads out our names from the paper.

I nod when my name is called but continue to look at the columns holding up the roof that shields the space where we stand, between the door and the steps. I'm sure this shielded space would be useful if it were raining, but it seems almost completely useless, just like the fancy dresses that the city girls wear even though they are bound to get dirty. Maybe everyone in the city that has money spends it on useless things?

"Please, do come in!" the short woman announces. I take my attention off the architecture and notice that the woman is now standing in the doorway, holding her arm out invitingly. Mother nods her head as a way of saying thank you. Florence and I recall her instructions and curtsy at the step of the door. The woman goes back outside, leaving the door open to the mid-morning sunlight and slight breeze.

Inside, my eyes adjust to the change in lighting. The house looks even more dignified on the inside! A few steps away from the front door is a staircase that one could only imagine is meant for a princess entering a ball. The floors are a dark wood and are partly covered by different rugs in each room. I follow Mother as she walks through the archway to what I assume is the parlor.

White wallpaper embellished with gold vines is plastered on the walls. This room is relatively big—much larger than the whole first floor of our house back in Lorretta. Not to say our house is small, but when compared to the gigantic homes of the rich neighborhoods of Brockschmidt, it seems like an ant next to someone's shoe.

A lovely couch sits between two windows on the far-left wall. The curtains appear expensive, at least to an untrained eye such as mine. A long table has been pushed against the wall on the opposite end of the room and holds may delicious-looking foods that for some odd reason nobody is eating. Finally, a dormant fireplace sits in the middle of the right wall. I am guessing that the furniture that is typically in this room was moved out for the soirée, since the imprints of table or chair legs are visible on the carpet.

Several young men who look to be Florence's age are already talking to pretty girls around the room. A young girl with copper hair steps into a conversation being exchanged between a handsome boy and short, plump girl who resembles the woman at the front door. The plump girl, most likely furious that her time with this boy was interrupted, laughs with a rather serious expression on her face. How silly this all is! Girls fighting over boys' attention is pure comedy. Some girls have gone so far as to wear a corset to appear thinner, but it's clearly unnatural. Some girls are wearing very inappropriate dresses that show far too much skin. How could their mothers let them go out in public in such outfits? It almost makes me think that Mother has been dressing us as nuns our whole lives.

"'Finally, brethren, whatsoever things are true, whatsoever things are honest, whatsoever things are just, whatsoever things are pure, whatsoever things are lovely, whatsoever things are of good report; if there be any virtue, and if there be any praise, think on these things.' the good book of Philippians says," Mother quotes to us. I try to find the message she is trying to convey in those lines, but every other word seems to have a different meaning to it. Florence does not appear comforted by the quote either, so Mother continues to soothe her. I would too if I had any advice, but nothing comes to mind. "Remember, you are the prize. Let them come to you, dear. And for heaven's sake, choose a rich one!" Mother whispers that last bit loudly enough for me to hear. I stare, rather perplexed at Mother's words. She ought to not be greedy and just hope that her daughter will find love!

"I bought these name cards for you at the Lorretta postal office before we left. I chose the best font and decorations for you. Now, you only have a dozen of them, so do not pass them out freely! To show that you are interested in pursuing a boy, you offer him your card. If he feels the same, he will return the favor with a card of his own. Mrs. Roast informed me on all matters of finding you a suitable husband!" Mother explains this so quickly that I feel like my head is spinning even though I wasn't acknowledged!

I catch a quick glimpse of the cards as they are handed to Florence. They are quite pretty, to be honest. The name Florence Stanton has been printed over a shimmering silver rectangle, and snaking up the corners of the rectangle are tiny green vines with pink flowers blossoming on their spirals. It looks lovely, but not quite what I would choose for myself. Florence, however, is starstruck at the sight of the name cards. She runs her fingers across them, verifying the reality of this moment.

This whole trip to Brockschmidt seems like a dream that I might awake from at any moment. I constantly find myself questioning if this is reality or just a figment of my imagination…

Florence clears her throat quietly and responds in the most ladylike voice. "Thank you, Mother. I shall bear those words in mind." She then walks off to join the party.

"Such a good girl!" Mother comments proudly. Even though it is not intended to be this way, I feel like this is a practice for my engagement season when I become of age. As if I will agree to an engagement season!

A pang of hurt stings my heart. Once again, Florence is the most perfect daughter anyone could ask for! She is, after all, marrying out of duty and not love; her marriage with provide our family name with connections and status.

"Azalea, you must go mingle with the boys your own age! They should be in the room to the right of the front door. Please, for Florence's sake do not make a fool of our name! Just give it a try. Talk to people instead of keeping everything in that head of yours. With any luck you might come out of this with an arranged marriage!" she declares.

I grimace, giving her my promise that I will make an attempt at conversation. My fake smile conceals the burning hate for this event that is growing inside of me. I follow directions and walk into the room that's to the right of the front door. This parlor room, though a bit smaller, is very similar to the one Florence is currently in.

I have no name cards of my own. I highly doubt it is necessary. After all, the boys I am to meet will not be able to marry for a few more years. According to Mother, the only girls that marry young are either pregnant or conveniently become widows shortly after the wedding.

It is a lot quieter in this room than the other, and there are far less people. There are four boys and only six girls (including myself), but that does not stop the girls from practically fighting over each boy.

I made a promise to start conversation, so I have to do just that. However, all of the boys are engulfed in conversation with the others. Everyone—excluding me and another girl my age—is already conversing about boring topics such as the weather.

"Not a fan of small talk, I assume?" I ask the girl, who is wearing a bright blue dress. She has chosen to stand in the corner of the room away from everyone else, so it's natural to assume there's a reason.

"How ever did you know!" she exclaims in fake surprise. We both giggle. "Yes, this is my fourth soirée this spring. My mom does not trust me to stay home all day because I am 'bound to make a mess or cause trouble,' so I'm forced against my undying will to go everywhere with her and my three sisters—all of whom are in the other parlor." She speaks as if this is all common knowledge to me.

"Three sisters? My goodness, I cannot imagine how crowded your house must be!" I laugh. The girl stares at me as if I am crazy. I then remember that the houses in the city are very large.

"Oh, you must not be from the city! That makes much more sense. Evelyn Puffin," she says, offering her hand as an introduction.

"Azalea Stanton." I gladly shake her hand. *See, Mother? I have already made a friend!*

"Azalea. What a creative name! If only I were named after something like a tree or a type of flower. It would sound so much more interesting than Evelyn. Before anyone tells you, my family is one of the highest on Brockschmidt's social ladder. Nobody ever talks to me for of that reason alone. It doesn't matter if they like or dislike me because in all the girls' eyes, I am a threat. And the boys think I am spoiled, but I could care less about finding a husband out of this group."

Evelyn Puffin is surely a kindred spirit! She mentioned her family's fortune not as a way of bragging but more as if it's a weight that she is shackled to and forced to carry around for life.

"I think Evelyn is a nice name! I have never been to a soirée before, although in these first ten minutes I cannot fathom attending four in just a few months. My mother and sister are in the other room trying to find 'a rich one' for my sister. My task is to enchant one of these boys so that I may 'secure an arranged marriage'. How ridiculous this all is! Honestly, I do not find a point in talking with any one of these boys because we are far too young to be married just yet! Wouldn't you agree?" I rattle on, my thoughts going straight from my brain to my mouth.

"I suppose." Evelyn shrugs, her entire demeanor suddenly different. No, no, no! I have just made a friend, and now I fear I have offended her!

"What I meant was that an arranged match would not work for me because we are from Lorretta! Anyhow, you said you have three sisters, right? I only have one sibling, and that is my sister Florence, who I mentioned before." I pause, anxiously glancing at Evelyn's face. "Evelyn, I fear that I have offended you. I am terribly sorry because I did not mean to. I have never really had a friend before that isn't kin," I admit, rather embarrassed. Surely, a girl who is high on this "social ladder" she speaks of has had many friends outside of her family, at least when they are not threatened by her family's wealth.

In the most shocking turn of events, Evelyn glances at me and lets out a laugh. She doubles over, laughing so hard that tears start coming down her face. The other girls and boys in the room look at us in annoyance at the sudden outburst. I awkwardly laugh, even though I have no clue what is so funny. Evelyn stands back up when she finally collects herself. She wipes the tears from her face.

"Azalea, in the few minutes I have known you, you have become the only friend I could ever be able to trust! I assure you have done nothing to offend me, but I do advise you keep those thoughts to yourself because if anyone else heard, they'd think you odd," she whispers with a smile. Through my bewilderment, I grin, happy that I still have a friend even if I am making a rather big mess of it. "Since you do not have much experience in the city, I will be honored to guide you. The first important thing to know is that these girls—besides me, of course—are not your friends. Do not fall victim to their trick of acting nice or friendly because it's only so they can figure out if you will be a threat when their engagement season comes. The second is that the boys couldn't give a hoot whether or not they talk to any of us! Their moms dragged them here in suits, so they are forced to converse."

I try my best to follow along as she points to the group of girls that flip their hair as they talk and the boys that smile out of politeness but remain quiet. "So, what you're saying is that I cannot trust any of the girls? How odd. They seem nice, though." It is impossible to tell if the reason they speak to each other is to be gracious or if it's for show.

"Yes, it's part of their trick. So do you really only have one sister? All of my sisters are here right now. Elizabeth is nineteen, Jean and Katherine are both seventeen, and I just turned sixteen last month. How old are you if you don't mind me asking? You look about fifteen years old." Evelyn mumbles monotonously when she speaks of her sisters, but I feel flattered that she shows genuine interest in talking about mine. I wonder if she too feels an undying jealousy when it comes to her sisters. Is it unbearable for her to live in their shadows, constantly being compared to them?

"That is very nice of you to say! My fourteenth birthday was in January. I love being born in January! Most of my birthdays there is a lovely amount of snow on the ground, so I go outside all day! Although, the only fault in that would be that my birthday is so close to Christmas that it's somewhat overshadowed. Not that I mind too much; I have become accustomed to it by now." I twiddle my hands as I speak. It's quite a challenge to be in the city. The noise will take a long time to become accustomed to. Almost every other minute I hear yelling, loud whinnies from nearby horses, or the rattle of wagons on the cobblestone streets. I wonder if Florence feels the same restlessness that I do, being around all these strangers? She appeared to be the face of calm before we parted ways, perhaps she is secretly nervous. "My sister is sort of the perfect daughter. She is the reason we came to the city—so that she may find a husband. Are your sisters like that? Undeniably perfect, I mean?"

Evelyn looks truly astounded at my talk. It strikes me as odd. After all, we're not talking in front of grown-ups, so there's no reason to be formal. I have taken her advice about not speaking of these matters to anyone else in the room, but considering nobody has come to the corner in which we're standing, I feel no reason to limit our conversation.

"Azalea Stanton, you are by far the most interesting character I have ever met!" She laughs loudly again. I nervously giggle, not knowing what she means by "interesting character." It doesn't sound negative, though. "To answer your question, I have never given much thought to it, but I suppose that, yes, having three older siblings does make it a struggle to become the favorite. However, my mom is very sensible, so she always says to us, 'You are all dearest to me! I could never choose one to put above the others.' I do believe there is truth in her words when she says that." Evelyn adjusts her voice to imitate what I assume is her mother's. It's strange that she calls her mother by the name 'Mom.' "Isn't your mom the same way?"

It would be terribly wicked to speak bad of my parents, but it's also sinful to lie. Deciding not to do either, I provide an excuse. "We ought to converse with the others! How about them?" I point to a group of three girls that stand near a window. Evelyn agrees and walks with me to join the girls.

It's rather difficult to tell their ages because of their lavish dresses and face makeup. The young lady to my right is by far the prettiest in the room! Her hair flows down her back in gorgeous waves of ebony. In fact, all the girls in the city seem to have very long hair. I have always kept mine cut to the middle of my back, and until now I had never given it a second thought. Looking at the dark-haired girl makes envy expand in my chest.

"Your dress is immaculate! What material is it made of?" I exclaim to the ebony-haired girl. She turns away from her conversation to face me, her skin a pale, unnatural china white. Compared to her, I look like an Indian child!

"Thank you? And your dress is so…mundane." She comments, her voice dripping in sarcasm. The two girls behind her giggle. She turns around, giving them a wicked smile.

"Mundane?" I whisper to Evelyn, feeling as though she would understand their strange talk.

"It means dull, ordinary, conventional."

"Oh." *Dull? Ordinary?* My heart cracks as if someone has broken it in two. The fact that I did not know the word the girl had used makes this even more embarrassing! "Well, I suppose it is a mundane dress!" I declare, trying to join in the laughing. But this is my Sunday best dress! There is nothing dull about it. My brown dress that I left at home is the very definition of conventional! Thank goodness it was not packed. "I do so love the Victorian era fashions! Queen Victoria was such a pretty queen in her youth. How tragic that she lost her beloved! I read once that Prince Albert was very handsome. She must miss him dearly."

The tense feeling does not subside, no matter how much I wish it would. Much to my relief, the topic is finally picked up by a skinny girl that had so far done nothing but laugh at me. "It would be sinful to say I do not adore the fashion, but Queen Victoria is not popular anymore! Sinful indeed that the lifestyle has not been properly adapted here in America."

I smile, happy that we are talking about something I am familiar with. "Most are lucky to live such lavish lifestyles due to the unemployment crisis last year. My Pa said New York still has so many unemployed men because of it! Have you ever been to New York?" New York looked so far away when I saw it on a map hanging on the wall of the postal office in Lorretta. Surely, America could not be that big!

The last girl speaks up. I want to ask her how old she is, as she seems a bit too old to be conversing with us. But since we are just now starting to get along, I decide to say nothing that might come off as rude. The older girl exclaims, "My family went to New York two years ago for my fifteenth birthday! A wealthy businessman begged for my hand in marriage, but my mother disagreed, for we had never met him before! But he clearly displayed a high level of class. There are ever so many proposals I have endured over these past few years. Such a hassle, am I right?" the girl exclaims, asking us all.

"Yes! It is heartbreaking for the men," the ebony-haired young lady says, as if it is a game to toy with these men's affections.

"I wouldn't know. I am only fourteen, so a proposal is out of the question!" I laugh. Their faces seem to turn in disgust by my outburst. I speak quickly to not lose their attention. "Well, I mean, a man has yet to propose to me! I assume it is from my age. Besides, I think it would be helpful to work for money before getting married, so you don't have to rely on your husband's fortune." Their expressions only worsen as if everyone has eaten sour grapes.

"I believe there is no other job for women besides motherhood," the older girl says, crossing her arms. I glance at Evelyn for help, but her face says it all. *I told you not to speak of such matters!*

"My mother says that if you are working a job, it is as good as being barren! No man wants a wife who works anywhere but in the house."

"Around here it's considered a show of wealth for a woman to have no responsibilities," Evelyn whispers in my ear. In this moment I want to bury my face in my hands to hide the red-hot embarrassment growing in my cheeks, but I know Mother would highly disapprove of me covering my face.

Our little group of girls disperses, snatching up the boys in the room, even though there is a short supply of them. Staying true to my word, I pull a breath of air into my lungs and walk over to a tall boy who is standing near the window.

"Hi, I am Azalea," I say, offering my hand for him to shake but quickly snatching my hand back when I remembered that it was improper. "Sorry," I mumble, hoping he did not notice.

"Charlie," he says, taking my hand from my side and kissing the top of it. His looks are not very pleasing, but I try not to focus too much on his awful haircut or awkward tallness. It seems impossible not to compare him to Russell St. Claire. Russell is dashingly handsome and a cowboy along with a gentleman. How can I not compare every other boy to him?

"Nice to meet you." I smile, but he appears rather bored by my expression. "Excuse me." I curtsy and scramble away to find another boy to talk to.

"Hi, I am Azalea!" I grin and curtsy.

The boy bows in return, giving me a flirtatious stare. "Azalea. Interesting name." His eyes scan my appearance. A sweat breaks out on my hands as he analyzes me. The whole moment is uncomfortable. "How much is your dowry?" he suddenly asks, leaning in to say the words.

I look back at him as if he is insane. His undying flirtatious stare tells me he meant what he said. "Excuse me." I turn around, walking hastily toward anything else. My past two conversations lasted only a few minutes but have already tired me out.

Mother pokes her head into the room, searching for me. Before her eyes even finish scanning the room, I am at her side. "How do you expect me to have an actual conversation with these people? That boy is a Bandersnatch! And he—over there—is an arrogant luftmensch!" I pulled the word Bandersnatch from one of my favorite books: *Through the Looking-Glass.* Luftmensch came from deep in my mind, back when I used to study the dictionary to appear smarter than Florence.

I protest my insults so loudly that both boys might have heard me, but the gramophone scratches as another record is placed on it. New music fills the room. My anger melts away at the beautiful ghostly violin sound. I see the magical device sitting on a table against the wall and immediately recognize it from when I saw one long ago in a newspaper. I had never heard nor seen one in real life until now. But I shall have to observe it later, for now there are more pressing matters.

Florence rushes into the room, joining us with a smile across her face. "Mother! There is a man named Lawrence Jones, and he is absolutely smitten with me! I handed him my card, and he handed me one back!" Florence holds out a tiny card with the words "Lawrence Jones" printed on the gray paper. It has no rectangle or illustrations on it, just this man's name on colored paper. It seems like a waste of money to buy such plain cards, but embellishments must not be attractive to the male species.

Mother turns giddy at the news. I am happy as well, but it would reassure me to know what this man looks like. Florence shines like a thousand suns as she tells us of this Lawrence Jones. She speaks directly, talking about how she was standing over at the table looking at the many different foods and trying to pick one to eat, "for it would be rude to eat more than one thing like some of the girls, including the daughter of the lady who is hosting the soirée. No men went over to speak to them." She talks profusely of how Lawrence came and stood a respectable distance away from her, talking about a food called chocolate. Florence explains the food as best as she can, saying it is a bittersweet square of candy that isn't sticky but rather almost melts in your mouth. My mouth waters as I imagine this delectable treat. I shall have to try and sneak into the other room where Florence had gotten the piece of chocolate.

"What a good girl! Now we must meet his mother and set up a super-vised meeting between the two of you! Dear child, what are you standing around for? Where is he?" Mother whisper-yells at us. Her dreams are about to come true; status and connections will soon be in her grasp. The pair of them walk away, and I trail closely behind as we enter the other room and push through the crowd of men and women.

Once my eyes catch sight of the table of food, I break off from Mother and my sister, setting my sights on the intricately arranged sweets. I peel back the wrapping, seeing the dark brown square that Florence vividly described. As soon as the sweet touches my mouth, a sweet flavor hits my taste buds, then a bitter taste that levels out the sugar inside the chocolate. Florence was right, this is unlike anything I have ever tasted before! My stomach growls as I realize that this is the first food I've eaten today. Glancing around the room, I make sure no one notices as I stuff two strawberries in my mouth, pulling the leafy greens off them first. I chew quickly with my back turned to the room.

"I think we got off on the wrong foot earlier," a voice says next to me.

I swallow, turning around to see the boy I had briefly spoke to in the other room. "You mean when I said hello and you demanded to know how much I'm worth?"

"Well…I did not mean it in that way! I think it's nice you think of me as a…what did you call it? Ah yes, a *Bandersnatch*. That means you're smitten with me, right?" he says stupidly. This boy obviously thinks Bandersnatch means something nice.

"Excuse me." I roll my eyes once again, walking away from him. I find Mother speaking to the prettiest woman I have ever seen. Mother's looks are well above average—Florence clearly inherited more than her fair share of them—but the lady she speaks to resembles royalty, her hair a stunning honey ginger wrapped up in eccentric braids that form a crown.

I curtsy deeply before them. Children are meant to be seen and not heard unless spoken directly to. I have co-existed with this rule for my whole life and right now is no different. My mouth remains closed as I stand behind Mother while she talks. Following along with a conversation and eavesdropping are two different things—in my opinion—so I see no harm in listening to what they are speaking of. Florence is vacant from the conversation, nowhere to be seen in the crowded room or hallway.

"There is a ladies' tea later this week. Thursday, I believe it is! My Lawrence and your Florence can meet properly. How perfectly splendid! The tea will be at Mel's Bakery next to the park, so they will be well supervised. We will have plenty of time to speak of the matter then. One o'clock sharp." Then, the short woman in the yellow dress intervenes in the conversation to whisper something to her, causing her to say, "If you will excuse me, Mrs. Stanton, I have to attend to an urgent matter." She must be Lawrence's mother! Even the way Mrs. Jones speaks is elegant, like she is soothing a child who has just fallen and scraped their knee.

"Of course, Mrs. Jones! It sounds splendid indeed," Mother answers in her best voice as Mrs. Jones hastily follows the host of the soiree into the crowd.

Sensing that we are about to leave—since we have found Florence's match—I speak quickly.

"Mother, may I say goodbye to a friend? It would be rude not to." I focus my eyes on Mother as she starts walking and searching around the room for my sister, who has been displaced in the crowd.

"What? Sure, Azalea. Make it quick," she replies, only half focused. I bow my head and push through shoulders and elbows to make it back to the room Evelyn is in. It does seem rude to not say goodbye to my only friend, but I also wish to ask if she will be attending the ladies' tea in the park that Mrs. Jones spoke of.

"Evelyn!" I yell as I break through the barrier of people flooding through the front door. Mrs. Jones and the host are trying their best to check everyone's invitations, but with the line of people waiting outside it will surely be impossible. This must be the urgent matter she had to leave for. It truly amazes me for a split second that so many people attend these soirées; maybe they are one of those city things that everyone knows and talks about.

"Azalea! I thought you had already left without saying goodbye!" Evelyn exclaims with a hint of hurt on her face.

"Of course not! I just wanted to ask if you are attending the ladies' tea in the park on Thursday? It will most likely be a boring and rigid affair, but it would be bearable if you came!" I shout above the gramophone, which is playing upbeat violin music.

"I shall have to ask my mom when I get the chance, but I estimate she will not pass up the opportunity. Do you want to come over to my house on Wednesday afternoon? We can play outside, and I wish to speak with you about something that I could use your advice about." She looks both ways to make sure the people entering the soirée do not hear.

There is something in her tone that makes me question what urgent yet secretive matter she could possibly need to talk about. I slowly nod, not knowing what kind of trouble I might be getting into by doing so. Evelyn scans the room, finding her target: a petite table holding a vase of red roses. She pulls open the drawer and digs around. Mother would have an absolute heart attack seeing me searching through someone's property without explicit permission, which somehow makes it more exhilarating! Mrs. Jones is occupied by all the guests, and nobody cares enough to notice two girls rummaging in a drawer next to the grand staircase. I act as a lookout to make sure no one—especially my mother, wherever she is—sees us.

"This is my address. Bring your mother when you come. She can keep my mom busy!" Evelyn says, hastily shoving the paper in my hand before walking away as if nothing happened.

Why would she want her mom to be occupied? The eerie feeling that there's more to this creeps over me. As if I am a foreign spy being handed the whereabouts of some valuable information, I tuck the little note in my pocket and rejoin my family.

Chapter 11

YOUR SIMPLE ELEGANCE CHARMS ME

MY LIPS REMAIN FASTENED TIGHTLY as we curtsy to the host, walk back to the hotel, and enter our hotel room. The rain begins downpouring just as we rush into the grand foyer. Thunder rumbles above as I shake droplets of water out of my dress at the door. Questions circulate in my head about why Evelyn wants my advice on something she clearly cannot tell anyone else about.

I am unexperienced in having friends. Nora was the sole person that I could count as a friend and look how that ended. Not to mention she is family, so that doesn't count. Florence and I have never been close; the barrier of competition has limited any bond that could be created. The children in Lorretta I once played with are strangers that most likely do not remember my name. For once I wish we would've had a schoolhouse. I could have met so many new people and learned so much more than what Mother taught us from her own knowledge.

I may not know much about having friends, but I do know that whatever Evelyn wants to talk about must involve lying, as she is being rather secretive about the whole thing. Lorretta has a church building, but the chapels here in Brockschmidt are positively beautiful—towering, painted white with holy glory, and complete with a shining wooden cross above each doorway. Unfortunately, Lorretta is a small town—if it could even be called that. A minister came through a few years back but did not stay as long as he had originally promised. We attended two services before the minister packed up to go somewhere more populated. "The Holy Spirit has guided me to another town where the children are in desperate need of God's grace and almighty knowledge," he had proclaimed whilst getting into a wagon. I whispered to Pa that it was most likely an excuse so that he could just go somewhere with more people to preach to. When Mother caught wind of my rather snooty remark, I was given a stern lecture of how sinful lying is and how "a man of the cloth follows the ten commandments by heart."

"Mother, a friend I met at the soirée—Evelyn Puffin—has graciously invited us to her house on Wednesday. She expressed that her mother wants to meet us, and Evelyn wishes to show me around her house." It is sinful to lie to anyone, especially one's parent. I silently pray, hoping God will forgive this one indiscretion. "Here is the address."

Mother gives an aggravated sigh as if listening to me for a moment took too much time away from Florence. She glances over the small piece of paper with a raised eyebrow. It is just a ripped-off corner of some fine parchment with an address written in black ink.

She unpins her tan hat, whose soft feather plume reminds me of a wealthy pirate. "Yes, I suppose it would be rude to not accept such a generous offer. The Puffins…Mrs. Jones mentioned them when we were talking…" Her eyes brighten, and her posture straightens. "The Puffins are very high society! Mrs. Jones spoke so fondly of Mrs. Puffin and how they often go over to each other's houses for tea. How perfectly splendid! We must start educating you on table manners. Oh, and your vocabulary!" She paces around the room, still holding onto the paper. Her hand gestures are frantic, but her voice is as calm as the ocean's waves on a windless day. The way she speaks about the Puffins is as if she's known them for ages and hadn't just learned about them in the past half hour.

I lift an eyebrow. "My vocabulary? My use of words is better than Florence's! I *profoundly* disagree. There is nothing wrong with my vocabulary." I fold my arms across my chest defensively.

"Azalea, there is truth in that, but here in the city you must learn to make sense of your *words.*" I squint my eyes, trying to determine what exactly she means. "You get so off topic! Florence will also be trained as fast as possible. We have all day tomorrow to prepare you both, then on Wednesday we visit Mrs. Puffin, and Thursday is the ladies' tea. I shall have to look for a dictionary somewhere around here. There was a bookshelf in the foyer downstairs. Azalea, you might turn out to be useful on this trip after all! Now girls, stay here, and I shall fetch the books!" Mother often thinks with her fingers, tapping her chin constantly. I have tried this method before to spark ideas, but it does nothing of the sort for me. She once again taps her fingers to her chin while speaking about how she's going to practically pound words into our heads over the next couple of days.

I glance over at Florence as Mother talks. She actually seems to be enjoying the idea of nonstop studying. I would be outvoted if I made any disagreeing remark about sitting inside all day tomorrow reciting words. I huff, admitting defeat as Mother races out of the hotel room in search of books.

It's very different to *want* to grow your knowledge versus having someone with power over you *forcing* you to do so. When I practiced difficult words to bring into conversations, it was mainly to compete with Florence. As the older child, you get a certain type of attention that the youngest doesn't receive. If you are the firstborn, you get the newest dresses and shoes that eventually get passed down to the next sibling in line—in this case, me—once they are outgrown. "Unappreciated" cannot possibly be in Florence's vocabulary because she has never experienced such a thing as being overlooked. Still, there is this rather nice part about being ignored: I can do whatever I want while she has to learn to sew and knit because she's older.

I contemplate the pros and cons of being the oldest and youngest child while walking to my room. It seems to be cleaner than it was this morning. The bed is freshly made, the many pillows on the bed have been fluffed and once again placed nicely on top, and the dirt from my dusty boots has been swept up from the gleaming floor. It is odd to have someone come into your room and clean up after you.

I pull open every drawer, searching for a paper until finally locating it in the drawer of the bedside table, then retrieve my fountain pen from my bag. With Florence in her room and Mother collecting the books, I kick off my shoes and curl up on the couch by the decorative fireplace. The raindrops patter against the windows, urging me to open them and smell the fresh scent of a midafternoon thunderstorm. 'Pride and Prejudice', one of my many personal favorites that I packed with me, provides a hard surface to steady my hand as I write. Still, my handwriting is rather messy and practically unreadable to someone that has never seen it before. An awful habit of mine is unintentionally tilting the paper diagonally and writing with my wrist bent awkwardly, making my words slanted at an angle.

Dear Pa,

Where do I begin? Oh Pa, this whole trip has not gone at all how we planned it! It would probably be better to tell you some of the details in person, for I fear that if you know it all, then you'll be sent into panic. Please do not fear because we are all perfectly healthy and safe. We just returned from the soirée…Pa, it was the most crowded place you could imagine and not to mention loud. I made a friend, Evelyn Puffin. She is so nice! She explained in detail the society they have here in Brockschmidt and what some words mean, like "mundane," for example, which is not referring to the one used in baking. Evelyn has invited Mother and me to her house on Wednesday, so as one would expect, Mother is thrilled. She has vowed to stuff our brains full of words suitable for conversation. Oh, and on Thursday we are all to attend a tea in the park. Guess what! Florence has already found a suitor. His name is Lawrence Jones. I suppose those soirée things actually have some sort of use to them! We are to meet him formally in the park at the tea. Mother has already talked to Mrs. Jones (she invited us to the tea), and she is the kindest, prettiest woman you could ever meet! We also met a young man named Russell St. Claire, but that story is for another time, preferably when we get back home. The buildings are so big here, the hotel is so peaceful, and my goodness is it deafening in the city! If I were not so plum-tuckered-out yesterday evening, I would have never fallen asleep. My greatest desire is for you to be here with us! I miss you, the quietness of home, my own room, the nature around our house, and especially Sense and Sensibility. That is all for now…I love and miss you.

P.S. how is Uncle Edward doing? I am sure he has found several things to talk about!

Love, Azalea

The ink flows from the fountain pen, signing the last "a" in my name as Mother barges into the hotel room. I leap to my feet, thinking something urgent has happened, but Mother is being overdramatic as usual.

"Girls!" she sings out as she kicks the door closed with her foot. The books make a loud banging sound as she plops them on top of the side table that is mere inches away from me. I grimace at the five books that are piled up high, all of them ranging from thick to thin. There is no excuse I can make now. I fold the letter, putting it in my pocket and making a mental note to ask Mother to mail it off later. Florence graciously enters the room, sitting down next to me on the couch. Mother, our self-appointed teacher, stands between us and the fireplace.

"Let's begin, shall we?" She thumbs through a few pages before finding a word. The title of the book is stamped into the spine: *Oxford English Dictionary*. Mother reads aloud, "Repeat after me: skilamalink."

"Skilamalink," we chorus back.

"The definition of skilamalink is 'secretive or doubtful.' Azalea, are you even paying attention?"

"Hmm? Oh, yes. Can I post this letter to Pa today? I don't have any envelopes or stamps here; I left my stationary box at home." I hold up the paper with my words to Pa written on it.

Mother gives me an annoyed side glance. "Yes, I can mail it later this afternoon. Now pay attention! This is important. We must make a good impression on Mrs. Puffin, Mrs. Jones, and the other ladies," she scolds.

After repeating approximately twenty words and their definitions, our lesson has still not ceased. We recite *esplanade*, *whinge*, *legerdemain*, and so many more useless ones until I have no clue which definition matches to each term.

"Now for posture! Florence, please stand. I want you to place these two books on your head and walk around balancing them! Azalea, you too. Follow along with Florence, please. No, no! Azalea, do not touch the books. They are meant to weigh your head down to teach you balance. Dear children, stop at once!" Mother cries as she bends to pick up the books that have just fallen from my head to their fourth death.

"Place the books on top of your head, right here, where your head rounds down." Mother demonstrates in front of us. "Keep your spine straight and your eyes looking forward, not at the ground! Simply glide from one footstep to another. See, it is as easy as that!" I am quite positive that she has used some sort of magic to keep the books on her head, as she takes several steps and the books do not fall off or even sway. Florence follows, instantly perfecting it almost as well as Mother has. I collapse on to the couch as they parade around the room.

Chapter 12

THIS IRIDESCENT CAGE

WEDNESDAY COULD NOT HAVE come soon enough! Mother mailed off my letter as promised, but she waited until yesterday evening, so my letter will not be picked up until this morning.

The rain is relentless, prevailing all night and most of the morning. Florence has been worried all morning about tomorrow's tea in the park. 'What if the rain does not stop and it gets canceled? What should I wear if it doesn't? What shall I talk about with Lawrence?' I make no comment on her inquiries because it would only end in me getting a scolding for increasing my sister's worries. Instead, I dressed, putting on the gown we made from the floral fabric I was gifted at Christmas so many months ago. To any other city girl, it would most likely appear a *mundane* dress, but I know Evelyn will agree that it is gorgeous! Evelyn seems to understand me so clearly. She is the first real friend I have ever had, and what a great friend she is! However, I cannot stop the questions regarding her secrecy from circulating through my head.

Within the next ten minutes Mother corrals the pair of us into the hallway proclaiming that we are 'already late' even though no declared time was set for us to arrive to the Puffins'. She walks next to me, perhaps rehearsing her instructions on how a young lady—in this case me, since Florence was not invited with us to Mrs. Puffin's house—should act when in the presence of a high-society woman.

"Are you alright, Mother? You seem awfully quiet. I am sure you and Mrs. Puffin will get along fine! I have not actually met her, but her daughter Evelyn is very agreeable! Evelyn told me all about the city girls at the soirée. My goodness, were they rude! You know what they called my Sunday best dress? Mundane! Also, Evelyn explained that mundane means ordinary." My mouth rambles on, every thought that pops into my mind is kept there for less than a second before exiting into the world.

Mother exhales, turns to face me, and holds my arm to stop me. Enormous raindrops hit the umbrella that she holds above us. "Azalea, I beg of you not to disrupt this Evelyn Puffin girl! She is high society, as is her family, so she ought to be well-taught in matters of etiquette and man-ners. You, however, are not well-taught in either of those. Do not ramble on and bore the poor girl to death. Behave perfectly in front of Mrs. Puffin, wait until she invites us inside, and then follow her instructions. Do you understand, child?"

Hooves clop on the cobblestone street next to us. The streets are rela-tively busy despite it being such a rainy day. A man dashes to the opposite side of the street, trying to escape the droplets pouring from the sky. The rain seems to bring out an awful smell in the city that makes me want to cover my nose.

A silent nod is enough of an answer to Mother, so she continues walking. Quickening my pace so as to not be left without the protection of the umbrella, I keep up stride with her.

As we walk past the house that held the soirée, the neighborhood only seems to spread out more and more. The houses become more lav-ish; the yards become bigger inside their fenced-in barriers. In the middle of the five houses on the street that branches off into the distance is the address of Evelyn Puffin. The houses surrounding it make it even more grand than it already is; giving one the impression of just how wealthy the

Puffins really are. Big iron gates tower above us, and a man stands on the other side. This man does not seem to mind the rain that is soaking his gray uniform.

"Name?" his scruffy voice demands.

"Margaret and Azalea Stanton." It is not that often that I hear Mother being called by her given name, so for a moment it strikes me as odd to hear it. Now that I think about it, I only ever hear Mother's name once or twice a year.

The iron gates squeak open, and we are directed down the long pathway to the French-style doors at the front of the stately house. Despite the rain, workers are sweeping, washing windows, and removing old flowers from the flowerbeds. I glance at Mother's face to find that she is almost as astounded as I am.

Evelyn Puffin told me when we first met that her family is rich and that she's often persecuted for that reason alone, but I cannot fathom why! Surely, any girl would attempt to gain Evelyn's friendship so that she could gain popularity, so why do they avoid her? So far, Evelyn seems pleasant, but is there another side to her? When we talked at the soirée, she seemed…normal, like we were one and the same. The house she lives in comes with status, servants, and popularity, and it is twice the size of my home. What could be so bad about all of that? I tuck these thoughts and sizzling questions into my mind. I will have to resurface them later to ask her.

Mother holds her skirts up as she walks up the shining white front steps and stands at the French doors where she places our umbrella. "It's nice, isn't it?" I whisper. She nods, quietly closing her mouth that was open in awe.

Perhaps it is her mission to not have me think vain thoughts or want more than what God has already handed us, but it's undeniable that this place has everything you could ever want for and more! Mother clears her throat, giving a polite knock that rattles the windows nearby. My eyes examine the house exactly as I did at the soirée. I want to remember every centimeter of this moment so I may revisit it sometime in the future. There are two windows on each wall facing the iron gates where the streets lay beyond. The foyer is just barely visible through the glass panes of the French doors, its classic beauty is undeniable. The garden out front is enviable. A snaking pathway travels from the front gates to the front steps, with flower beds on either side of them. An archway with snaking vines and blossoming flowers wrapped around it leads somewhere to the backyard, and all of this—the house, the pathway leading up to it, and the grass around it—is caged in by a stone wall about my height. It's unbelievably perfect! I suppose the massive unemployment last year had zero effect on rich city people.

The sound of clicking heels comes forth from somewhere inside as a woman walks around the corner. The woman—who I assume is none other than Mrs. Puffin, for she is not dressed as plainly as the workers that are outside—swiftly opens the door with a smile. With the numerous servants I am quite shocked that Mrs. Puffin would open her front door, but the thought is shaken away.

"Hello! You must be Mrs. Stanton. Evelyn told me you were coming today! Oh my goodness, you must be Azalea! What a pretty dress you have on! The fabric is so exquisite yet sensible," she coos in admiration. My smile becomes even brighter knowing somebody as important as Mrs. Puffin admires the dress that the other city girls would likely mock and label as dull.

I curtsy quickly and blush at the fact that I forgot Mothers instructions to do so sooner. "Thank you, Mrs. Puffin," I say clearly enough for her to hear. Without looking at Mother I could feel her embarrassment of me. Maybe she is secretly wishing that Florence was invited along instead of me.

"Pleasure to meet you, Mrs. Puffin!" Mother says with a saccharine smile, waiting for Evelyn's mother to invite us inside.

Perhaps Mrs. Puffin notices the subtle hint or just by her good nature decides to exclaim at once, "The pleasure is all mine! Please, do come inside. Azalea, Evelyn should be upstairs in her room. It is up the stairs and down the hall to your right. Mrs. Stanton, I had some refreshments prepared for us this morning!" All in one minute Evelyn's mother has invited us inside, given me not only permission but directions to go upstairs, and offered food to Mother! The stiff formality that has existed in almost all the city folk in which I have become acquainted with, does not linger within Mrs. Puffin, for she is the embodiment of sunshine.

The French front doors swing open to mahogany floors with a small table and empty vase next to an archway that leads you further into the house. After curtsying again, I travel up the nearby staircase. I run my hand up the banister as I hike up the steps without missing a detail. The stairs are covered in fluffy tan carpet that urges me to take off my shoes and feel it with my bare feet. I round the corner and walk to the end of the hallway as instructed before finally reaching a bright blue door that stands out from the other white doors in the hall.

I softly knock and jump at the echo it makes. "Evelyn? It's me, Azalea."

The blue door swings inward. "Azalea! Thank goodness you came. Is your mother downstairs with my mom?" I nod quickly, eager to get the greetings over with so we can discuss the secretive matter that has been consuming my thoughts since the soirée. "Good. Please, come in!" she offers, walking away from the open door.

Her room is almost as big as the loft in our barn! Blue is definitely Evelyn's favorite color; it has been plastered everywhere from the dark blue walls to the teal blankets on the bed. Her room is also covered in the fluffy carpet form the stairs. I suddenly notice that Evelyn is walking around barefoot in her room, so I slip off my shoes too, placing them neatly by the door.

"Evelyn, your room is so…beautiful!" I whisper in awe as my feet touch the carpet and I gaze around even more. On her desk lie newspaper clippings with illustrations of expensive dresses, a photograph capturing the sight of a city with some weird structure that sits on four legs and points up to a starry sky, and a drawing of a person who looks like Evelyn. Numerous books remain tucked into their place on a bookshelf that covers half of the wall. I skim my fingertips along the shelf while my eyes read the titles printed on the spines of Evelyn's books. One book in particular stands out to me the most. I notice the leather spine as I pull it off the shelf. The other books beside it fall into its place. The cover of the rather large book has a sketch of little boys and girls outside of a sod house. I read the printed words that sit below the drawing aloud. "*Uncle Tom's Cabin.*"

"Hmm? Ah yes, *Uncle Tom's Cabin* was the book that started the Civil War. That is what my mom says, anyway. I read it a few years ago when I got it for my fourteenth birthday. It was very enrapturing! That book has both volumes one and two in it, so you do not have to buy both of them separately. You can have the book if you want. I am not into reading as much as I once was," Evelyn admits, half-interested in the subject. I turn, amazed at her generosity. She stares at me, serious about the offer, as she settles down in the middle of the floor.

"Thank you! I have never been gifted a book before by anybody but my family. Did I tell you that my sister is to start courting? His name seems to have slipped my mind…the last name is Jones." Evelyn gasps loudly, causing me to stop talking altogether and wonder what made her inhale that much air.

"Your sister is courting a Jones?!"

"Yes, I just said that. Lawrence! That is his name: Lawrence Jones. We are to meet him tomorrow at the ladies' tea in the park! Why?" I raise an eyebrow as Evelyn collects her thoughts before releasing them to me.

"Well, the Joneses are very popular. Lawrence has attended two engagement seasons including the current one! He does not seem like the marrying type, if you catch my meaning," she mumbles loudly enough for me to hear. I do not catch her meaning, but I am not quite sure if I want to. Mother and I will meet Lawrence tomorrow, and I do not want gossip to soil his image. He may, after all, become my brother-in-law.

Wanting to change the subject, I speak of the first thing that comes to mind. "I had a question I thought of while walking here." Evelyn nods, bringing forth my thoughts that fly out of my mouth unfiltered. "Your house is so bewildering and amazing! At the soirée you said the other city girls judge you harshly for being rich. But I mean, look at all this!" I announce, gesturing around the room. "Do excuse my ignorant question, but I just don't know how there could be anything horrible about this?"

Evelyn eyes scan the room anxiously as her cheeks turn pink. She turns her face away, hiding from my stare. I blush from shock when she turns back to me in tears. "You do not understand, Azalea. Although this extravagance seems wonderful—not to say that the servants, prepared sandwiches, generous amounts of space, and enough money to buy any-thing your heart desires is horrible—time after time I have been used because of it and have felt trapped by it all! That is part of what I wanted to talk to you about." Her slow tears bemuse me. Even though I have never experienced riches like this, I can see that there is some sort of truth to her words, to why she could feel trapped by the pressure. "The other city girls are jealous of this. I have been wrapped into fake friendships just so that they can brag about being friends with 'the rich princess of Brockschmidt, Wyoming.' The constant attention is overwhelming! I can barely just be myself out of fear that no one will like me!" I sit on the floor, facing her as she wipes the tears away messily.

"I am sorry. My ignorance! Mother has often scolded me for it; now I understand why," I say with a laugh. Evelyn sniffles a laugh as well, for-getting what happened as we sit in silence for a moment.

"Anyway," she says, wiping away a delayed tear that spills out of her eye. "I invited you here because I trust you more than anyone else.

My sisters aren't in their bedrooms right now, which is rare. Jean and Katherine are in the backyard practicing their French, and Elizabeth is out shopping for a dress. I arranged all of this today by telling my mom that Jean's French needed work. So Mom directly instructed Katherine to help her study. Oh, and Elizabeth's dress happened to 'tear.' I do feel guilty about that, along with telling a lie about it. Azalea, you seem like a very circumspect person, so I request that you seriously consider what I am about to ask of you!" Evelyn inspects the room and lowers her voice as if someone is secretly listening. I have no idea what circumspect means, but it does not sound bad, so I nod, wanting her to continue. "I need to make a sort of…peregrination out of the city. At the soirée, when you spoke of how you have no intention of getting married at this age…when you saw my reaction to it, I was positive you could see my intentions!"

"Intentions? About what? I had just assumed you thought differently on the matter."

"I am going to tell you something, and you must swear to keep it a secret! I need you to be completely honest with me about it, though, because it probably sounds foolish." Anxiety begins gnawing away at me as Evelyn hesitates, twiddling her hands. "I have been planning to run away to marry the love of my life, Percy Willards. He's lived next door to me for four years, but we only started talking two years ago. For the past year and a half, we have been secretly courting!"

My mouth pops wide open and only seems to grow with every word Evelyn says. Running away! To be married at sixteen! There's no doubt that it is incredibly romantic, dangerous, and downright insane! "I do not understand. Why can you not just get married here? Why would you elope?"

Evelyn's eyes seem to glow at the thought of this Percy Willards. "Well…the thing is, my family has forbidden us to be together because they want me to marry higher up on the social ladder and spend my days talking with the other ladies about boring topics and ordering servants to clean my house! I need your help, please. You are the only person that has looked at me as a friend and not because of how much money my parents have. Help me run away! If I don't get out now, I never will!" She grabs my hands, begging me profusely to aid her.

Considering she told me this after meeting me two days ago, fully knowing that if I disagree, I could march downstairs and tell her mother, the amount of trust she has in me is enormous. But what will I tell her mother when she realizes her daughter has mysteriously disappeared? It would be a violation of my morals to agree to this, but it might be an even bigger violation to refuse.

"What's the plan? You will need money and a place to go, preferably outside of Wyoming, and your mother mustn't know anything about this, right? How romantic! Like a modern re-telling of Shakespeare's *Romeo and Juliet*!" I note, rushing to grab a piece of paper and pencil off her desk. "We must map everything out. You two will only have one shot at this. If someone finds out or sees you escaping, your parents will never let you see him again." My hands go to work, mapping out the city from what I remember of the ride in on the stagecoach, walking to the soirée, and walking here to Evelyn's.

"Oh, I am so glad you have agreed! Thank you, Azalea, you really are the truest friend. I solemnly swear that you will not be found responsible for my disappearance!" She holds up her right hand while swearing her allegiance.

"I shall do everything in my power to help you, Evelyn Puffin, run away," I promise with utmost loyalty while mirroring Evelyn's posture. For a few moments, we sit with our right hands parallel, palms out, a bond of friendship growing between us, until Evelyn breaks the silence at last.

"I have all my savings; it is about six months' worth. Percy will surely have money saved, too." She gets up, walking over to a book on the shelf. Flipping it open to a certain page, Evelyn dumps out the bills on the floor. She bends down, counting out the money and folding it neatly. "Ten dollars!"

My eyes bulge at the sight of that much money. "Ten dollars," I repeat in awe. Then my mind snaps back to attention. We surely have no more than an hour to have this plan set in motion. I understand now why Mother was to come along with me; we need a distraction to keep Evelyn's mother occupied. "The train will be faster than hitching a ride or stagecoach. How far is the train station? We passed the train tracks on our way here, so it must be close."

"Seven blocks, maybe? You are right about the train. If only I'd thought of that sooner! Say, how do you know so much about this?" She pauses, giving me a quizzical expression.

I grin childishly. "Let's just say I have read about it in a few books. Of course, I have never thought of running away myself, but it is quite interesting to read about!" I admit with a laugh.

After thirty minutes, we have formed a proper plan to execute this escape flawlessly. The next step is for me to sneak down to the servants' quarters, which has a kitchen and rooms that are accessible by ladder. Evelyn goes downstairs beforehand, and I follow a moment later, quiet as a mouse.

"May I bring some food up to my room? Azalea has never tasted oranges before and wants to try some!" Evelyn's voice follows our script perfectly. She was to ask her mother for food both as a distraction—so I could duck into the servants' quarters—as a way to collect food for her journey.

Tiptoeing across the floors is no easy task but one that I eventually master by the time I arrive at a white-painted door with a silver knob. To anyone this would seem like a closet door, but when opened it reveals a ladder that leads down into a dimly lit room. I follow my instructions directly. I need to close the door, descend the ladder to the below-ground kitchen, then locate a servant's bedroom to steal clothes for Percy and Evelyn.

My bare feet hit the tile with a cold smack as I shiver from the chilly air. A single lightbulb dangles from the ceiling, but otherwise there are no candles or windows to allow light. The walls down here are made of brick stones, so no sound will be able to travel upstairs where Mother sits talking.

"Servant's bedrooms," I repeat over and over, looking for them. A few feet in front of the ladder is a wooden table adorned with pots, pans, fruits, and vegetables. Against the wall on the other side of the room stand two stoves and a water pump.

Suddenly, the door opens, alerting me that someone is coming. Panicked, I whip to the left and see a doorway. I dash through it into to a room with three doors on each side of me. To the right the doors are painted bright blue and to the left they are a faded pink. Across the room from the doorway is a washroom. I quickly race inside the first pink door. Footsteps on the ladder echo, bouncing off the stone walls as I slide the door shut.

I press my ear to the door, listening for any sign of the person that climbed down the ladder, but there is nothing. The door swings open, sending me flying to the tile floor with a pathetic smack. I lie spread out at someone's feet in defeat. My eyes glance up, embarrassed, but I find Evelyn's face looking down at me and holding back a laugh.

"What ever are you doing?" she asks, helping me off the floor.

"You said to find the servants' bedrooms! I assumed you might be someone coming back to retrieve something from the kitchen, so I hid in the room and was listening for a sound," I admit while rubbing the arm that I fell on.

"Azalea, you are quite the character! I was supposed to ask my mom for oranges as a snack, so I did. Where do you think we would get the oranges from?" She gestures to the other room where the table has fruits piled on top it. "All of the servants are busy working right now, so no one will come down here until the day is over."

"Oh," I say, my cheeks glowing red. "Well, come on! We do not have much time! You get clothes for Percy, and I will find something for you." We exchange a nod and disperse to rummage through the trunks.

I reach up into the darkness until I feel a lightbulb and a metal cord hanging from it. I pull the cord, and it the light flickers twice before glowing with electricity. I shall never overcome my amazement when it comes to electricity! Each of the servants' bedrooms is only big enough for a bed, a small trunk, and a few square feet of open space. How awful it must be to live in such a small room with no space to even breathe!

The first servant's dress is too big for Evelyn, the second's too small, and the last has no spare clothes for us to use. Evelyn finds a pair of trousers and a shirt for Percy, but we are still left at a dead end. Evelyn will either have to go in an extremely baggy dress or a tight one, either of which would make movement impossible as she tries to make her escape. I look around for another option but cannot find one. Evelyn is much taller than me and has more weight than me, but it's not as if she is so plump that we cannot find anything for her. I debate whether or not to give her my dress made from the fabric I was gifted on Christmas, but it would be too suspicious for me to go back home wearing a different dress or to have Evelyn spotted while running away in my dress. That would definitely link me to her disappearance.

"I am almost positive these will fit him. What do you think? Percy is the same height as me, but he is very muscular," she asks, holding up the trousers and shirt. Suddenly, a brilliant idea pops into my head.

I run to the man's trunk from where Evelyn pulled the trousers, grabbing the other pair, then go to the next room for a bigger shirt. "Perfect!" I whisper to myself while holding up the outfit to Evelyn.

"I already got the clothes for Percy. What are those for?" she questions as I take the clothes out of her hands.

"Shhhh! They may hear you." I keep my voice low. Evelyn's hand flies to her mouth as we wait for several moments, trying to hear if someone is coming. "These clothes are for you too! If you are spotted, someone will assume you are a boy. It is absolutely splendid! Quick, you must grab the oranges, apples, and loaf of bread. Can you get in contact with Percy so we may give the clothes to him?"

She follows along with my words, grabbing the food and wrapping it in a red-checkered cloth. "Yes, we developed a code a few months ago so that we may met each other when no one is watching. The only problem is that we always meet at the gazebo in the backyard, but that is where the twins are studying French right this very minute! Our windows face each other; perhaps we could find a way to give him the clothes and information that way?" I consider the idea and promptly agree. We could contemplate it more, but first we have to sneak back to Evelyn's room before anyone realizes we are gone.

The ladder creaks as we climb up, the door closes quietly, and the carpet softens our footsteps as we sneak back to the room. I can hear Mother's sharp voice asking Mrs. Puffin about the flowerbeds outside, and I feel confident that this conversation alone will allow us enough time. If I did not know any better, I would assume that Mother is in on our plan since she's kept Mrs. Puffin occupied for so long.

Once we arrive back in the haven of Evelyn's room, phase two of our plan commences.

We peer out the window for a moment until Evelyn sees him inside. "That is Percy's window right there. Oh, I see him! He appears to be reading. Do you mind grabbing that rope?"

Rope? I look around my feet until I notice that something is sticking out from under the bookshelf. The four inches between the carpet and bottom shelf are just enough for me to reach my hand through and pull the rope out. It is downright genius!

Evelyn reaches over to her desk, scribbling the information on a paper. Then she pokes a small hole in the corner with a pencil and loops a piece of ribbon through the hole to tie the paper to the rope. The space between the two windows is only about seven feet, so the rope will easily reach. The window squeaks open as I push it up and hold it for Evelyn.

"Can you also hand me one of those pebbles? Thank you, Azalea!" A quick glance to the right reveals a handful of small, smooth rocks sitting on a few papers on the desk. I noticed them earlier and wondered what she possibly could use them for, but my question is now answered by her actions.

With a winding toss, the first pebble hits the wall about a foot away from Percy's window before falling to the ground. The second one hits the window with a small tap, alerting him to look over at us. Evelyn waves urgently, and he promptly opens his window.

"Evelyn? What are you doing? Who is that with you?" he whispers while gesturing to me. Percy is certainly not the handsomest boy but is definitely one of the best-looking boys I have ever seen. Even from where I stand holding up the window, I can tell he has an admirable face, is very tall, and is a skinny boy for his age. No wonder Evelyn has fallen for him! He of course cannot compare to Russell St. Claire, but I shake the thought away before any more ideas come to my mind.

"This is Azalea. She is going to help us escape! Do not worry; you can trust her. We've already made the most splendid plan. I'm going to throw the rope over with a paper tied to it." Percy glances over at me again with skepticism. I offer a small wave, but he does not return it. Well, clearly his manners could use a bit of work!

She gently tossed the rope, and Percy caught it quickly, untying the note whose contents I assume have something to do with the servants' clothes and train station where we will all meet later today. He nods to no one in particular, looking around his room. I wonder how often they have spoken of this moment, the one when they can finally be together forever? Evelyn has most definitely considered this a great deal, or else she would not have so much money saved.

"The clothes, Evelyn! He mustn't be seen walking out of his house in any clothes but the servant's!" Evelyn looks down at the first pair of boy's clothes that lies by our feet.

"Percy, wait! Here are the servant's clothes we got. Azalea says to put them on. Try not to let anyone see you! We are to meet at the train station within the next hour. Azalea will help us from there. Be careful, my love!" After verifying that all of Evelyn's instructions were correct, I give a nod of approval. She tosses the clothes individually without dropping any. Percy nods once more, then disappears into his room. I make a mental note to tell Percy to cover his platinum blonde hair, which is sure to make him stand out otherwise.

"You must hurry and dress. If we only have an hour before the three o'clock train, we must use our time wisely," I explain.

The train schedule is foreign to me, but Evelyn informs me that the three o'clock train has never been more than five minutes late, so we have to rush to make it on time. The door closes behind me as I step out of her room and into the hallway so she can change. My ears listen closely to every sound coming from downstairs or any of the other rooms in the hallway. As far as I can tell, all her sisters are still occupied, and our mothers are still engulfed in conversation.

This whole situation is absurd! Me helping a city girl—one I'd only met two days ago—run away with her secret love! How I wish I could tell Pa about this, but nothing can ever link me to the disappearance of Percy Willards and Evelyn Puffin, two kids from Brockschmidt's richest and most popular families. There must be more to the story for the Puffins to not approve of the Willards family, but I would never directly ask Evelyn for fear of stirring up unpleasant memories.

A moment later, Evelyn opens the door to her room so I can examine her disguise. Covering my mouth with my hands, I have to hold back a laugh at the sight of her. Instead of her fancy day dress, she is clothed in dark brown trousers that halt before her ankles due to her tallness, a baggy black shirt that hides her bosom, a matching black cap that her hair is tucked into, and brown boots that I have never seen before.

"How do I look?" She laughs, spinning in her room with outstretched arms.

"I barely even recognize you! You do appear to be a worker boy, practically the spitting image of one. The only problem is your face. If anyone looks at you directly, they will recognize you."

"What about charcoal? We could dirty me up a bit. Jean has a small fireplace in her room," she offers. I imagine Evelyn's face with streaks of black on it. Of course, the charcoal will not perform miracles, but it would make sure she does not look like a rich city girl.

"Yes, that shall do nicely! You will have to put it on because it will stain my fingerprints and my mother shall notice." In these cases, one must think outside the box. I know Mother would notice if my fingertips were black, then ask how they came to be like that. Lying is not something I do regularly nor with much ease. I pull on my shoes, then followed Evelyn to Jean's room.

Each of the sisters must have color-coordinated rooms. Evelyn's is decorated with a range of blues, and Jean's is yellow. The bare walls are painted the color of sunshine. A bed has been pushed into the left corner, a trunk and side table with a lamp next to it. A fireplace sits cold in the middle of the wall next to a window that looks outside. Jean's room is smaller but definitely messier than Evelyn's. Several books lie in piles along the floor, open to pages written in foreign languages. Papers containing pronunciations, notes, drawings, and mathematical equations are scattered haphazardly. A desk stands near the fireplace, purposely away from the window, with even more stuff on it! From this alone I get the impression of just how studious Evelyn's sister really is. I watch Evelyn as she bends down, brushing her fingertips amongst the coals and instantly turning the tips black.

"I would have never imagined that this day would actually come!" she says, laughing as she wipes the coal dust on her cheeks and upper brow. "Do not get me wrong, I have contemplated this a number of times.

It's just something that I sadly thought would never happen. How do I look now?"

A laugh escapes my lips at the sight of this girl that I met at a soirée wearing a fancy dress now wearing a boy's outfit with a face streaked in coal dust.

"Nobody will ever be able to recognize you now," I remark proudly. Yes, this situation will cause me to lie, deceive, and help my friend elope—going against everything I have been taught about what is respectable and proper—but it is exciting in an odd sort of way. "I guess this means I'll have to attend the ladies' tea without you tomorrow. What a shame! At least you can be free and no longer a bird trapped in a cage, even if it is a quite beautiful enclosure."

"It really is, isn't it? You seem to match words so well to one's circumstance. I just want to say—before we really go through with this—how thankful I am to you! Percy and I are forever in your debt! I suppose we will go down south. Percy always spoke so highly of learning some sort of trade, but I think I would like to open a store of some sorts. There are, after all, so many things I have never experienced and a world out there to see!" Evelyn holds a glowing amount of gratefulness in her eyes when she speaks to me. She really is a bird finally being set free to fly away as far as she pleases.

"Of course! I wish you both the best of luck in your future together." I look around, running over to Jean's desk and writing on the corner of a blank page. Ripping off the corner on which I'd written, I hand the piece to her. "Here is my address back in Lorretta. Send a letter once you are safe, under a different name."

"I will, Azalea. Thank you." She engulfs me in a hug that I gladly reciprocate. I shall always cherish the memory of my first real friend, Evelyn Puffin, who treated me with such kindness. She is truly a kindred spirit.

Chapter 13

DEPARTURE INTO A LIFE OF THE UNKNOWN

EVELYN STAYS SHUT IN HER ROOM as Mother and I kindly depart. The rain is downpouring down from the gray clouds above. The hem of my dress is soon soaked, and my boots squeak with every step I take. My mission to meet Percy and Evelyn at the train station pulses in my mind with every breath. Mother is quiet as usual, focused on tomorrow's itinerary. Not a word is uttered until we reach the hotel lobby. The lady behind the counter is nowhere to be seen. Another woman sits on a chair near the doors that lead to the path and greenhouse. She flips through a book, constantly stopping to peer outside.

Mother shakes the raindrops out of the umbrella and abandons it at the doorstep. *Uncle Tom's Cabin*, the book Evelyn gave to me, remains safe in my hand.

"Mother?" I whisper to her as she steps inside. My heart pounds rapidly in my chest. Evelyn and Percy are most likely already on their way to the train station, but I cannot tell Mother this, so the greenhouse seems like an acceptable excuse. "May I spend some time in the greenhouse? It is such a nice image outside when it rains. I've never been in a greenhouse while it is raining before! Please, Mother? May I?" I plead, grasping my hands together.

Mother is rather young to have two teenage daughters, but some days she looks much older than she really is. She has no wrinkles nor frown lines, unless she raises her eyebrows up, which she does now.

"Why in the world would you want to go outside in the pouring rain? What an odd child you are sometimes, Azalea." She rubs the spot between her brows as I await her answer.

What would the pair of them—Percy and Evelyn—do if I am unable to accompany them at the train station? Would they wait for me and surely be caught, or would they attempt to leave? I am no expert in running away, but I know for sure that if you don't have help, it makes it ten times harder to escape.

"Fine. You may go sit in the greenhouse; this will at least give me some time to ready your sister for the ladies' tea tomorrow. Take a coat so you do not catch your death in that coldness!" Mother calls after me, but as soon as I heard her agreement, I dashed up the stairs to our room.

Florence opens the door after I repeatedly knock. Slipping past her, I set my book down on the bed, tug my coat on, then skip out the door and back down to the lobby.

Mother walks softly up the stairs as I run down them, skipping at least three steps at the end. The sound of thunder rolls above as the French doors swing open. Without bothering to grab the umbrella, I twirl into the downpour, feeling free for a moment before I remember my mission. Walking past the greenhouse—which seems to call my name, yearning for my presence—I follow Evelyn's directions to the train station, which she gave to me not long before I departed from her house. I stroll through alleyways and along the street, looking everywhere for the station.

"Are you lost, little girl? Do you need help?" A scruffy man asks, taking my wrist in his dirty hands. The smell of him burns my nose with every panicked breath my lungs take in.

"No, sir. I am perfectly content. Please unhand me!" I shriek, hoping someone will see my struggle and help me. His grip remains steadfast and only seems to tighten as I try to pull away. My strength quivers, and I start tiring easily as he remains standing.

His few crooked teeth show as he talks with slurred speech. "What a pretty thing you are! 'Content.' Odd word, that is. Where are you trying to go, little miss?"

An image fills my mind. The robber stands in front of me, running his finger down my face as if to feel my blood pulsing before he kills us. His breath is next to me. Dark black eyes are all I can see, his face hidden by the bandana.

I will not stand here again and let myself be put in mortal danger! My eyes focus on the man as he tugs my arm, trying to pull me away from the street. A wagon driver goes by without noticing my panicked expression. If I scream, what would this man do?

My knee jerks up, hitting the man in the groin. He collapses the ground, letting me go. His arms grasp his stomach as he lies scrunched up in a ball. He yells foul words that make my ears ignite and gazes at me poisonously with the devil in his eyes.

I quickly look around, watching as people start to notice a grown man lying on the ground with a girl standing over him. My legs start moving before my mind can comprehend what has just happened. Refusing to stop for anything, not the questions from women that calmly walk past me or the people that I nearly collide with, I run. Before long, the rain slows, and when I finally skid to a stop at the train station, I am soaked to the bone.

My eyes skim the faces of the people waiting on the platform by the train tracks. A girl my age stands nearby, constantly glancing up at the clock that hangs above the doors to enter the station building. The train is due any minute.

A woman cradles a crying baby, trying her best to rock it to sleep. A little boy dressed in a suit runs around his mother's skirt, trying to tag his older sister. A man perches on a bench, reading the newspaper, and two boys sit across from him. For a second, I almost keep walking, but I notice a familiar black strand of hair sticking out of one of the boys' caps. I quickly sit down beside them in the most normal way possible, looking around to make sure no more attention is brought to me.

"Were you able to get the train tickets?" I mumble, not daring to take my eyes off the train tracks.

"No, the conductor in there will recognize us instantly. He has been working at this train station for a long time, and my family has bought their fair share of tickets from him when we travel," a small voice whispers to me. "You can come with us if you would like. I know the circumstances aren't ideal, and we will all most likely be poor, but think of the adventures we'll have!"

My breath catches in my throat for a split second. Here Evelyn is, offering me a way out, out of always being the disappointment and the runner-up to my sister. A way to follow my dream and go west, where I won't have to abide by anybody's rules or regulations. A way to feel the prairie grasses against my hands and see the ocean on the western coastline roaring with power and slamming into rocks. A way to witness with my own eyes a herd of bison stampeding across the land, to move to a lovely, close-knit town, and to be led by my own freewill.

What about my family? I have not hesitated for a moment to think of all that Percy and Evelyn are giving up just to be free and together, which only makes it all the more romantic. My heart beats with the love I hold for my family; could I really forget that just to follow my own desires? Some might say it is a moral quandary, the second one I've found myself stuck in today. And this moral quandary requires a decision, and a rather tough one at that.

My eyes search the platform, rapidly thinking. The seconds seem to tick by slower, as if the world and time itself have stopped spinning. If I went with Evelyn and Percy, I would never see Florence married and walking down the aisle in the white dress that I would help make. I would forever miss Mother teaching me to sew, Pa watching the cows graze…

brushing my hair at my vanity back in my room…all the small but beautiful moments in my life that make it perfect the way it is. Even though new memories, friendships, and perfect places would be created if I went with Evelyn and Percy, how much would I lose just trying to achieve something that could hypothetically happen—a perfect life out west? And even though only a moment passes by in the time that a million thoughts of the future whirl through my head, I realize that this is not a future I truly want!

"I am sorry, but I cannot. It would be a wonderful adventure to travel alongside you both, nevertheless, I would never forgive myself for leaving my family worried about what happened and would become of me. Best of luck to you both on your life together, and Godspeed. I will get the tickets for you."

"It's okay. Here are five dollars. Please hurry, Azalea! The train is due soon!" The five dollar bills are shoved into my hands. The paper is smooth from the many hands that it has probably touched in its lifetime.

The clock shows that the train is two minutes late as I push my way through the doors and into the station building. I locate the old man, who I assume is the conductor, standing behind iron bars just like the ones at the postal office and stagecoach station. I clear my throat, and the old man's blue eyes glance up at me from the papers that he is reading.

"Well? Where to?"

My mind tries its best to figure out what he means, but I come up short-handed. He blinks, pointing to the board hanging next to me. The list isn't that long, and the handful of destinations on it are not familiar to me. The name Boulder, Colorado, rings a bell in my mind, so I instantly say it aloud. The man gazes at me as if I am an annoying child that will not stop talking. The whistle of a train rings throughout the station as all the people on the platform lean forward simultaneously.

"Two tickets, please." I slap the bills on the counter, sliding them under the bars. The man tells me the cost of the tickets, but I am not paying him any attention.

The train squeals to a stop as its bell rings three times. People begin to rush off the train as the conductor steps outside, ready to punch holes in everyone's tickets. I watch this from the window and can clearly see Percy's worried expression. I look down, seeing my change and two gleaming tickets on the counter.

"Thank you, sir!" I dash out of the station building, grabbing Evelyn and Percy on my way to the platform. I skid to a halt at the back of the small line of people climbing aboard the train.

"Your tickets," I offer. "Make sure to get off the train before the next stop. When people start searching for you, the first place they will look is the train schedule from today. Please stay safe, both of you." Not wanting to risk it, I do not wrap them both in a hug but instead imagine it in my head. Their eyes shine like a thousand suns as they nod, and Evelyn whispers another thank you. Percy shakes my hand, and I take my leave, stepping away from the line and walking back to the street, constantly glancing back at the two of them.

The conductor watches as they step forward. He glances at Evelyn, who is looking down at the ground and holding their food wrapped up in the handkerchief, and Percy, who also refuses to peer at him directly in the eyes. In a quick motion, he grabs the tickets from Percy, verifies they are real, punches a hole in each, and then moves on to the next person in line. Their faces adorned with shock, the couple dressed as poor worker boys steps onto the train, and into their future. Through the train's glass window, I can just make out the image of them both sitting down on one of the plush chairs. In my head, the truth shows as if written in the sky by God himself: I made the right decision in staying.

The train lets out a high-pitched whistle, which is followed by a slow forward movement along the tracks. Raindrops cease as the gray clouds roll away, revealing their fluffy white tops, and sunshine smiles again on the world. In the distance is a small rainbow showing God's promise to never flood the world again. The puddles on the streets gleam with light from the sky as horses trot along and wagons rattle past me. My wet shoes squeak all the way back to the hotel, and my dress is heavy from the water it holds. Even though the sunshine is warm against my face, I shiver from the coldness of my wet clothes. The greenhouse looks positively radiant in the sunshine after a rainfall, but I have already spent too much time away from the hotel room. I press my fingers to my lips and blow a kiss to the greenhouse as I enter the hotel, dripping water.

"Dear child! Azalea, why, you're soaked to the bone! Please tell me you did not go galivanting in the rain! Let us get you into warmer clothes before you catch a cold. We cannot have you sniffling all day tomorrow at the ladies' tea," Mother exclaims loudly when she opens the hotel room door. Florence jumps up from the purple couch, where she was reading one of the dictionaries, to help tug my soaked jacket off me.

Teeth chattering, I peel off my wet dress and change into my night-gown, which is still wrinkled from being jammed in my bag. Exhausted from today's events, I collapse on the feather bed in my room and fall into a deep slumber, leaving my dress in a puddle on the floor next to my bed.

⸺

My eyes open several hours later to darkness as my stomach rumbles within me. I can see that it is well into the evening now, as the sun has dipped below the buildings in the distance, leaving only a trace of light shining into my room. I pull myself out of the warm, comfortable bed, my feet slowly touching the cold tile floor. I step around my wet dress, which lies in a crumpled heap on the floor, and walk into the main space of our hotel room. Florence once again sits on the purple couch eating from a china plate, mainly focused on a book labeled *Proper Etiquette of a Lady*.

I look sleepily at the silver cart next to the door that holds platters covered by silver dishes. Uncovering one platter reveals a china plate with gold vines around the rim of it and an array of delicious-smelling foods. Mashed potatoes, buttered green beans, and part of a grilled and seasoned pork chop are piled high on the plate. It looks like enough food for a king!

I grab my plate and utensils that sit on top of the cart, carrying them to the purple couch, where I settle down next to Florence. "Why do you focus so much on what people think of you? Honestly, some stranger's opinion should hardly matter, you should not let it push you over the edge!" I remark while scooping a forkful of mashed potatoes into my mouth. The buttery flavor hits my taste buds instantly, causing me to grab even more forkfuls. I was so nervous to go to Evelyn's house this morning that I have not eaten more than a few bites of food all day.

I hardly notice Florence's questioning and slightly offended stare out of the corner of my eye. "Are you speaking of the books?" she asks, holding up the one in her hand. "I am doing nothing of the sort! Can't one simply enjoy reading something that genuinely interests them? Besides, you really should not be stuffing your face full of food; it is very unladylike." Florence says, giving a huff before returning to her book. The plate that holds her food has barely been touched and instead has been placed atop the pile of books on the side table. The lamp beside her gives the room a little light, but shadows roam around freely everywhere except the couch on which we both sit.

I swallow a mouthful of green beans with a spark of fire burning inside me. "Fine. I am just offering my opinion. I'm allowed to do that, right?" I sneer sarcastically. Florence responds with a glare, returning to her book as if holding back everything she wants to say. "The food is really good. You should not waste it so. That can be seen as unladylike." Even though my last few words are spoken at a whisper, they are still heard.

"Nobody asked for your opinion Azalea! I'm off to study in my room since you are pestering me so much. Goodnight." Florence slams the book, leaving the vicinity. Her plate still sits on the side table, growing colder by the minute. Feeling guilty, I place mine on the other side table and return to my room. Mother must be resting for tomorrow, so there is no use in finding entertainment talking to her.

I pull a book out of my bag but end up reading for no more than a few minutes. Lying back down on my bed, I feel some of the warmth left from where I slept less than ten minutes ago.

Sleep is not on my side tonight, as I stay awake for most of the evening tossing and turning. The noise of the city finally gets to me as I stare into the nearby shadows of the room. Homesickness creeps into me once again, and more than anything I wish to be back in my own room at home. My lack of sleep is also due to the constant bundle of nerves in my stomach. It grows each time a worried thought about Evelyn and Percy comes to mind.

At some point my thoughts turn into nightmares as sleep takes over. *The train comes to a lurching stop as policemen get off their horses and board it. They're given permission to search the luggage and people aboard. Evelyn, dressed like a worker boy, looks worriedly over at Percy. The policemen disperse, each choosing a train car to look through. An officer slowly opens the train car door. He focuses on the worker boys, who deliberately refuse to make eye contact. He studies the boys. One wears a cap that hides his face carefully, and the other boy, the one with an oddly dirty face, looks up at him with a frightened gaze.*

"Papers?" his voice rings out. The boy wearing the cap almost seems to jump at the word, a movement which does not go unnoticed by the officer.

"We have no papers with us. Just on our way to the city to find work," Percy *squeaks out. The anxious bounce of his foot is soon noticed by the policemen.*

The officer peers closely at their faces, trying to figure out who really hides under their imposter disguise. In a moment of weakness, the boy that has been looking out the window glances over, revealing their identities with a single action.

Every detail of our plan is ruined as I watch the scene unfold before me. I am stuck in the narrator's limited view. With shouts of disagreement from Percy, the officer rips off the cap that hid a girl. Her hair falls from where it was tucked up as she stood, clearly humiliated. He yells to his fellow comrades, and they soon join him in laughing at the girl with charcoal on her pretty face and commoner clothes on her body.

I am useless to help and cursed to watch as Percy struggles against an officer. Evelyn, now revealed, is dragged away without so much as a parting goodbye. Her fear-stricken eyes only make everything worse as she disappears behind the train car's door. It slides back, locking everybody in the train with a slam.

Chapter 14

THE JOYFULNESS OF THE PRESENT CANNOT AFFECT THE FUTURE

MY EYES OPEN, instantly scorched from the light coming through my window. I sit up in my bed and look around, puzzled. I am not on the fateful train where my friend was found. Instead, I am exactly where I fell asleep, my hotel room in Brockschmidt. My fingertips rub my face in an attempt to awaken my conscious. Once I realize that Evelyn is okay and most likely somewhere in Colorado by now, I fall back onto my bed, scrambling to pull the covers back over me. The warmth lasts only a moment. Mother barges into my room, standing at the foot of the grand bed with her hands on her hips.

"Azalea!" she yells as I cover my face with a pillow and let out a groan.

This clearly disrespectful display earns me a frown from Mother and is put to rest by the covers being ripped off me. The blankets fall heavily onto the floor. My nightgown is worn and thin on account of it being handed down to me from Florence, so I huddle into a ball, climbing further into the mountain of pillows atop the bed.

"Honestly, it is just about afternoon, and you are still curled up in bed! I thought you would be excited for the ladies' tea and already changed into day clothes, or wide awake at the very least." This comment strikes me as odd. How can Mother possibly and truly think that I have any interest in attending a tea party in the park?

The only thing that would encourage me to go is to put a face to the name Lawrence Jones. That, or see Mrs. Jones again. She seems like a kind soul that could become a lifelong friend, especially if she is a sort of mother-in-law to me and Florence. Not to say I do not love Mother just the way she is, but I can't help but dream of a mother that finds adventure in climbing a roof to watch a sunrise instead of a mother that finds constant ways to change me into someone else.

Mrs. Jones seems to have a softer, kinder approach to children. I'll never forget her purposeful tone of voice that made me feel like the adult I am on the inside when she addressed me as she said goodbye to Mother.

"Is that Puffin girl coming? Emily? Her name seems to have slipped my mind. I figured you two got along just fine when we went to Katherine Puffin's house yesterday. You certainly would not stop talking about her when we returned from the soirée! I am grateful that you managed to not offend Mrs. Puffin yesterday. Can you imagine insulting one of Brockschmidt's wealthiest families!" Mother seems to shout her sentences when she is excited, even if she's asking a question.

A panicked breath catches in my throat at the mention of Evelyn, but it goes unnoticed. From a hole in between the pillows, I see Mother digging through my bag that sits on the floor not far from the wet dress I wore yesterday. Realizing it useless to hide any longer, I slip out from under the pillows and walk with caution over to the dress that lies in a sopping mess on the ice-cold floor.

Mother's back is to me as she digs through my bag trying to find a dress that is sensible, not as wrinkled as the others, and not too attention-grabbing—not that any of my dresses are very attention-grabbing compared to Florence's or any city girl's. Swooping down in one motion, I grab the dress and hang onto it for dear life, hiding it behind my back. I do so without taking my eyes off Mother, who is holding up a plain white dress with sleeves that go to my wrists, buttons from the collarbone to mid-stomach, and a collar at the throat that folds over. I forgot it was even packed and dearly hoped it wasn't. It is by far the worst thing I have ever owned! Boring and plain…a mundane dress, if you will.

Mother turns around just as I stand up from the floor. Without noticing my grimace at the dress that she holds up to my chest or my arms tucked behind my back holding the dripping outfit, she smiles at me. It is the smile of a parent who so dearly loves their child in their own way.

"Yes, I will be very glad to see Evelyn at the tea party!" Fake enthusiasm oozes into my voice but goes undetected by Mother, who is now smoothing the ugly white dress on my bed. "Shall I help Florence get ready after I have changed?"

"No, no. I will ready her. There is no need to annoy or distract her from the task at hand today: securing a marriage proposal!" With that she leaves the room in haste to make sure I do not suggest again that my help could be used. The only reason I even suggested helping her was to get her out of the room in the first place!

While she strolls away, I keep my fake smile and hold my hands behind my back until she is completely out of sight. Once the click of her shoes is far enough down the hallway, a sigh of relief escapes my mouth. I hang the wet dress in the washroom to dry, then change out of my nightgown and into the frock picked out for me.

The knots in my hair are a hassle to pull through this morning with the brush, but I manage just fine on my own. My locks are once again braided awfully and messily due to the nervous pit in my stomach that returns from another thought about Evelyn. How will I keep this charade up even after we leave the city?

When I step out of my room, closing my door as I go, I get to see the finished masterpiece that is Florence. Wearing her cream blouse with her off-white and light blue vertical-striped skirt, she looks positively gorgeous! Her hair is styled in a braid and her eyes seem bewitchingly soul-piercing. Even if she weren't wearing a speck of white on her, it would be practically undeniable to anyone who lays their eyes on her beautiful image: Florence appears bridal. The young ladies of Brockschmidt shall have to hold onto their beaus because my very own sister is sure to capture every boy's heart today. It is strange to think that Florence is courting this mystery man that swept her off her feet at a soirée and that wedding bells are not that far off in her future!

Mother wraps her cream shawl over Florence's shoulders, pinning it at the front with a simple metal brooch. When I am older, I'll be sure to own many beautiful brooches with golden vines or flowers so I can pin them on my shawls for all to see!

I have come to find out that afternoons—matched with perfect weather—in the city lead to a bustle of people on the streets. The park, which I saw when we first rode into the city, is only a fifteen-minute walk from the hotel. A train whistle blares in the not-so-far-off distance as we stroll past the towering gates of a factory. I jump at the sound, remembering once more the events of yesterday. *Keep it together, Azalea!* the voice inside my head yells.

In an effort to distract my racing mind, I focus on the factory next to us. Through the window I can just make out the image of a girl not much younger than myself spooling yarn on a machine. Her hair is tied firmly back, as is the hair of each of the girls beside her who watch the machine work the yarn. The pipes above us spill thick white smoke into the atmosphere. It feels uncanny and unnatural to see it obstructing the view of the sky in such a hideous way.

The park is just as I remember it. A large pond sits in the middle with a short wooden dock. A few dispersed willow trees, a dirt path that loops around the outskirts of the pond, and a few benches placed sporadically along this path just waiting for a conversation to be had on top of them. I can smell freshly baked bread and candies before we even set foot inside Mel's Bakery. As we enter, we walk under a long black sign with silver letters spelling the bakery's name.

Inside, many women stand in line, and the others are bent over, pointing through the glass case at some of the baked goods. My mouth waters at the sight of the food. Each treat is set on a plate next to a tiny card with a handwritten label describing what it is and indicating how much it is. Steaming hot cornbread is shoveled out of an iron skillet all in one piece.

As we join the back of the line graciously, I read the menu, which is a blackboard that has all types of foods listed in categories on it. Cream puffs, strawberry tarts, and queen cakes are all written in fancy handwriting under the sweets category; next to it are bread steaks, crumpets, and egg fritters. All the foods have been dubbed names that are almost impossible to say! I try my best to understand the almost foreign dialect the mothers in front of me speak, but it appears quite impossible. We are finally next in line when I realize I have no clue what to eat! Florence seems too distracted to properly focus on the menu; she starts biting her nails, remembers that it is a nasty habit, starts twiddling her hands, then restarts the whole process by biting her nails. Mother examines the other young ladies in line as if one of them might snatch Lawrence Jones from Florence at any moment. The lady in front of us steps away with her "croissant," as she called it, and I stare blankly at the aproned middle-aged man at the cash register.

"Welcome to Mel's Bakery. What can I get for you this afternoon?" He speaks in a monotone voice without so much as looking me in the eye.

"Croissant," I say, just as the woman before me had. My finger points against the glass case where the U-shaped pastries sit on a large plate. "Please." He stares blankly at me, then grabs a saucer, placing the croissant on it. He slides it over to me on the short counter, directing his sleepy-eyed gaze at Mother.

"One cup of black tea, sir. That will be all." She reaches into her tiny purse, which is tied with two thin ribbons around her wrist. The coins slap on the counter unintentionally and ring out their quick song before going still. The man nods, pushing open the swinging door to the kitchen and returning with a pink teacup filled to the brim on a matching saucer.

"Next!" he yells out before we have even stepped away from the counter.

The bakery is small, but the windows on the wall facing the vast park make it feel joyfully roomy. A small clock straight out of a child's story book hangs on the wall, revealing that it is ten minutes until four o'clock. The door through which we entered is bright blue and has a bell that rings each time it's opened. Bright tile floors gleam as sunlight leaks into the bakery. A few tiny paintings hang along the yellow walls, giving the room a much-needed cheerful glow.

If only Evelyn were here. She and I would be talking up a storm about the contents of each dish. Perhaps she has tasted some of these items that are so foreign to me. My heart longs for a friend to talk to right now!

The few unoccupied tables are missing chairs, as they have been pulled to other tables. Every inch of the bakery is packed with people. With the heat from the oven, which is barely visible behind the swinging door, and the hot breath from the many strangers, my blood grows warm and sweat breaks out on my forehead.

Mother suddenly notices Mrs. Jones sitting outside on one of the teal-colored iron tables on the sidewalk near the windows. Mother is quick to pull Florence and I along with one hand. The other holds her chattering cup of tea that almost splashes over the side. Mrs. Jones, who is taking the most ladylike sip of tea, places the teacup back down on its saucer when she notices us gathered around her table, taking care not to sit at the three empty chairs without her invitation.

"Mrs. Jones! How nice it is to see you here. Always a pleasure! Are you drinking black tea? Me too. I have had a great fondness for it ever since I was a little girl! Where is that dashing young man of yours? Azalea and I have yet to meet him, but my daughter Florence has talked so much about him."

As soon as her name is called, Florence steps forward, offering a curtsy with a smile plastered on her face. The other ladies standing and sitting around us whisper as Mother speaks. Mrs. Jones is by far the most popular woman in all of Brockschmidt; her name is on every-body's lips.

Mrs. Jones returns the smile with the compassionate, loving gaze of a mother. "Nice to make your acquaintance, Florence. My son should be joining us momentarily. Please, do sit!" Mrs. Jones takes yet another sip of her tea after speaking. Mother beams like a ray of sunshine, and even Florence seems to forgo her nerves, replacing them with a lady-like qui-etness. We settle in our seats, not letting them remain empty for another second.

Two women near in age to Mrs. Jones, most likely their late thirties, suddenly pull up chairs in unison. I can see that Mother does not approve of her time with the lovely Mrs. Jones being cut off by these women. Nonetheless, she opens her arms, inviting them to the table and the con-versation with a fake smile.

In an effort to keep the attention on us, Mother looks to me, asking her question indirectly so the rest of the ladies can hear her clearly. "Where is Mrs. Puffin?" Noticing the other ladies' eyes on her, she turns to them, saying, "Just yesterday she invited us to her house. She is the most gracious host!"

The other ladies appear rather jealous at the mention of a coun-try family such as us having direct contact with the elite families of Brockschmidt.

"Didn't you hear the news? Well, I guess you did not, being so out of touch with the comings-and-goings of the city. I am Miss Hackenberry, and this is my dearest friend Mrs. Epperson. I pride myself in knowing the latest, juiciest news in all of Brockschmidt!" she sneers, flipping her dreadful rust-colored hair over her shoulder so many times that one might think the movement is involuntary.

Miss Hackenberry, for some reason, is unmarried—my guess is that it is because of her dreadful looks, which makes me pity the poor woman—and she is quite the gossip. Her hair is cut very short or perhaps has never grown long. It stops just before reaching her shoulders, and since it's not long enough to put up or style, she just wears it down with uneven waves in it. She continues, "What a scandal indeed! Mrs. Puffin called for her daughter Evelyn—I have always looked down on the name Evelyn but never expressed it until now. Anyway, she didn't come down from her room. Mrs. Puffin heard her daughter in there, but in order to 'respect her privacy,' she just let her be! I'll tell you right now, if a child of mine did not come when they were called, I would beat them with a switch, not just leave them be! Anyway, Mrs. Puffin later found out it was actually a servant cleaning in Evelyn's room when she thought her daughter was in there. This caused, as you would imagine, a panic! Even after searching everywhere imaginable, they could not find the girl! She has been missing since six o'clock yesterday afternoon.

"And I just found out this morning—when Mrs. Puffin told me all of this—that their next-door neighbor's son has been missing since around the same time! When I suggested they had run away together, Mrs. Puffin severely disagreed, but it is practically fact now. The girl and boy have gone without a trace! No one has seen them in almost a day. The police already ruled out Evelyn Puffin being taken because there are no clues nor ransom notes. I knew there would be heaps of trouble right when I heard that that Percy Willards boy fancied none other than Evelyn Puffin! Wasn't I right, Mrs. Epperson?" Miss Hackenberry's speech has surely left everyone at this table sitting on the very edge of their seat.

The croissant that I have been eating until now sits untouched on its saucer. Miss Hackenberry sees this as a waste and points at the pastry. Being unable to digest any more food—especially when I have just found out that the police could be following Evelyn—I nod. Miss Hackenberry pulls the dish closer to her, picking at the buttery pastry and putting the pieces in her mouth.

Mother quickly turns to me with the most blood-chilling, shocked expression. You would think that somebody has just told her that her own daughter was involved in Evelyn Puffin's disappearance! I shift uncomfortably in my chair. Florence, who has never met the Puffins, is completely dumbfounded by the news. Miss Hackenberry thoroughly enjoys every moment that goes by silent from the shock. She continues picking off bits of the croissant with a smug smile.

"It is true. Miss Hackenberry did say that boy was bad news! It has never been much of a secret that Mrs. Puffin severely disagreed of a courtship of a Puffin girl by a Willards boy." The timid Mrs. Epperson would never say anything like this aloud, but the implication is there: nothing is ever a secret because of Miss Hackenberry's mouth! "You see, there has always been some sort of turmoil between the two families. Nobody really knows how it started, but Mr. Puffin's father's father swore to never speak to the Willards family as long as he lived. This evidently was the case, as he was laid cold in his grave without speaking a word to a Willard for eighteen years! As you would think, the Willards family also vowed to do the same thing. They have always been more of followers than leaders, so it would only be natural for them to make the same vow.

"When the two families moved into those two houses next to each other on Pineheart Road, it only fueled the long-lasting argument! There cannot be two families vying for the spot of Brockschmidt's wealthiest household. After a few years, they came to discover that ignoring each other and going about their lives was easier then fighting over where their two land plots ended or began. That is also why the wall barricades the two homes."

Our mouths gape wide open as she speaks. It is interesting to hear these backstories, even if we have no idea who the people in the story are.

Evelyn has only ever told me that her mother disapproved, but this is far more exciting to hear! Mrs. Jones herself appears so shocked at the news laid before us that she has not touched her tea recently. It's probably ice cold by now.

⤻

The two ladies make quite the pair. Mrs. Epperson's moderately pleasant appearance is made downright gorgeous when compared to Miss Hackenberry's rather abrasive one. Mrs. Epperson is shorter, nicer, quieter, prettier, and less of a gossip—but only barely—than Miss Hackenberry. Miss Hackenberry's looks, as I mentioned before, are hopelessly behind the times. But the awful hair, along with the crooked smile, are things you cannot change. She is a lengthy thing, and her legs barely fit all the way beneath her skirt. Her ankles show freely, and if Mother notices this, she will most likely pull us far away so we will not be soiled in talking to her. More than once Mother has expressed that if anywhere from your knees to your ankles showed, then you are a prostitute in her books.

At least twenty minutes have passed by since Mrs. Jones said Lawrence would be arriving momentarily. *Where is he?* Just as I think this, a cluster of voices directs my attention to a crowd of a dozen boys walking toward the front of the bakery. The mothers in the bakery rush outside with their daughters, giving them orders to stand up straighter or tuck a curl of hair over their shoulder.

Conversation halts altogether as Mrs. Jones stands. The rest of the women at our table follow closely behind as if she is the Queen herself. Mother stands and gestures for me to follow suit. The dozen boys locate the girls they were matched with at some point this engagement season. A young man with medium-blonde hair steps forward, kissing Mrs. Jones on the cheek. As his eyes land on Florence, he grins and kisses her hand with a bow.

"This is my son, Lawrence," says Mrs. Jones.

Mother, ecstatic at the sight of this handsome young man court-ing Florence, beams like a thousand suns. Mrs. Jones introduces each of us to him, saying our names as our hands meet. Lawrence firmly shakes my hand before greeting Miss Hackenberry and Mrs. Epperson like old acquaintances. Without anyone seeing, I massage my wrist, which still hurts from when the disgusting man grabbed me yesterday.

"How about we go for a stroll in the park? It is getting awfully crowded here!" Mrs. Jones remarks joyfully. Mother nods profusely and says the most excited goodbye to the two gossiping ladies that we're leav-ing behind at our table.

Does Florence look tense? She walks side by side with Lawrence, speaking in polite tones. Mother and Mrs. Jones stroll a few lengths behind them, commenting about what a cute couple they would be, and I stand at the very back of our group.

But I do not mind walking slowly behind the two mothers with nobody to talk to. It gives me more time to let the day's events sink in. Lawrence seems like quite the gentleman, which is the exact opposite of what Evelyn had implied. He walks with his arms behind his back and untucks them when he speaks, which is quite often. Besides the useless hand gestures, there is nothing alarming about him as far as I can observe.

My estimation of people's ages is never too far off, and Lawrence appears twenty or even twenty-one years old. My inquisitiveness (a word I learned during Mother's vocabulary study session the other day) tends to take over my mind rather forcefully. Why had Lawrence not married a year or two sooner if he is dashing, handsome, and wealthy? The topic of their conversation must certainly be interesting, for Florence has forgone the stone-faced, "lady-like" expression and replaced it with a subtle smile. What if they become betrothed this very day? The thought crosses my mind before being quickly dismissed.

There was a time when I wanted to be taken back to when a man and woman would be engaged after only meeting once or twice, but now I am not sure if that is to be considered romantic or foolish. On one hand, it is incredibly romantic to find that you already know that the pair of you are fated to be together, but on the other it is incredibly foolish because something is bound to happen that ends the betrothal, or you find out that you two were not destined after all. Marriage has never seemed like much of a possibility for me. It is something that I cannot truly decide if I desire. I feel as though time is going by too quickly, for my decision is demanded out of me by my family more and more in each moment that passes by.

Russell is the only boy I have ever truly considered marrying, but that, of course, will never happen! Russell kissed me, and the feeling still lingers on my lips, but it is rather foolish to imagine we should ever see each other again.

Russell leaves my mind as I focus on my sister and her new beau. They walk in the same stride, even though Florence takes smaller steps. How perfect they would be together! His hair is not the same exact shade as Mrs. Jones's honey ginger, but his medium blonde matches Florence's hair. He is much paler than us, a common trait I have noticed in most city folk.

When Lawrence and I shook hands earlier, I stole a quick glimpse into his eyes. He has the most bewitching gray eyes that seem to take on the color of whatever mood he is in. For example, they appeared almost blue when he kindly shook my hand and then green when he bashfully began walking beside Florence. Surely, with their blonde hair and gray or blue eyes, Florence and Lawrence's children would be very handsome.

The park is quiet for such a fine day as this. A family of four—wife, husband, and two young children—walk past with smiles that I gladly reciprocate. I have come to find out that the city is not exactly the spawning point for friendliness. Most passersby are content with a simple smile instead a full conversation, which is positively foreign to someone from a small town such as me. For example, if you are going into a small town to stop by the mercantile, you would most likely strike up a conversation with half of the population of Lorretta before you have even started on your journey back home! The city has undeniable perks, such as electricity, running water, and new foods, but the community is clearly different than that of Lorretta.

As the group of us keep walking, a lady's booming voice yells out repeatedly, "Votes for women! Women's rights!" A madame around the age of forty stands next to a small table with books and pamphlets piled on top of it. The table is barely a foot off the dirt path, so it cannot be easily missed, especially with the constant shouts. She wears a sash stamped with the words, "It's time for our voices to be heard." She holds up a pamphlet in her left hand as she extends her arm to its full height. Her dark skin stands out amongst the sea of white. "Let us keep fighting for the rights of all women in every state, not just Wyoming! Take a pamphlet! Educate yourself on the women's suffrage movement!" she continues yelling even after I stop at the table and stand directly in front of her.

Mother, Mrs. Jones, Florence, and Lawrence all continue walking without so much as a side glance at the women. I, however, remain interested in the subject of women's suffrage. It is common knowledge by now that the movement has been going on for almost fifty years! Our very own state of Wyoming granted women the right to vote decades ago when it was a territory, but many other states in America have only granted partial rights.

"Here, little lady, have a pamphlet." The woman snatches up one of the folded papers and jams it in my hand. She watches me with prickling eyes as I open the paper and begin to read the paragraphs of words, facts, and predictions:

"Black women's rights are equal to those of white women. If all men are created equal, why can't women be? Why does Congress stand by and let us be persecuted in certain states and be given the leftover scraps in others? Sign the petition that already has thousands of signatures so that we may present this before Congress!"

The information seems to jump off the page in every direction, snapping your attention from one place to another. As I continue reading, I find myself raising my eyebrows one minute and scrunching them together the next. For once I wish I paid attention like Florence did during Mother's corrections of complex English sentences! The words are printed in bold and italics to be even more eye-catching. I look up at the woman, who has gone right back to yelling the information out for all to hear. The rest of the people in the park keep walking by, as my own group has, without giving a moment of their valuable time to this worthy cause! The rest of the people in the park keep walking by, as my own group has, without giving so much as a moment of their valuable time to this worthy cause! What does this woman hope to achieve? Why have this display in a park of Brockschmidt, Wyoming? We have already won the right for women to vote, so why not have this display in a state that hasn't? I cannot withhold these questions for long when I covet the answer to them. Mother has always told me that I must think before speaking. The only problem is that I do think, but in those few moments of contemplation I usually see nothing wrong with my thoughts.

"Why not have this booth in Washington? Why here? We already have the right to vote here." My voice becomes small next to the booming, intimidating woman standing in front of me with her vocal cords of steel.

She stops shouting as if someone has stolen away her voice in the timespan of a second. "Well, child, I offer this information to you in the kindest of fashions. Look around this park. What do you observe and notice about this city? Are the people welcoming to a country bumpkin, a black woman such as me, or any type of foreigner?"

My humor comes at the worst possible moment, causing me to laugh due to the obviousness of the answer, though the question was clearly serious without a hint of comedy. My face straightens out instantly from the woman's glare. She probably thinks I am mocking her when that was never my intention!

"No, ma'am. The society here is different, but that is to be expected of a city of this breadth and quality!"

"Aha! So you do have a mind of your own. Not just another lady that follows, a blind mouse following the tomcat hoping it does not swallow you whole. You are correct in that sense but misled at the same time! Look at it this way: you are a little girl with big ideas, but nobody shall respect your opinion because of where you come from. Why is that?"

What might have come off as rude does not to me. Being called a country bumpkin or blind mouse certainly stings, no doubt about that, but it also makes me think outside myself and the box that I have been put into unwillingly.

"Rhetorical question," the woman interrupts just as my mouth opens. "There is no need trying to come up with an answer, because I assure you there is not one. Yes, we do have the right to vote, but do you know how many women actually use the right that our fellow sisters have fought for? Less than twenty-five percent! That is out of all the women in this very state. So mark my words, for someday they will aid you. That I am sure of. You must not try to change what people think but instead present them with the option and opportunity for greatness. Now I could spend my day running up to men and spilling countless facts about women's suffrage, hoping they will change their minds and support us, or I could stand here yelling—*presenting*, if you will call it that—the option for ladies such as yourself to come to me and be better educated!"

I stand here dumbfounded by my own nearsightedness. I have always prided myself in thinking outside the box, thinking anything in life is simple to figure out if you thought hard enough, but even the metaphor of the tomcat and blind mouse she used is baffling!

Without wanting to appear as a child with no real concept of life or real hardships, I simply thank her, though my true intention is to ask more questions on not only the subject of women's suffrage but also on the contents of her mind. If only we as humans shared more of what we thought and the ideas that run through our heads! If I had forgone my stubborn, embarrassed ego and asked the woman more about this, then my knowledge would surely have increased even more! It amazes me that I care so much about what this stranger thinks about me that I would not ask her what she meant in simpler words!

"Umm. Thank you, ma'am. I will think on that." My question has been answered, and I have been polite, so both duties are filled. Mother and Mrs. Jones are stopped far ahead, occasionally glancing back at me. Lawrence—to whom I have not spoken a word in the thirty minutes I have known him—and my sister keep taking tiny steps and speaking every couple of moments. Without wanting to hold them up any longer, I duck my head sheepishly, running to join them. I arrive out of breath at the side of Mrs. Jones, Mother on her other side.

A bird swoops by the short-cut grassy ground, chirping joyously. The pond has the most beautiful water lilies growing near the bank! I resist the urge to go pick one, knowing that Mother would scold me tremendously if I were to fall into a pond while Florence has her new beau walking alongside her. Even though this is not quite enough to convince my mischievous spirit, Mrs. Jones's presence persuades me to stay on the path. I truly want her to think of me as a good little girl.

A frog croaks loudly before jumping into the water with a splash after I come too close to it. The dirt path is just big enough for two people to walk side by side on it, with Mother and Mrs. Jones, there is not enough room for me to stand next to them. I stray off the trail and onto the grass that still holds little dewy drops from the morning mist. At the hem of my ugly dress are bright green grass stains. It might be wrong to even think this, but I do so hope it is permanently stained so that this dress might be "put out to pasture" for the good of the world. I sure would not mind never laying eyes on it again! The dress gives me such a square shape, which, as you would expect, is not at all common in a city filled with the tiniest waists and most confining corsets.

"What an awful business Miss Hackenberry spoke of!" Mrs. Jones finally breaks our silence. By her awestruck face, Mother never expected Mrs. Jones to say this aloud or even think it for that matter. "Please do not misunderstand me, but Miss Hackenberry is the city's most infamous gossiper. Even the minister has reprimanded her multiple times about how sinful the business of gossiping is! Multiple times, I say! She continues to attend church every Sunday without fail but cannot seem to keep her mouth filtered when it comes to a rumor. Poor Katherine Puffin must be worried sick thinking nonstop about her daughter!" Mrs. Jones is undoubtedly a kindred spirit! She speaks her mind in the plainest of ways without a care for what Mother thinks! I aspire to become just like Mrs. Jones, and even if my looks could never be half as perfect or my personality a smidge as outgoing as hers, I still desire to be exactly like her!

"Why…yes, I suppose that is true. But I—" Mother pauses and stutters, unable to comprehend the sudden outpour of reality. A grin emerges at my mouth, the glimmer of a laugh brimming my lips.

"Perhaps, we should probably take a break from strolling for a while," I shyly comment.

We have finally made a full loop around the dirt pathway and found ourselves standing back at the entrance of the park that gazes ever so cheerfully at Mel's Bakery. My stomach growls at the thought of food; I did not get to eat much of the croissant on account of Miss Hackenberry's gossip about the Puffins. My nerves are unsettled at the thought of police searching for Evelyn, Percy, and quite possibly me. Our visit to the Puffins' house, so close to the time Evelyn disappeared, could be misconstrued as suspicious.

"Quite right you are! Look, these tables seem to be clear and waiting especially for us." Mrs. Jones promptly takes her seat at a table with three chairs. Another table with only two chairs sits a few feet away, and this is where my sister and her beau take their seats. Mother rushes off to look for something on the menu that she can eat whilst carrying on a proper conversation with Mrs. Jones. The breeze is truly wonderful, whisking by delicately and lifting the stray hairs from my braids.

Once we are alone, I decide that if Mrs. Jones and I are truly like-minded, then she must understand my vain thoughts. "I wish my hair were a pretty honey ginger like yours is! Mother tells me it's vain to wish to look different because God made us this way for a reason. But my brownish hair could never compare to blonde *honey ginger*." The words "honey ginger" are effortlessly beautiful when spoken aloud. I say this statement in the most affectionate tone so it will not come across as envious.

Mrs. Jones clearly understands me better than I ever thought possible because she eases my every worry of coming across as envious. "Well! I do believe there is truth in that. When I was a little girl, my hair was every bit the color that yours is now, if not darker. Darker hair seems to be hereditary on my father's side of the family, but it was not passed down to Lawrence. After years of praying, my looks slowly started changing, but only when I had become perfectly happy with my appearance! Do not find faults in your appearance, Azalea, because I assure you that you are already beautiful." She tucks one of my braids over my shoulder so that it is parallel to the other braid. My heart swells with pride at her words. I will never again spend a moment of my time comparing myself to Florence— or any other girl, for that matter! "Here." She unclasps the pearl necklace that hangs around her neck. It glimmers like stars when she holds it above my hand. Reaching down, she takes my palm, opening it and letting the cold string of pearls fall into my clutches.

My mouth drops open at what lies before me. I noticed the strand earlier but would have never thought I'd actually be touching it now! The beads are imperfect circles with a string through them and a clasp at the end.

"Ma'am, I couldn't! These must be extremely expensive! You see, we live in the small town of Lorretta, and I have never seen a pearl cord clasped around the neck of a woman until we arrived here. The city seems to have an abundance of pearls for whatever reason, but I could never expect to hold one before me much less own it! It must be some family heirloom entrusted to you by a dying aunt or other family member, therefore giving it too much value to bestow to a poor girl from Lorretta of all places!" The words do not seem to stop coming out of my mouth until I glance back up at Mrs. Jones and realize that I haven't looked at her once throughout my whole speech; I have been so rudely focused on the cream-colored pearls!

Mrs. Jones stares at me for a moment blankly. It turns dead quiet at the table as my cheeks grow red and my palms break into a sweat. Suddenly, Mrs. Jones bends over, laughing hysterically, which only makes me turn from cherry red to ghost white.

"Dear, you are by far the funniest, most creative person I have ever had the pleasure of encountering!" she finally says after wiping away the tears that spill from her eyes. Lawrence continues talking quietly to Florence as this happens, but my sister glances over during Mrs. Jones's laughing fit and assumes the worst has happened. Florence gives me an alarmed glance, then returns to the conversation to answer some question Lawrence asked. "I have two other necklaces at home, neither of which are from this dying aunt or any rich family member you have spoken of, though I dearly wish their origins were as interesting. My first cream pearls, for which I saved up for a long time before my twentieth birthday, are from myself. Most people in Brockschmidt do not care to investigate other folks' backgrounds, but mine is a sad one, indeed, if you don't mind hearing the reason."

I nod without daring to utter a word. Mrs. Jones is truly the kindest person I have ever met, and I am positive that will remain a fact until I am an old maid!

"My family—maiden name Torranca—is originally from England, and my great-grandparents eventually migrated before the Revolutionary War to what soon became America. My parents raised us in a small town back east, which was humbling. My parents moved me and my five other siblings after my father lost everything in a business deal. We came to Wyoming Territory shortly after. My sisters and I worked in a factory while my three brothers went to work each morning with Father. So, when I turned twenty, I used all of that money I'd made working at the factory to buy that piece of jewelry. That strand, in fact, was what caught Mr. Jones's eye when I wore it to a friend's party. Without those beads I probably would have never met Mr. Jones or talked to him. He complimented the necklace's beauty, and we started having a conversation that ended in him getting down on one knee and proposing with not a ring in sight! We had only known each other for three hours before he proposed marriage. He called it love at first sight, but I am positive God had something to do with it!"

"How romantic!" To think the very string of pearls that I hold in my outstretched hand had caused Mrs. Jones to become… Mrs. Jones! She smiles at my comment and continues.

"The second rivière is pink and was given to me as a gift from my husband on our wedding day. The last one, which is a deep gray, I bought for myself for no other reason than because it reminded me of the night sky on a cloudy evening. I am bequeathing this set to you. It is your choice whether or not you keep them. If it makes you too uncomfortable, I will take it back, but what a shame it would be to not see you wearing them. I think this will help you see your beauty even if you think it isn't perfect. I would be pleased to have you as a sort of daughter-in-law." She whispers the last line as if it is poetry that's too delicate to be said in common tones. My eyes just about spill over with tears of happiness.

"I shall never know how to properly thank you, Mrs. Jones! It is one of the most beautiful, sentimental things in my possession." I stare down at the gleaming beads in the palm of my hand. My dress does the necklace no justice; nonetheless, I reach up and close the clasp, letting the cool pearls surround my throat, endlessly gleaming. The beads are quickly warmed by the sunshine that mimics my blissful smile.

Just like a mother looks at her daughter, Mrs. Jones gazes at me. For once, I am not compared to Florence or seen as just a child in somebody's eyes. In some ways, Florence's potential marriage to Lawrence really is a blessing. Based on their conversation, which has yet to end, it is clear to any of the other girls that pass by with looks of envy that my very own sister and Lawrence Jones are deeply and unconditionally in love. It shall only be a matter of time before a proposal will be made and wedding bells will ring!

I whisper a quick thanks to God; Florence has found a happy match in which she can be loved instead of married in name only, which seems like such an empty life. When she said that she was marrying for the good of our family, there was no doubt in my mind that those words were out of truthfulness and duty. But now it would be sinful lie to say that her intentions remain the same, and I am glad about that.

"And do not fret, for Florence will be presented with gifts, too. She will make a wonderful bride, wife, and mother," Mrs. Jones whispers, as if it were a secret, gazing fondly at her son and my sister. I smile, glad that she understood my thoughts even if they were not expressed clearly.

Mother finally comes back with a plate of the most scrumptious strawberry tarts in existence. The conversation between the two mothers resumes quite naturally at a table just outside of Mel's Bakery. I make a decision right there and then to look at this moment as an opportunity for growth. Mrs. Jones does not treat me as a child that is to be seen and not heard, so I will take advantage of that!

An engaging conversation is held for the next hour. In every spare moment, I make a comment or ask a question about the latest fashions. This was very much appreciated by Mrs. Jones, who encourages my questions by turning and talking to me directly. Mother has firmly told us that when adults are speaking, we should not be. She goes on talking when the conversation comes to her, but she looks at me with an inconspicuous glare that says, "Remember your manners and your place." I, however, ignored the look and keep speaking with full enthusiasm.

The sun soon dips below the buildings, and the sky is coated in orange, blue, and purple, colors which the clouds so gladly took on. The streets are relatively empty, only containing the people that are walking back to their homes. The bakery soon closes, the waiter stacks up the chairs and sweeps the hard workday out into the streets. The few remaining mamas—a word that, as I have recently learned from Florence, means mothers—beaus, and young ladies outside the bakery wave their goodbyes before dispersing.

We all stand on the sidewalk as our mothers bid goodbye to each other without ever really ending the conversation.

"We will have to convene again soon! Are you to attend the end-of-season ball? I, personally, look forward to it every year. Mrs. Zerkel organizes it each year at her house. I shall speak with her and make it known that you are coming as a personal guest! The invitations will be mailed to you. The Grand Hotel, I presume?" Even though Mrs. Jones speaks directly to Mother, she pauses for a moment to give me an imperceptible wink.

Mother, who is flattered and clearly ecstatic at the invitation, avidly replies, "Of course! Yes, the Grand Hotel. We shall patiently await the invitation! Until next time, Mrs. Jones." She nudges both mine and Florence's arms as she holds up her dress skirts by an inch to curtsy. Mrs. Jones smiles affectionately and strolls away with her son, who towers over his mother.

Once we are alone, Mother bursts into beams of smiles, already planning out in her mind what to expect out of the invitation we were just metaphorically handed. "Lawrence seems like a nice young man, even though his clothes were less formal than I would have preferred." A proper

Mother compliment could not go without a remark of something she would have liked to see changed, but Florence and I walk on either side of her, quietly listening. "I must admit I am most confused as to what made Mrs. Jones so impressed by us!" For a moment it seems as if her line of eyesight is directed at me, but I anxiously stare at our surroundings as we continue to step forward along the sidewalk.

The electric streetlights, which I had not noticed until now, form glowing a path for us along the empty street. Piano music spills out of the Public Pub, which is one of the only open businesses at this time. Men laugh, each of them waving a glass filled to the brim with brown liquid before downing the whole cupful and slamming it on the counter. Mother grimaces at the sight and marches us forward at an even faster pace until the pub is out of sight. The restaurants seat only a few people, most of them finishing off their meals, and besides the occasional person walking or homeless family, there isn't anybody in sight.

"Yes, Mr. Lawrence Jones is a proper man. Most of what he talked about was incomprehensible, I must admit, but it is natural for someone who is raised in the city to be taught more things," Florence admits shyly, looking to Mother.

The awkwardness hangs between us all for a moment. Florence and I are grateful, of course, to have had our Sunday schooling with Mother back in Lorretta, but there is a great deal of things that Mother herself has no knowledge of. It is unspoken of—but clearly visible—that country girls are at a disadvantage in the matter of general knowledge of city school studies.

"Well, he is a highborn young man! He has probably received the best education imaginable. Darling Florence, I am sure you made a perfectly suitable impression. Weren't we just invited to sit out the rest of the engagement season and attend the ball by none other than Mrs. Jones herself? You must not worry too much over it. He is not, after all, looking for a wife based on her knowledge of history or mathematics!" Even though what she says is meant to soothe her daughter's worries, it does not seem to have much effect on Florence's newfound insecurity. I does give me pleasure to see Florence's faults; after years of thinking she is undeniably perfect, I finally get to see another side of my sister. I, however, remain quiet on the subject because my opinion would probably send Mother into a rage. "We ought to learn more about Brockschmidt's culture…I heard one of the other ladies talking of a famous art gallery not far from the hotel. Next weekend we shall make a visit there before our arrival at the ball."

The door to the hotel squeaks open, and we spread out, finding comfort in our rooms after a long day. On the floor next to the door lies a white envelope addressed to none other than me! I scoop up the letter, already aware of the sender's identity. I run to my dark room, jump on my bed, and turn on the lamp that sits on the bedside table. Flipping over the envelope, I tear into the back of it using what little nails I possess. My nails always seem to break whenever I do my morning chores at home, but I have never really cared until now. My short, ridged nails made it all the more difficult to rip open the letter and read its most anticipated contents! However, I was finally able to messily tear off the envelope and pull out a thin piece of paper that holds words written in a fountain pen similar to mine. The letter read:

Dear Bluebird,

There is certainly some worry in my heart when you tell me the details of your trip so far would "send me into a panic." You have captured my attention, and I will now be checking the postal office for your next letter. Your Uncle Edward was momentarily delayed but arrived four days after you left. He has been a great help with the chores around here and has had lots to talk about. I hope all is well, my little bluebird. Before you ask, yes, Sense and Sensibility are doing well, but I am sure they secretly miss you!

Lawrence Jones sounds interesting, and I am sure he is a fine lad. I can't wait to hear all about your travels and the city when you return, which, hopefully, is soon. Tell everyone I miss and love them. Until next time, my bluebird.

-Pa

Pa's letter, though short and sweet, holds so much love in each word. It is so ordinary and happy that it makes me miss home even more. For the first time since we arrived here, I truly take a moment to look around the room. A ceiling that is over twice my height, an enormous bed with feather pillows, electric lamps adorning the bedside tables, and a dresser that could hold three times the amount of clothes I own…As wonderful as it all is, with fancy teas and hotel food that is unlike anything I have ever tasted before, a feeling of emptiness lingers inside me! This is not where I am meant to be! I have my cows in a small wooden barn; my room back home with my vanity, where I sit each morning and brush my hair; my own bed, which is not made from the softest feathers but is still the most comforting place for dreams to be created and experienced; and my own house that, compared to a hotel room, is quaint but still holds the warm-hearted feeling of home.

I came here for Florence but instead found out something about myself along the way. I have experienced so many things here already. Strength in the face of adversity, stubbornness to admit certain things, jealousy that has slowly faded out of my heart, happiness in my sister's successes instead of seeing them as a challenge, loyalty to an unlikely friendship, newfound hope for the unknown future, and finally, contentment in being myself. I do not have to be in competition with Florence nor turn into her to be her equal. Because for once in my life being Azalea is enough! Maybe Nora changed because she felt trapped in trying to be like me, somebody filled with hope for the future and an undying will to go against the boundaries set against her. My grudge against my sister's endless perfection and the death of our sisterhood, along with the anger of Nora leaving me alone, is swept away like a roaring sea after the thunderstorm. My heart becomes lighter at the resolution that I, Azalea Bree Stanton, am good enough to just be myself!

Reaching into the bedside table's drawer, I pull out a piece of paper and my trusty fountain pen. Pa's letter lies on a pillow with the ripped-open envelope next to it, giving me inspiration to write.

This place is not so empty when you look at it like an adventure that you will embark on, then return home in the end. And so I do. I write about the stagecoach robbery, the hotel—the beauty of the greenhouse, the regal woman in the painting on the wall, and the marble floors covered in red velvet fabric—the soirée where I met my first true friend Evelyn Puffin, and the ladies' tea today when Mrs. Jones gave me the very string of pearls that are around my throat. I also write about my hope for my future, about being happy with myself even if there are other girls that are more charming, more sharp-witted, or taller than me.

Even though I feel the growing need to write about the quest that Percy and Evelyn set out on to escape their lives and find new ones with my help, no soul can ever be aware of my part in their disappearance. Putting it in writing would only incriminate me if anybody ever found it.

In the end, I use up at least twenty full pages of just my adventures in the city. I have never written anything of this nature before, but when I have all these ideas fresh off my mind it becomes like clockwork to scribble down my memories of our first week in Brockschmidt.

My eyes grow weary, and I reluctantly fall into a deep slumber after placing the pages on the table and clicking the lamp off. With every beat of my heart, I know that today was quite possibly the best day of my short-lived fourteen years of life. Whatever the future may hold, I will meet it graciously....

Chapter 15

REMINISCING ABOUT THE PAST AND THE ART OF TODAY

IT IS ANOTHER CLOUDY, rainy day outside of our hotel room when the mail is slipped under our door. I rush to pick it up, expecting the response to my last letter to Pa, even though Mother mailed it for me only five days ago. A rectangle piece of paper about the size of my hand sits elegantly on the floor, looking up at me with excitement. I know in a moment what this paper holds.

You are cordially invited to:

Brockschmidt's fourth annual end-of-season ball

This year's theme is Flowers of Spring

Wednesday, April 25th

Ladies, wear your best bright-colored formal dress, and gentlemen, wear well-cut, tailored clothes adorned with carefully knotted neckties! Each lady must adorn her hair in either curls or a bun with her choice of flower. Gentlemen must have well-groomed hair cut at the appropriate length. This year's location will once again be Mrs. Zerkel's house on 482 Grandiose Drive, Brockschmidt, Wyoming. Refreshments will be provided for all that choose to attend! Please bring your invitations so we can verify that you are invited (we would not want a repeat of last year's fiasco!). We look forward to meeting the newcomers and witnessing the new matches of Brockschmidt!

It is written in the most technically perfect calligraphy, with every line is curved into spirals at the tips of the letters. The paper, along with the blue ink on it, is clearly expensive. A few moments pass by of me admiring every detail of the card before remembering where I am.

The Holy Bible lies in its rightful spot on the couch's side table from when Mother read us today's sermon. Mother and Florence sit on the purple couch, Florence enraptured yet again by *Proper Etiquette of a Lady* and Mother holding up the latest newspaper. Today's headline is another article about Evelyn and Percy's vanishment. From today's paper, I have gathered that the police checked all stagecoaches and trains that left that day but never found any new clues. It is by far the most interesting topic in Brockschmidt, besides the proposals that have already been made, to which there's an entire page dedicated!

Mother is quick to point out my awed expression and the card that I hold before me. Her expression promptly transitions from almost relaxed to the most euphoric face I have ever witnessed. She stands, snatching the paper out of my hand, an action which grabs Florence's attention most deliberately.

"It has arrived!" Mother exclaims for all to hear as she keeps her eyes on the paper.

Florence sits holding her book, which shut in her confused excitement from Mother's shout, causing her to lose whatever page she was reading moments ago.

"What is it, Mother? What has arrived? Oh, please do tell us!" Her eyes catch just a glimpse of the words "Brockschmidt" and "Annual Ball," which sends her into a frenzy of panic and excitement. "What does it say, Mother! Do not leave me waiting a moment more for my whole future to be revealed! When we met Mrs. Jones and the other ladies last week, Miss Hackenberry told me that the ball is when the most proposals happen, particularly on the terrace that overlooks the rose gardens and the grandest fountain in all of Wyoming! In Wyoming, she said! Mrs. Zerkel must be as rich as that Mrs. Puffin to have rose gardens, ballrooms, and the grandest fountain in the state." Florence's endless chatter goes in one ear and out the other without registering with Mother for a mere second. For we are well aware that the reason my sister is chattering is to conceal her nerves for what might be a proposal in less than a week.

"We must fix you a new dress! All the eligible young ladies of Brockschmidt will be there, and their wardrobes outshine ours by a mile!" I have never heard Mother place Brockschmidt girls on a higher pedestal than us, even if that might be fact. "The seamstress will already be piled high in work. The entire city knows when the ball will be, so I'm sure there will be the most absurd prices imaginable! Wednesday, April 25th. That gives us almost a week to polish you girls up to be high-society ladies. Get your things together, girls, for we must hurry along and buy some fabric for Florence's new dress! After that, we will visit the art gallery so you both may see some of the city's culture and have something to talk about at the ball. Well, do not just stand there, Azalea! Hurry along, child, and get ready to leave." I nod without actually processing her command. It is not until Mother waves her hands that I rush along to my room to brush my hair, which is still in knots.

I look high and low, in my bag, and in all the drawers of the dresser for my hair ribbons, but I cannot find them anywhere! I almost collide with the cart holding the plates from the breakfast that we had eaten earlier this morning. The taste of the syrupy buttermilk waffles is still fresh on my lips as I narrowly miss the cart on my way to Florence's room. Mother stands next to the hotel door tapping one foot under her dress and crossing her arms. Just as I am about to knock on the door, my sister swings it open and rushes past me in search of the missing shoes that she had been yelling about for the past five minutes. Slipping past her, I immediately locate my purple hair ribbons on the top of her dresser. My Sunday best is the only thing proper to wear today, and the purple ribbons pair very nicely with it. I tie the last ribbon around my braids as my sister slips on her last shoe. The three of us exit the room with grace and no hint of the rush that we all surely feel to get to the store before every woman in Brockschmidt buys out the fabric for their dresses.

In our short time in the city, I have already noticed sure changes in not only my personality but in my appearance, for my hair has become just a tad bit lighter versus the chestnut color it was before. My personality, however, has changed a great deal, to be honest! Every time I walk past a girl my age, I stand a little straighter and hold my head higher, for I am proud to be a country girl. My string of pearls does not go unnoticed by anyone, including my family members, who asked the most invasive questions about its whereabouts and origin. Once I explained that Mrs. Jones herself had bequeathed (a word she used that I have become quite fond of and made a mental note to use whenever the possibility arose) it to me, Florence seemed so very disappointed that it caused me to feel embarrassed that I'd accepted the gift. I promised that Mrs. Jones said she has an even better gift that is intended for Florence, but it was useless; my sister was already aware of the fact that I was given something much more sentimental to Mrs. Jones than she would be gifted.

We catch a break in the endless morning rain when the three of us step out into the city, only for it to start again within a few minutes. Despite the rain, Brockschmidt is abuzz with news of courtship and of engagements that have been made so far. A man passes by me, asking his wife which of the Clyde brothers she thinks a woman named Kenova would choose to marry. A newspaper boy stands on a street corner shouting the headlines along with the price of the paper. He is no more than thirteen years old, which is a pattern I have seen in the city—children seem to find any type of work they can to help support their families, and if they can't, they all become homeless.

The seamstress's store is located less than five blocks from the hotel. The city's streets are a bit uneven and have winding, looping roads. Even if I'd lived in Brockschmidt since birth, I would never be able to go more than a block without getting lost!

The bell rings as Mother pushes open the door, leading us inside the small store. Just as Mother predicted, the seamstress is in a flurry of fabrics. We watch as she overlaps and pins a hem, then runs to fetch a measuring tape. To the right of the door is a sparkling glass window with lifeless mannequins showcasing the few dresses left in the store. The wall that meets the glass window is just one big shelf full of horizontal poles with different fabrics wound on them. A short counter stands in front of us when we enter the store, but it faces the shelf-wall. At the far side of the room are three mirrors hanging on the wall with a stool in front and a tiny dressing room shielded by a brown curtain. A man, somewhere near thirty years of age, with a bushy red mustache stands behind the counter, adding up prices and using sharp black scissors to cut six yards of blue velvet fabric for a tall, dark-skinned lady in a poufy pink dress. The cash register dings each time it is opened, the coins ring when dropped into place, and the bills are weighed down with metal clips.

The seamstress is dressed plainly compared to the other ladies in the room. She bends over a dress worn by a girl no older than my sister, pinning the hem so that it is long enough to cover the girl's shoes yet comfortable to walk in. The girl is equipped with a serious expression as she gazes at the dress—as if it is not the best thing in the world! A smirk appears on her lips when she notices how I stare at her dress, and she flips her unnaturally red curls over her shoulder. Florence takes notice of this dress-in-progress, making a mental note of how the seamstress pins the bottom, for it is no secret that Florence has a passion for sewing everything from dresses to socks.

The dress is a lovely deep indigo, made from the very velvet fabric that is being bought by the tall lady at the counter. It has puff sleeves that reach the elbow then become tightly fitted down the rest of the arm before stopping at the wrists, which drip lace. Several white buttons are at the wrist for decoration and match the buttons at the stomach of the dress. A V-neck reveals the cream-white blouse the girl wears. The skirt cascades down like an elegant wave of deep blue, then hovers mere centimeters above the floor, the same lace at the wrists stitched onto the bottom of the skirt. And the outfit is complete with a hat made from the same material. It has two red fabric flowers tucked between its rim and curved top.

It is positively beautiful—and worth a fortune, no doubt about that! Everyone who lays their eyes on the dress knows this, and the girl herself is certainly aware. She takes much delight in the jealous stares from the other girls in the store.

Mother is quick to notice the girl and the expensive dress that is in the process of being made. She takes each of our hands in hers and leads us away from the girl and over to the shelf that contains an array of fabrics. Different types of denim, lace, velvet, silk, wool, taffeta, and lightweight cotton are wound around poles that can easily be pulled out so that you can inspect whichever one you want to. A tray of spooled thread sits on a shelf filled with books on sewing stitches and patterns.

Mother focuses her attention on finding some fabric that could be made into a wonderful dress for Florence. I skim my fingertips across some soft velvet, wondering what it would feel like to wear something made from such fine material. Velvet is certainly more expensive than other materials, such as the wool that most of our clothes are made of. It is not like we could not afford it, but there would have to be a sacrifice for a few yards of velvet. All of our money cannot go toward a dress, no matter how beautiful it may be. Pa and Mother have always had a head for finance as far as I can tell; after all, we were barely affected by the hardships of last year, so I count my blessings.

Sometimes I wonder how empty people like the girl being adorned in a stunning velvet dress feel. Evelyn, for example, was at the height of society and never had to want for anything because she could have it in an instant, yet she described it as a cage that she was forever trapped in. But having bountiful amounts of cash has never been important to me, for it could never buy my most valuable possession: my family.

"How about this one?" I hold up the first fabric that I speculate Florence will like. It is a soft, white material I have never had the pleasure of seeing before. It's slightly shiny and has daisies dotted all along it. I hold it up to Florence's skin to see how it would appear with her features. In my eyes, my sister would surely be the belle of the ball in a dress made from this. "What do you think, Mother?" Florence smiles as she turns to face Mother with the fabric held up to her chest, waiting for approval.

Mother adjusts the daisy fabric in all different ways as if it will magically change in different lighting. "Hmmm. Yes, it should do very nicely if we do a cinched waist, a floor-length skirt—of course—and perhaps cap sleeves. It ought to be hot with the amount of people attending the ball and summer soon approaching, so the sleeves will do nicely, I imagine! Luckily, I brought a sewing pattern just in case we were to need it! Dear me, is that really the price per yard? It is nearly twice as much as the textiles back home! Fifteen cents per yard, my goodness." My sister's smile falters instantly upon the mention of the cost. We would need at least five or six yards to complete the dress. By the time that added up, it would be almost a dollar! Mother bites her lip, deciding what to say to her doe-eyed daughter with the daisy fabric tossed over her shoulder.

Near us stands a lady with her two daughters, who appear to be identical twins around the age of seventeen. She catches wind of our conversation and seems to take a mental note of the fabric held against Florence. She leans over to whisper to her girls, who have been picking up every spool of sewing thread and placing them back down. They stop quickly, gazing jealously at the daisy textile. The lady nods when she notices her daughters' expressions and marches over to where the three of us stand.

"My, what a gorgeous girl you are!" the lady exclaims, throwing her hands up at the sight of my sister. Florence graciously bows her head, acknowledging the compliment, but her uncomfortable stare is clear as day. "I think I shall take what is left of the bolt. Looks like there's only enough for one dress. If you do not mind stepping out of the way, darling! Or were you going to buy that? It seems awfully expensive for...*common folks*." I glare at the woman without taking a step away from the shelf. The woman's fake smile turns into an evil glare at my disobedience.

"You are mistaken, madam. I am just about to buy this very fabric for my daughter! You ought to run along and find something else for your children," Mother declares, stepping forward. She towers a whole head higher than the woman, who seems to shrink down but does not forgo the evil glare directed at us. For a moment I expect a few more insults to be thrown or the woman to tear the fabric away from Florence's hands, but nothing happens for several anxious seconds.

"I suppose I am mistaken. Good day, then." The woman turns back to her daughters, who still stand together looking enviously at my sister. She guides them to the other side of the shelf-wall, searching for another flowered fabric for the ball.

"Thank you, Mother!" Florence bounces up and down as soon as the woman is out of earshot.

Mother smiles meekly, possibly regretting the impulsive purchase she has just agreed to make. "You are most welcome, darling. Let us get in line before we are stuck waiting for too long."

By the time the coins are counted out three times over and handed to the clerk, Mother seems a bit more relaxed that the purchase is over and done with. The fabric is the sole reason for the jealous stares from the other ladies behind us. The clerk offers the delivery of the fabric to our hotel, and Mother quickly agrees to it, writing our hotel's name on a piece of paper.

The theme for the ball is "Flowers of Spring," so the shelves have already been bought up of every fabric containing a simple embroidered flower. This may just be the last flowered fabric in all of Brockschmidt! Although it would be nice to have a new dress for myself, I do not mind wearing my Sunday best or even my floral Christmas dress to the ball. It is such an exciting thing to imagine Mother, Florence, and me going to the ball at the end of the Brockschmidt engagement season! How far we have come from our town of Lorretta, Wyoming.

The bell rings as we step out of the shop with the intent of locating the art gallery. A single-seated wagon rolls by with wooden crates filled to the brim with apples, oranges, and exotic fruits. Mother asked the man behind the counter for directions to the gallery, and he gave them without missing a single detail. It appears the people of Brockschmidt have some-how become accustomed to the streets' twists and turns.

"Florence, do you think once you and Lawrence get married you will both move to Lorretta or stay here in Brockschmidt?" I ask as we cross the street to the other sidewalk.

Several moments pass by without an answer from my sister. I stare at her blankly as we continue to walk along the street. She bites her nails, avoiding the question for as long as possible. "Well, I do not know for sure. Lawrence likes Brockschmidt, but we have not talked about the future besides what he intends to do for a living. I would love to stay near to you, Pa, and Mother, but I am sure Lawrence must feel the same about Mr. and Mrs. Jones." It is a dignified answer, but a boring one at that. Florence sometimes seems to answer a question only to make me think of a thousand more during the process.

Mother leads us around a corner, then brings our conversation to an immediate halt. "Girls, there is no need to worry until we come to it! Lawrence Jones has yet to even propose, and if he does not at the ball, then we may have to wait another whole year for him to do so!" Mother seems to become stressed over just speaking of the matter of a ring on her daughter's finger, but Florence, however, does not seem too worried about the topic at the moment. We blankly nod without speaking another word of the matter for the day, but I will be sure to ask Florence privately about it soon.

The bell rings as we step out of the shop with the intent of locating the art gallery. The endless rain showers let up when we were in the seamstress's shop, and now only light gray clouds shield the city from the much-needed sunlight and blue sky that lies above. My shoe splashes into a puddle on the sidewalk as I try my best to keep up with Mother, who is trying to recite the directions we were given by memory. Stopping at every turn or corner, she goes over everything the man from the shop said, then tries to figure out where we are.

Brockschmidt is a grand city, but like every place, there are two sides to the story. The Puffins live on the privileged side, which is full of people who have worked hard to get where they are now. But as we walk along the one-room houses, I get a real glimpse at the poorer side of the city.

A girl not much younger than me throws a bucket of foul-smelling water onto the street and wipes the sweat from her brow with the back of her hand. She looks up at me for a second, possibly thinking of the hundred different things she must complete before the day is over. She wears a simple, short-sleeved black dress that barely reaches past her knees and patched up in several different places. A white cloth has been cut haphazardly and tied with two strips of cloth to make an apron around her waist. Her hair looks as if it could use a proper washing, but I highly doubt she has the means to do so. If only I had something to give this poor girl, who has likely faced unimaginable hardship!

With the dented metal bucket in one hand, her other arm is clearly visible, and I get a good look at it as we continue walking past. Dark purple and blue bruises dot her skin in no particular pattern, but it is obvious this was caused by the hand of someone else. She notices my endless stare and shields her arms from view, fearfully gazing at me one last time before ducking into her house. My heart aches to see her leave in a fearful manner, but there is nothing I could do about it.

Mother snatches each of our hands, pulling us along closely as we pass by disgusting men who whistle as we stroll by. Their smiles reveal missing teeth, and they point at us with mischievous grins. The houses are crammed together, providing little room for the inhabitants living inside of them. Most do not have paint, and even the ones that do are so worn down that we can see the moss-covered wooden planks that the homes are built of. Simple slanted rooves sit on top of the homes with the infrequent pipe poking out, letting the smoke from a stove into the atmosphere.

Soon we are walking along the serene streets again, eventually arriving at a place where the streets intersect. The square is just a place tucked in between a few buildings that cuts it off from the busy main street. A big fountain sits in the middle, spraying water up into the air only for it to fall back into the fountain. The building on the other side of the square is the art gallery. Mother is quick to comment on "the horrendous journey through the slums" that the man sent us on but is ultimately glad to have finally arrived at our destination.

The art gallery is a towering, red-bricked building with three rows of front-facing windows, and it has a huge archway in the middle with a dark wooden door. With the gallery in front of us, another wide building to our right facing Main Street, and two more buildings creating the four-sided square, it feels rather crowded. Water splashes quietly into the fountain, creating the only noise in the peaceful square.

At the archway is a tall man that stands steadfast, watching the occasional horse cart go by. Mother pulls out three tickets that she had bought this morning from the lady that stands behind the hotel counter. With a nod, the man reaches over, opening the heavy wooden door that slowly reveals the flamboyant gallery before us.

I step into a giant room that has an endless array of paintings hung in an orderly fashion on the dark scarlet walls. White porcelain tiles adorn the floors, reflecting the light back up at the dome-shaped glass ceiling.

The art gallery is as quiet as a mouse, no one speaking louder than a whisper or more than a sentence at a time.

As far as my eye can see, the gallery continues room to room with even more paintings along the walls. It seems like something out of a story book where the girl is transported to a foreign kingdom only to find out she is secretly the princess, and when she wanders around the enormous palace for the first time, she comes across this very room, which holds paintings that are forever marked in history books and rich with the artists' points of view! For a disappointing moment I must remind myself that I am not a lost princess in a fairytale land with a palace containing huge libraries, ballrooms, or art galleries.

Florence appears flabbergasted by not only the room but also the paintings along the walls that each seem to call out in a different voice. begging you to take a moment of your precious time to be enchanted by their oils, pastels, and watercolors. Mother is the face of calm, but I know better; it would be an understatement to say that on the inside she is equally or even more shocked than I am by the beauty of it all.

A bachelor stands over near the archway to the next room, gazing seriously at a painting of a solider going off to battle riding the most beautiful white horse. The man holds his hands tucked behind his back, giving the painting careful consideration before slowly walking into the next room as if his life has not been changed by the sight!

Immediately, I march over to the painting and mimic the man's serious stance, holding my hands tucked behind my back as I critique the artwork. The soldier's fearful expression is captured in a specific way that almost makes one feel pity for him as he stares into an endless sea of mounted, spear-wielding men. The soldier's white horse seems like the same horse from Revelation, as if Jesus himself is riding it. The man is staring at his fellow soldiers, who seem to await his command to charge into a battle from which some of them would not return. How could a person take one look at this art and not be forever affected?

I press my fingers to my lips, blowing an unseen goodbye to the soldier in the painting before rejoining Mother where she stands gazing at a different picture.

This other painting appears to strike Mother in an odd manner. Her face softens at the sight as if she herself has lived it. "*Sunshine Through the Trees,* 1861, by Robert Sandlock," the silver tag reads in black letters just below the painting's frame. A young woman sits on a rope swing attached to an overhanging branch, and her beau pushes the swing from where he stands in the shade of the forest. The woman is frozen in a smile, hanging onto the two ropes as she looks up at the sky above. How interesting, indeed!

"It is a very nice painting. Reminds me of a memory from when I was a little girl, we had a swing just like that at my childhood home in Maryland. Your grandpa built it for me when I was all but seven years old. Grandma Flora would push me on that swing for hours on end just to see that smile on my face each time I went up into the air," Mother whispers to nobody in particular. Her eyes are still fixed on the artwork as her mouth speaks the thoughts that run through her mind. She gives a sad smile before taking a deep breath and moving on. I watch as she moves a few steps away, gazing at the next art with less fondness.

When I look back at the woman on the swing in the middle of the forest, I do not see it for what it is but rather as an unknown memory of Mother's. She does not speak that often about Grandma Flora, but when she does, it is always about the most heartfelt things that could possibly be mentioned about a person. One could only wish to be spoken of that highly when their own time comes.

I will never forget when the news of Grandma Flora's passing reached Mother and Pa. It was a windy day back at our house in Colorado. That was the house that me and Florence were born in and had lived in for quite a few years before moving to Lorretta. Back when we were two peas in a pod, we did not care for jealousy since we were always too busy playing cat and mouse.

This time I was the mouse, and Florence ran around the uneven ground close to the front porch where Mother sat knitting a winter scarf. She was much younger then, although she still looks the exact same now, just with a few more worries placed on her shoulders. Pa had just arrived back home after taking a day to travel to the nearest town to get supplies for the coming winter. He dismounted his bay horse, leading it over to the hitching post, his face bearing a frown that made our hearts stop altogether.

My sister and I ran over to him with smiles of laughter, greeting his long-awaited return home, but we were waved away as he slowly walked up the few steps to where Mother sat. Her smile soon faded when she looked at his face, knowing that no good could come from that creased brow and worn expression. Without saying a word, he handed her an opened letter—a letter whose contents I was never told, for I was much too little to know of such private matters. Her tears came shortly after she read the first word written on the paper.

Less than two days later, Grandma Flora was placed in her forever resting place back east in Maryland. Without sooner notice, Mother was unable to attend the funeral, but Aunt Nancy, Uncle Edward, and young Nora attended despite the miscarriage that Aunt Nancy had endured three weeks prior.

Even though it was many years ago, I still remember Mother's tears, which seemed to last for days on end at the thought of Grandma Flora being gone from this world. Each night Mother slept—after falling asleep from exhaustion—with her very last letter from Grandma Flora, which said she had been planning to visit us in Colorado for Christmas in a few short months.

Artwork should depict a wonderful, immense, growing nature instead of what the average unimaginative person sees as dead. Nature is vivid and powerful and is God's great creation! Art should express a memory, place, point of view, or even what cannot be seen but rather imagined, an analogy between humanity or nature itself in all its wild beauty.

An oil painting labeled, "*Mankind and Creation*, 1834, by Unknown," is next. It appears to be the Garden of Eden. A soft sunlight comes from all directions, and trees bear exotic and undiscovered fruits that hang in the lavish sunbeams, gleaming with a certain angelic quality.

Adam and Eve, from whom mankind was birthed, stand wearing the clothes they made after eating the forbidden fruit. With their eyes open to the sin of the world around them, they are disobeying God by hiding in shame and trying to deceive him. All-knowing God walks into the garden with outstretched arms, glowing like a thousand suns and wearing pure white clothes. The oil painting shows the very sight which we all have so often imagined, the sight of God meeting Adam and Eve after they have eaten the fruit, the snake that is the devil in disguise slithering down the forbidden fruit tree with a fork-tongued smile of satisfaction for having undone mankind. *Mankind and Creation* sets forth the image of what the artist's mind envisioned as he or she read Genesis, and it can now also be seen by anyone else who lays their eyes upon it.

"I was never too interested in art until now if I am being truthful. My mind has always seen it as a most complex thing that can never convey a bigger message. Now it is much more than that indeed! Most of these paintings are physical proof of that, but I suppose it would not matter how good a work of art is if the viewer gaping at it cannot see it for its true meaning," I say aloud, addressing nobody in particular since not a soul is near me. Florence stands on the opposite side of the room looking up at a portrait of an English nobleman, trying to figure out if there is meaning behind it or if it is truly just a portrait. Mother is slowly walking around without stopping to gaze at anything; the memory of the swing is proba- bly still fresh in her mind.

Passing under an archway, I enter a room that almost mirrors the first one but has fewer paintings and instead has more sculptures, which all stand in glass cases or on pedestals. A stone woman leans against a broken column, reaching up and wearing nothing but a piece of cloth over herself.

It is something from the ancient civilization of the Greeks or Romans. The illustration behind the sculpture is a thunderous sky with bolts of lightning striking a hilly countryside. Darkness looms dangerously over the landscape, reminding us that perils, although unforeseeable, can come as quickly as a midsummer's storm.

Chapter 16

A BROKEN MIND VERSUS A BROKEN HEART

EACH MORNING FOR THE NEXT five days Mother works tirelessly to perfect Florence's daisy dress. My ongoing pleading finally broke Mother's stubbornness, and she has finally allowed me to help her make it! I am only allowed to stitch places where it would not be visible to anyone, for my sewing is in much need of reforming and practice.

My sister stands in the middle of her room, and Mother bends over at Florence's feet with a needle and thread. It is a mere twenty-four hours until the ball, and so far, the dress is more than halfway done. The parts that are already complete include the cinched waist, the bodice with the short sleeves that will sit on top of her shoulders once she tries it on, and the skirt. All that is left to do is sew all the pieces together and hem the skirt, which Mother is currently working on.

I sit on Florence's perfectly made bed as I stitch the final part of the bodice. My weary eyes glance over at the tiny clock that ticks quietly on the fireplace. I squint until I see the hands pointing at five and eleven. Considering we all went to bed at ten o'clock last night and awoke this morning at five, a mere fifty-five minutes ago, I would call our progress a great improvement! Florence stifles another yawn as she stands with her arms stretched out. She eyes the mirror on the wall, which reflects her face to where I sit.

I tie the last knot in the thread and use the fabric shears to cut off the excess. "It is coming along nicely! The bodice is finished now. I do wish we could have made the sleeves better, maybe even puffed out! Oh, how lovely that would look on you." My feet hit the marble flooring as I jump off the bed, rushing to place the bodice at Mother's feet.

She glances over at me, stopping her work on the skirt to check my sewing. "Yes, you have done very well on the bodice—I dare say that it is better than I would have done if I'd had to complete it in addition to the skirt! The puff sleeves would have looked very fashionable on Florence's dress, but we haven't enough fabric to waste on them. Do not fret, for the current sleeves will look just fine! I admit it was foolish of me to give into temptation and buy such an expensive fabric, but it has turned out better than any of us expected!" She acknowledges the work that we each put in over the past few days, giving a tired smile to each of her daughters.

Florence puts her arms down, twiddling her fingers before opening her mouth to speak. "Do you truly think so? Is it wrong to be this nervous waiting for the inevitable? I can hardly contain my excitement for the ball tomorrow, and just the thought of Lawrence proposing provokes a hundred new worries. If only I could just go forward in time! How can I even enjoy the delicious food we will be served if there is a growing pit in my stomach?" Her eyes dart to each of us, waiting for someone to say something to soothe her, but we come up short-handed. Mother opens her mouth twice but ultimately closes it and continues working.

"Well, I….do not fret, dear sister, for I am quite certain your beau will propose within the next twenty-four hours! He may be picking out a ring as we speak! Imagine a gleaming silver—or even gold—ring on your finger tomorrow. How lovely something like that will look on you. Mother, how did Pa propose to you all those years ago?"

Mother stands once again, brushing off her dress and giving a meek answer. "Well, your Pa was incredibly nervous. We were back east on a trip to visit Grandma Flora and Grandpa Judd. There is this mountain range that I do not recall the name of that was not far from the house. He took me out there, intending for it to be sunset, but had lost track of time, so the stars had already come out. Your Pa was so nervous that it took nearly fifteen minutes just to get past the promises of being a good husband! Once I was certain he was proposing, I simply said yes, and we got married a few months later." Although it was funny to think of Pa as being so nervous to the point where he could not speak, the story does not sound as romantic as one's engagement story should. Florence just nods, taking the story into consideration, perhaps hoping her proposal will be better than Mother's.

"There! All hemmed and finished. You can step out of the skirt now, Florence. We can finish the rest tonight, then see if anything else needs to be altered. We must start wrapping the curls in your hair or else they will not be ready tomorrow night."

Neither me nor my sister have ever had our hair wrapped in curls because, before now, there was never much of a reason to. Florence obeys, stepping out of the skirt, changing back into her nightgown, and then sitting in a chair next to the fancy vanity in her room, which I had not noticed until now.

Mother brings the pitcher and bowl over to the vanity. She pours the icy cold water onto Florence's hair little by little while I hold the bowl underneath to catch the excess water. Once her hair is completely wet, I am ordered to round up all the hair ribbons we own between the three of us. I run off, finding two handfuls of ribbons that clash with each other, being the many colors they are.

I watch closely as Mother wraps Florence's hair tightly around one ribbon, then spins it slowly up until it reaches her scalp. She then ties the ribbon and moves onto the next one. So this is how the city girls get those unnatural, beautiful curls! Once Florence's and my curls are wrapped up and finished, the three of us sit down on the purple couch, eating the strawberry scones, slices of bacon, and scrambled eggs that were delivered to our room on a cart.

Just as Florence said earlier, she has lost her appetite, only taking a few bites of her scone before placing it back down on the plate. The only comfort to her is studying *Proper Etiquette of a Lady*, which she already finished reading yesterday. The whole day passes by in a blur of needles, thread, alterations to the dress, and compliments on the final product.

It is the middle of the night when I strangely awake to the silence of the evening. I close my eyes, rolling over and trying to find my dream again, but it is no use, for I am already wide awake. I sigh, sitting up straight in my bed and leaning against the mountain of pillows behind me. My stomach growls loudly, begging for just a bite of the food left over from the dinner cart.

My feet touch the floor silently, and I tip-toe to the door in the darkness of the night. The knob rotates slowly as I grimace at the thought of waking up my sister or Mother when their sleep is very much needed considering the important day that is tomorrow.

In the darkness, I can just barely make out the dinner cart that sits by our locked hotel door, our dinner plates piled high and waiting to be taken by the hotel cleaners in the morning and replaced with breakfast. An apple sits atop a bowl of uneaten fruit, begging me to take a bite from it.

My stomach growls once more as I bite into the apple. I then freeze because my ears hear a different sound coming from down the hall. A light comes from under Florence's door, which sparks my curiosity. I set down the apple, swallow, then knock as quietly as possible. I hear a whisper of a, "Come in," and the door creaks open.

Florence sits in the middle of her bed reading a book with her lamp-light turned on. She turns her head, which is still tied up with the hair ribbons, only it is now dry after so many hours of wearing what I imagine are now painful things. My own tied up curls itch profusely, begging to be let down.

"What are you doing awake at this hour, Azalea?"

"I could ask you the same thing! Why in the world are you even bothering reading '*Proper Etiquette of a Lady*'? It will only drive you crazy with worry if you are persistently thinking about the ball."

She nods in agreement, closes the book, and sets it down on the table. I close her door, stepping back out into the darkness of the hotel room and debating whether to go back in her room and talk to her.

My conscious wins in the end, and I reenter Florence's room, this time crawling into her bed. When we were children and one of us had a nightmare, we would crawl into each other's bed at any hour of the night, finding comfort knowing none of the imaginary beasts we dreamt of could attack us if we were together.

Several moments of silence go by, and my sister does not say anything about me returning to my room, for she does not want to talk. Instead, she turns off the lamplight and pulls the blanket closer to her, causing my side of the blanket to be yanked over to her. I shiver in the cold night air, pulling the soft blanket back over to my side, a laugh escaping my mouth.

"Do you think you will say yes to Lawrence?" I suddenly ask, bringing the blanket war to a stop.

"I do not know. It is much more complicated than that. You will understand when you are in my predicament," her voice whispers into the darkness of the night.

I turn over to see her face in the moonlight that streams in through the window next to my side of the bed. She seems properly conflicted by the question I asked, and she still gave a horrible answer.

"Don't do that."

"Do what? Give you an answer to the very question you asked?" She stares at me, her blue eyes filled with sarcasm.

I give her a playful glare, then become serious. "No. Don't act like I am a child—because we both know I am not anymore. Tell me the truth, sister. Do you love Lawrence? If he gives you the most romantic proposal known to mankind, would you accept or decline? You must know these things when you are courting him!"

Florence shifts, uncomfortable with my intrusive questions, but they are genuine. What will she do in less than twenty-four hours when Lawrence gets down on one knee? "I...I don't know," she says without caring to whisper anymore.

I peek over at her face, fearful that I have made her mad, but there is not an ounce of anger, only utter confoundment. "What does love even feel like? Mother has never spoken of her and Pa courting until today, so it is not as if I have had any information to go on! What if he does propose? What do I do, or even say, for that matter?" She throws her hands up, letting them fall back to the bed with a thud, speaking solely to the ceiling.

"I don't know. I figured you would understand what love feels like since you are older." I pause, waiting to ask the question that has been aflame inside of me ever since I met Russell St. Claire. "Have you ever been kissed by a boy? Russell St. Claire kissed me the morning we walked to the stagecoach station. He gave me that chain with the gold ring on it, saying that he had promised to give it to someone special. What does that mean, Florence? When a boy says, 'someone special,' what does that mean?"

Florence becomes dead silent for several minutes. It gets to the point where I must turn back over and look at her to make sure she did not fall asleep while I spoke. "Russell St. Claire kissed you!" she whispers loudly when I finally look her in the eye.

"Shh! You might just wake Mother talking that loudly. Yes, he kissed me, but it was not how I had always imagined kissing to be like. Kind of gross, to be quite simple." My sister bursts out into a fit of laughter, which causes me to laugh as well. We both clutch our stomachs due to the immense pain, wipe the tears from our eyes, and shush each other continuously since when one of us becomes quiet, the other one seems to start back up again.

After gaining control of herself, Florence finally answers my question. "Yes, Theodore Roast kissed me one time during a game of hide and seek maybe ten years ago. Mrs. Roast just laughed up a storm when I ran back to her and Mother, wiping my mouth over and over again. But Mother was furious, saying he had practically stolen my virtue, which I now realize is a bit too dramatic, for it was only in childhood innocence." She giggles, as do I, but then faces me with a look of determination. "Are you in love with Russell? How tragic that would be if we never see him again. To answer your question, I think that to him, 'someone special' probably means his future wife. The ring was most likely meant for his proposal. Gold is rather expensive! He must be rich to have that in his possession. I thought Russell was very handsome—much more then Lawrence to be truthful, even though he is by far the best young man in Brockschmidt—but since I had to catch a city boy, I knew it was out of the question. Do not tell Mother, but most nights I still have nightmares of that day. Seeing two people die might well be the most traumatic thing to ever happen to us!"

I nod, thinking back to the time when we were moments from death. A shiver prickles up my spine just revisiting the recollection. "Me too. I do not know if I can ever unsee it all. If only it could just be permanently erased from my subconscious! Do you truly think it was for his future wife? I wonder why he gifted it to me, unless he…" My sentence trails off, leaving the thought for both of us to contemplate.

Florence clears her throat, then speaks quietly once more. "I think I like Lawrence. He is a nice young man, and I wish we had spoken more about our interests at the ladies' tea, but he spent half of the time just talking about perpetual motion, which I know nothing about! He shall make a fine husband and father, though. I wish to not speak so plainly, but it is definitely comforting to know that he can provide for his family. Love will come later, I hope. Being in a loveless marriage will not last long, but that is what I had in mind when we came to Brockschmidt."

Florence speaks in such a quiet, soothing voice that the thought of sleep overpowers any objections I would normally have about my sister entering a loveless marriage. "That is nice, Florence. We ought to get to sleep or else you will be too tired out for tomorrow. Good night, sister. I love you." Ever since I was little and realized how precious life really is after Grandma Flora passed, I've said, "I love you," to my loved ones before going to sleep. Those three words may someday be the last I speak or even the last words someone hears, and what fine words they are to hear before you die. It may be morbid, but it is never guaranteed that any of us will wake up in the morning the night is an unconscious day filled with uncertainty for what is to happen when you are not awake.

"Yes, you are right. Good night. I love you too."

Chapter 17

NIGHTS LIKE THESE

"Honestly, Azalea! I told you to leave your curls in all night, and now you come to me within just five hours of the ball to tell me your hair is messed up?" Mother exclaims as she smooths out her dress. The dress does not contain any hint of floral pattern or so much as an embroidered leaf, for not a thing Mother owns looks like that. Instead, it is her Sunday best, which she bought last summer after Pa sold a few of the chickens and we had a few coins to spare. Florence, Pa, and I decided that the money would be put forth for Mother to finally buy fabric for a new Sunday best since her last one had been through many years of use, and it clearly showed.

This one, however, is a great improvement! It is a simple, white bodice with long sleeves and a navy-blue skirt made from the leftover yards of fabric from Pa's Sunday shirt that we had made that summer for the upcoming winter. The dress's extravagant folded-over collar, which reaches mid-shoulder, is made from the same navy-blue material. The dark blue makes the white cotton that much more elegant!

Each week when Mother came downstairs wearing the pretty dress it always reminded me of her smile that morning, after we came back from town and carried in the white and blue fabrics. She was standing over a pot on the oven, boiling that night's dinner while wearing her old best. Turning around to see her husband and two children grinning and holding out the newly bought goods, she was so properly stunned at the sight that she had to sit down and give the wooden spoon to my sister so she could take over the cooking. Florence craned her neck just to see Mother running her fingers over it. Tears brimmed at her eyes, for little had we all known that this was the very thing she had wanted.

Mother clears her throat, yanking me out of my thoughts, whilst awaiting my response. "Yes, Mother. They are not too bad, I must say, just a bit frizzled! Can I please take them out now and gaze at the waves in my hair?" Today is the day, and the ball is less than five hours away, the ball where all our futures will change at the bend of a knee and the joyous yes that would soon follow. Florence is about to become the new Mrs. Jones and marry into one of the richest families in this city!

My bead strand is already waiting to be clasped around my neck and worn to the party for all to look upon its shining beauty. And it was decided that I will wear my Christmas dress and have my hair in curls for the night. Mother demanded that I not take them out before going to the party, but I have awoken to find that one wrapped-up curl is halfway unraveled, and the others are a frizz of hairs sticking out!

Our dinner cart arrives, carrying fried ham, buckwheat cakes, baked potatoes, and a tea set with fresh black tea. Mother graciously takes the cart from the hotel worker, rolling it over to the purple couch and pulling up a chair to the other side of it.

The room is silent as knives cut through the ham, forks carry the food up to our mouths, and tea is poured into the light blue china teacups. Florence forces the food to go down her throat, but on a day such as today she can barely eat one bite of food. My mood is rather solemn due to the heavy cloud of worry hanging over all our heads. Even Mother does not seem interested in the prospect of eating the food, even if it is the most deliciously cooked dinner that ever graced our stomachs.

With a piece of savory ham still in my mouth; I voice the thought that pops into my head. "Oh! We must hurry down to the gardens before we disembark to the ball. A lily will be an appealing sight in your hair! If you want a bit more color, there are red roses growing on a bush inside of the greenhouse. The greenhouse is the most exquisite place I ever did see with my own eyes! There are ever so many plants that don't even seem native to Wyoming. Either that, or I have never seen them before! From what I recall since last being in the greenhouse, there is this purple and white iris planted in a very oddly colored clay pot. Of course, it would not look too lovely with your dress, but I thought it was worth the mention since I have never seen nor heard of a plant of that nature before. It almost looks half-dead, all wilted down, but I suppose it is meant to look like that! Maybe God had a sense of humor and created a flower that wilts every day, although now that I speak of that out loud, it sounds sad to hear of a wilted iris." The words fly out of my mouth in a rambled-on fashion. In most cases I would have just stopped talking after mentioning the red roses, but today is different, for we all need something to take our minds off the ball. The duty fell upon me to start some sort of conversation—even if it is something like rambling on and on about the flowers outside in the greenhouse.

Mother takes notice of Florence's constantly biting her nails, which have been scrubbed clean along with the rest of her visible skin. Her face is the cleanest I have ever seen it and seems to glow in the sunlight that streams into the room. Tonight, we are no longer country bumpkins (not that we ever really were) but instead two country girls blending in and taking on the mien of city girls. Or rather, young ladies, on account of that sounding much more refined and proper.

Mother turns to me after taking a sip of her tea. "Yes, that sounds like a good idea, Azalea. Before we leave, you are tasked with picking out a flower for each of us to wear in our hair. Mind you, nothing too frivolous or colorful! We cannot walk into the ball looking like island savages with awful flowers in our hair, so nothing of this wilting flower you speak of. Something sensible that will allow your sister to stand out amongst the other girls that are sure to be overdone in their looks."

I nod happily, grabbing another bite of the wheat cake. My mind is already racing at the thought of which flower I will choose for each of us! If only I knew some of the names of the flowers; it would sound so much more elegant at the ball! *Oh, this flower is called the Yellow-Valley Orchid, and the one my sister is wearing in her golden locks is none other than a pink Gardenia.* The words seem like they would just roll off one's tongue, don't they?

Once dinner is finished, we disperse into our rooms, each finding something to worry about and contemplate. Mother is surely overcome by Florence's proposal and unable to aid due to her rather unconventional proposal from Pa, who could barely say two sentences without stammering! My sister is obvious in her fearing the worst for this evening, which we are all quite certain will not happen. I, however, am concerned about my looks, even though I swore to myself to never again be vain about my unchangeable appearance.

I stand in front of my mirror, agonizing over every detail, such as the hair that sticks out of my impermanent curls in an unruly manner. In all my fretting, I have not once thought of myself as ugly, for I know I am a pretty girl but not the prettiest. Sometimes when I just happen to look in the mirror, I catch myself in quite a beautiful moment thinking about how perfect I look sitting on my bed with an open book in my hands.

It is not as if those moments have stopped, but instead they seem to happen less frequently in the city. Could it be because of the other girls around me, who appear exemplary at everything? Or is it just because I do not feel as though I truly belong in Brockschmidt? Lorretta shall always remain my home.

Speaking of which, I have not received a reply from Pa in a while, which makes me think that something has happened to him, but no word has been sent to us by Uncle Edward, so I am forced to go on assuming he is fine.

I reach over to touch the necklace that Mrs. Jones gifted me. It lies on top of the dresser, and just feeling the cold pearls touch my fingertips makes me remember Mrs. Jones's words after she unclasped it from her neck and put it in my hand. *"After years of praying, my looks slowly started changing, but only when I became perfectly happy with my appearance! Do not find faults in your looks, Azalea, because I assure you that you are already beautiful."* The words echo in my mind, taking me back to the ladies' tea party and the exact moment when she said them.

"Azalea! We are leaving in two hours so that Florence may get there early, so do start getting ready!" Mother's voice calls out from the other side of my door.

I jump at the sound, as I was lost in my thoughts, but quickly regain my composure. "Yes, Mother. I will be out promptly!" I call back, but the only reply I receive is the echo of her footsteps as she saunters away.

Water splashes over the edge of the bowl, getting the top of the dresser wet as I continue to pour the rest of the icy liquid from the pitcher. I shiver while splashing the water onto my face, wiping the dirt away and scrubbing my face clean. The soft towel soaks up the remaining water. I then stroll over to my dress, which has already been laid out on my bed for me. Even if my Christmas dress is not the prettiest or fanciest, it will still be equally, if not even more, special than anything else worn tonight at the ball.

I unravel my messy curls to reveal the waves in my hair, except for the one strand that is half flat. I slip on my shoes, then start walking out of my room before realizing that the most important piece is missing.

When I put it on, the cream-colored necklace gleams round my neck and catches the light in interesting ways, making me shine more than before. My eyes glance at the mirror, and it is obvious that right now is one of the times when you find yourself in a truly beautiful moment. Not because of how you look, but instead because of how you feel inside.

A knock comes at the door. "Azalea?" a small voice asks.

"Yes, Florence? Come in."

Florence creaks the door open and slips into the room. The sunset leaks through my window, its orange light shimmering along the marble floors until reaching Florence and bathing her in the sunset's glorious light. The daisies cascade up the skirt of the A-line dress beautifully. Her hair is no longer in the uncomfortable hair ribbons but now let down in a waterfall of gold. The curls stream down to her mid-back, on account of Mother pinning the top half up in a carefree swirl of a bun, creating a half-up half-down look—unlike my hair, which is much longer and let down. Two small pieces of hair have been pulled out, framing Florence's face and making her seem even more innocently and unknowingly dazzling.

"Oh, Florence, you look so beautiful! I can only hope that I might look just like you when I'm eighteen. Mrs. Jones has such pretty honey-ginger hair, almost like yours, but she told me that it used to be a similar shade to mine, and it ended up lightening over the years! Oh, what a hopeful feeling that sparks in my heart!" I spin around the room, looking up at the ceiling, which is an array of hand-painted blue skies, cherubs, gold vines, and doves, before stopping to see my sister's complex expression. "What is wrong, sister? Are you unwell?"

"Azalea, I have tried to remain composed as Mother told me to, but the nerves have finally gotten to me! I do not know if I can even attend the ball at this point. What if I trip and fall down the staircase or otherwise make a fool of myself and our family name? I still don't even know what to say to Lawrence when I see him, but I am positive no words will ever be able to escape my lips when I'm in his presence!" She floats over to my bed, spreading her arms out and falling back on the springy mattress.

I walk over, her worries bringing a smile to my lips. I have clearly noticed these worries, but I know they are not as confounding as she thinks they are. "My dear Florence, do not think too much about the little things or else you will miss the whole moment in the here and now! Just focus on seeing Lawrence instead of on what he may or may not say. I am sure that once you are in each other's presence all these worries will go away. I'm quite certain of that! Now, I must pick the best flowers from the greenhouse for all of us, so I will be back in a moment. Then we can leave." My sister gives me a meek smile, understanding what I have spoken about but also persistent about not letting go of her thoughts. Florence and I have always had a bit of Mother's stubbornness, which is both a curse and blessing in moments like these.

⌣

The sun begins dipping below the rooftops as I fling the glass doors open, skipping to the back of the greenhouse.

The sudden presence of an older lady makes me stop dead in my tracks. Staring melancholically at the fading sunshine, she sits on the bench near the fountain. With her gaze turned in the opposite direction, I start sneaking backward to the door, seeing that this moment was meant to be spent in solitude.

At the worst possible moment, I bump into a pot sitting on a metal stand, sending it crashing to the floor. The pot breaks apart in a hundred pieces at my feet, causing the woman to be disrupted from her sadness and eye me with a questioning gaze.

"What are you doing, child?" her hoarse voice croaks as I open my eyelids.

"Sorry, ma'am. My mother tasked me with finding three flowers to put in our hair for the Brockschmidt ball tonight. You looked so sad, and I figured you might want to be alone. When I tried walking away, the pot fell and broke at my feet. I did, after all, knock into it, so I suppose it is my fault there." I wave my hands rapidly as I explain my being here and the commotion I have just caused. But by the time I finish, my face a cherry red from the humiliation, the old lady just bends over laughing.

She stays bent over on the bench in an uncomfortable position even after several moments of me awkwardly glancing around.

"Come sit, child." She finishes laughing and waves me over.

I cautiously obey, sitting next to her on the bench. Her face is wrinkled with age but still shows a sense of happiness and humor in her laugh-lines. "I am the garden keeper who takes care of all the plants in this here greenhouse. Oh, don't look so terrified! The pot is nothing. It happens all the time, though never under circumstances such as that. As you said, the annual Brockschmidt ball is tonight, and it stirs up memories of the past. Mrs. Zerkel has been running the annual ball for four years now, but it has been a timeless tradition. Mrs. Zerkel certainly has a way of making the ball the event of the year. Nothing wrong with that…until everyone becomes focused on just getting invited and never enjoying it! My husband—may his soul rest in peace up in heaven— proposed to me the day before our ball, which was nowhere near as friv- olous as they have it now, and that is where we announced our engage- ment. Every year it stirs up those things and gets me all teary. How old are you, child? You cannot be younger than seventeen if you plan on getting proposed to tonight."

I hold back a smile, but my toothy grin peeks through as I speak. "I am fourteen years old, ma'am. We are attending for my sister's sake; she is eighteen, turning nineteen this August, and her beau is bound to ask for her hand in marriage tonight. She is just a bundle of nerves right this moment. May I ask how you did not know I was already engaged?" The very topic of me being engaged humors a certain side of myself.

"There is no ring on your finger." The old woman grins as she points to my left hand. I laugh at myself for not noticing something as obvious as that. "I can help you pick out the flowers if you'd like. Everything you see in here was started out from a wee little seed by me." She stands up from her spot next to me on the bench without waiting for my answer and limps over to the array of bushes, pots, and planters on the other side of the fountain. I leisurely follow the woman and join her as she stares down at the many flowered plants that gaze up at us, hoping to be chosen.

"Hmm. There are the basic daffodils, tulips, carnations, and gerbera dai-sies, but half of the city will have those. A dahlia will look nice in your hair; after all, they are known to signify when someone is entering a new phase of life! Yes, that will do." The old woman points at each plant as she talks in a hushed tone. When coming to the brilliant red dahlias, which have hints of white at the ends of the petals, she stops and tries to bend down but is forced to remain standing due to her age.

"Allow me to pick the flowers," I interject. "You can just tell me which one, and I shall pluck it." The old woman smiles and nods to a dahlia, as she called it, then croaks out more of her thoughts. The dahlia gleams in the orange sunlight as it sits in my hand.

"Roses are such common things now. In my day they were hard to raise up in the cold climate we've got here in Wyoming. The white anem-one right there was shipped here from some state back in the southeast. Now, a rose form white begonia is very nice and not so much to the point when everybody wears them. Snow-in-summer, that is the one! Yes, right there. Shirley poppy, certainly a colorful option. And a lily should be very personable choice, yes, that one to the left." I bend over, picking the last flower and ending up with a wonderful bouquet consisting of a dahlia, some snow-in-summer (which I mentally note because I wish to remem-ber such a distinctive name), a white anemone that will be a lovely picture in Mother's hair, and lastly, a rose form white begonia that I can already imagine matching nicely with Florence's brand-new dress.

I stand, brushing the dirt off my dress, then look the old woman in the eye. "Thank you, ma'am! I must run off and deliver these flowers to my family. I daresay you have sparked a new interest in me for plants!" I exclaim thankfully as the old woman smiles once more.

"Have fun, darling girl. This night may just be one of the most important ones of your life, so do keep every detail in that head of yours! Oh, and child, it is called botany." she advises, then turns, starting to limp away into the shadowy side of the greenhouse. Without so much as a glance back, she disappears into the darkness in mere moments without waiting for my response.

I carefully ponder her words as I walk back to the room. Upon my arrival, the door swings open as Mother and Florence stampede out into the hallway. Mother is the first to glance at my surprised expression, but then she turns her devout attention to the flowers, already determining which ones were good enough to be worn to the prestigious Brockschmidt ball.

"This one for Florence. Azalea, which one did you pick out for yourself? I suppose this one will do perfectly for myself. Are you prepared to leave? We must make it to this Mrs. Zerkel's house early." I am quick to grab my dahlia as she starts pulling the flowers out of the bouquet. Mother has gotten the white anemone, as I had thought she would, and Florence is handed the begonia, which really does look like a white rose. "Wait, have I forgotten the invitation? Oh, here it is! Come, children, we must quicken our pace if we are to be on time. I made arrangements with the lady at the front counter for us to arrive by carriage. We mustn't have our dresses dirtied by walking across town in the dead of the night."

Mother tucks my flower behind my ear as she did with hers. In all her franticness she has just a moment to give me a smile of admiration, which I so gladly return. My sister's begonia is placed in the middle of her perfectly done bun, making it look like the flower is emerging from the curls.

My head turns ever so elegantly as we step down the staircase and into the hotel lobby, where a grand carriage awaits us outside. I wave a quick goodbye to the portrait of the lady as we walk away from her, and for a moment it seems as if her simple smile is meant for me alone. Her eyes, which match the blue dress she wears, watch my family exit the hotel lobby.

The carriage sits just outside the hotel's entrance, and a Belgian draft horse swishes its tail as it is hitched up to the black hackney carriage. Two small wheels are at the front of the carriage, and the two in the back are larger. The top of the carriage is down, revealing a starry nighttime sky that has not a cloud in sight. A firelit lamp hangs near the driver's seat up front. The driver stands beside the opening, ready to offer his hand when we step into the carriage.

I take Florence's hand with a smile as we climb up to our seat in unison, Mother settling in the seat across from us. With a click of a tongue and the crack of a whip, the horse trots away, sailing us smoothly over the cobblestone streets. The moon is full, shining on us as we travel down the winding streets, waving royally at every person we pass by. Many other fancy carriages ride alongside us, all going to the very same destination of Mrs. Zerkel's house. At some point the cobblestone street transitions to a dirt road, leading us to the quieter and more expensive side of the city. I glance down at my right palm, stroking my scar, wondering what it would be like if Russell were here, but the thought is put out of my mind once we arrive at Mrs. Zerkel's house at 482 Grandiose Drive.

The horses whinny joyfully as we step out of the carriage one by one. My eyes are focused on Mrs. Zerkel's house in all its angelic beauty, glowing like a beacon in the night as I step out of our carriage with my mouth ajar at the palace before me. Rocks crunch under my feet as the three of us walk side by side with everyone else in the late April night air up the way to the grand front door, which is painted a burgundy color. Lights glow in the evening from the lightbulbs inside the house, and streetlights line either side of the path.

This path leads straight to the burgundy door, which is wide open. Two men stop each person to check the invitations. I catch just a glimpse of the inside as I pick up my skirt to walk up the steps before finally reaching the door. Mother offers our invitation with a certain air of importance, giving a smirk of confidence as the man waves his hand for us to enter the building. A glance over my shoulder reveals the crowd of people standing in the line anxiously waiting for their chance to join the party.

⌒

Closed white and golden doors lined the hallway, and portraits of unfamiliar people hang on walls that are so tall they seem to reach the heavens. Even the portrait of Abraham Conway—a man who was a part of the Lewis and Clark Expedition—dressed head to toe in a travelers clothing, seems to look down on me. Mother had once told us in our Sunday schooling about how he bravely fought off a bear from attacking his fellow traveler with no more than a knife and spear! On the ceiling is artwork that must have taken hundreds of hours to complete based on the detail in the forest and castle scenes. Candlelit chandeliers hang from the hand-painted ceilings, adding even more light to the grand hallway! The hallway continues into a dark, unlit gloominess, but Mother leads our group of three away from it, following the crowd of people in front of us that sing out their own praises, which are very much alike to mine. I, for once, choose not to speak, instead enjoying the observations in my mind.

In the middle of the hall are two staircases chiseled from limestone. One leads up to a second floor, curving out of sight, but the other goes straight down to an open room filled with the gentle hum of voices. Heels click their sweet ring as skirts are lifted and hands stroke the railings. I hold my breath, internally praying that I do not fall down the thirty stairs. I remember at the last moment to look up instead of at my feet as I walk down, the spitting image of grace. Florence's smiles coquettishly at me as she walks on the other side of Mother. Her eyes are soon taken off my coy grin and directed at the awe-inspiring ballroom before us.

The theme of the ball is clearly visible by the sea of floral prints: enormous hidden hoopskirts and petticoats, puffed-out sleeves, feathered hats, waists contracted by hidden corsets, trains long enough to be intended for wedding gowns, colors ranging from a moss green to grape purple to lemon yellow and everything imaginable in between!

The staircase finally ends at a wide limestone floor filled with men and women of all ages. Two blooming bouquets of exotic flowers stand in dark red vases atop stone pillars on either side of the staircase's end. On the ceiling above, which is painted in heavens of blue and white clouds like our hotel room, hang even more candlelit chandeliers spiraling down in an array of white crystals reflecting a glowing warmth. In the corner closest to Florence sits a string quartet playing violins and violas as hands are taken to the middle of the floor for the night's first dance. A few tables along the left wall hold bountiful amounts of foods, including roasted ducks, browned bread loaves, an assortment of berry scones, jams, jellies, cakes, dishes of baked and boiled vegetables, and finally, a tray of chocolate truffles (a word I hear one lady call them as she pops another in her mouth). Fans flap in the hands of the young ladies who have not been asked by a man to join them on the dance floor.

"Mrs. Jones! How divine you look this evening!" Mother sings out, walking over to Mrs. Jones, who stands talking to a few other women dressed in expensive textiles. My sister and I stand on either side of our mother as we saunter closer to the group of ladies.

At the sound of her name, Mrs. Jones tosses her honey-ginger curls and turns to us with a genuine beaming smile. "Mrs. Stanton, Florence, and Azalea! How perfectly sublime to see you all here, and in such good spirits! Dear Florence, your gown is amazing, wherever did you get it?" The ladies behind her coo their halfhearted compliments to accompany Mrs. Jones's praise. Mrs. Jones is the north star of the night, wearing a dark sapphire ballgown with lace at the neck, off-the-shoulder sleeves, and pink and white roses patterned along it. Her hair is tucked up like Florence's, adorned with a pink rose to match.

Florence steps forward, curtsying at her name. The way her skirt flares out as she rises makes her look like an angel. "Thank you for your words, even though they are truly too kind! We went to a seamstress's shop just last week before we attended an art gallery. If it were not for Mother's trained sewing and Azalea's help, it would have never been finished in time for tonight!" she exclaims with a smile, then flinches at the realization that she has just admitted the very dress she wears was handmade by us. The women behind Mrs. Jones's shoulder quickly pick up on this and start whispering to each other behind their fans. Florence glances worriedly at Mother, who is most likely having a stroke behind her calm face, then looks down at the ground, ashamed of messing up only twenty minutes into the evening.

Mrs. Jones moves forward, lifting Florence's chin with one of her white-gloved hands. "It is beautiful and nothing to be ashamed of. I must ask you for the pattern sometime soon, for I am sure I know a handful of ladies who would love to use it!" Upon this remark, the ladies behind her chime in with their admirations of a job well done, which make Florence's face morph into a smile once again only to falter a moment later at the mention of my name.

"My dear Azalea, please do tell us of this visit to the art gallery! You do have such an expert way with words for a child your age, and I must say your jewelry looks wonderful." Mrs. Jones remarks quite marvelously. My hand flutters to my neck, as do the eyes of everyone around us. I glance at my sister's face, which appears hurt and only interested in what I am about to say because she has to be. The nods and stares of the ladies make me break into a sweat as I begin with a quiver.

"Well, I…the paintings—there were ever so many to look at—and the sculptures were breathtaking. How interesting it is to see our American culture through unbiased eyes, which I found out are very much needed in an art gallery if one wishes to see the artwork through different…perspectives." I bite my lip as the impact of my words settles into everyone around me, and several conversations are struck up at once.

"Was it the gallery on Melody Lane?" one of the women asks as the lady next to her comments on a painting she saw two years ago by a famous artist.

"A gorgeous oil painting called *Peaceful Underfields*…valley of red, purple, and yellow tulips," someone else remarks. My head turns to find where the voice came from but is unsuccessful due to the number of conversations overlapping with each other.

"Interesting! I will have to keep that in mind next time I attend a gallery viewing. Mrs. Stanton, have you met Mrs. Zerkel? Here she comes right now!" Mrs. Jones declares, waving over the infamous Mrs. Zerkel.

Someone would have to be blind to not notice Mrs. Zerkel's extravagant lavender purple dress adorned with lace from the hollow of her throat to the floor. Satin flowers blossom up the train, and she wears a purple hat with genuine bird feathers pluming at the top.

Mrs. Zerkel takes her time walking over to the group of us, stopping every now and then to greet a friend or accept another compliment on her attire. When she finally stops in front of us, she clasps her hands together and exclaims, "Mrs. Jones, you look enchanting, as always! I daresay tonight has already been proclaimed a success. That man over there"—Mrs. Zerkel points at a scrawny old man that appears to be in his fifties and holds a notepad in his hand, scribbling down words at a rapid speed—"is a writer for none other than the Brockschmidt Gazette! I made sure to ask what he is writing. It is, of course, high praises like every year! There has already been an outstanding quantity of proposals, and the evening has barely begun! This season has been such a boring one, but the least I could do was throw the most marvelous ball that has ever graced this city. Has your son picked a wife yet? All the young ladies here are anxiously awaiting his arrival. I have had three girls tell me that already. I am sure he will find someone tonight!"

Uncomfortable looks are directed at Florence, who has profusely fought to maintain a smile but is failing miserably as Mrs. Zerkel rambles on without caring or noticing the pain that she is causing. Mrs. Zerkel continues, "He is a handsome boy. A wife will surely get that notion of traveling studies out of his head—"

Mrs. Jones clears her throat in the most ladylike manner, bringing Mrs. Zerkel's ignorant words to a halt. "Mrs. Zerkel, you seem to be mistaken because Lawrence is already courting Miss Florence Stanton. We are all positive that a proposal will be happening soon, but indeed there is no need to rush something as life-altering as this! As for my son's arrival, he is walking down those very steps as we speak."

The violins match every beat as Mrs. Jones speaks, creating a speech that just fills you up with adrenaline as the words are processed through your mind. When she releases the last word, the string quartet finishes, and the dancing couples retreat to the tables full of food. Mrs. Zerkel is so positively shocked at the display that she spends several moments in utter silence and confusion just waiting for somebody to object the claims made against her, but nothing of the sort happens.

Mother seems absolutely and positively ecstatic at Mrs. Jones's claims of a proposal, but everyone's attention is soon turned to a young man with blonde hair walking in our direction. Nobody notices as Mrs. Zerkel's cheeks flush red, her posture straightens, and her head tilts high as she searches for party guests who will appreciate her gossip, which is as bad as that of Miss Hackenberry. Florence swiftly brushes off her dress and tosses a curl behind her shoulder as her prince walks into the ball to sweep her off to the dance floor for the next waltz.

"Florence, may I have this dance?" Lawrence asks, bowing and taking my sister's hand, guiding her to the middle of the room, where all the other couples stand and applaud the quartet as it starts up again.

I notice a certain blue velvet dress on the dance floor. The girl I saw at the seamstress's shop stands smugly next to a tall light-haired young man. A woman next to me whispers that she is none other than Kenova, the girl that the man on the street spoke of that day as we walked to the shop. I lean in closely, listening to the woman's hushed conversation with her husband.

"Kenova finally chose between the two Clyde brothers. Understandably, she chose the oldest, who is to inherit the family fortune!"

Florence floats across the floor on the arm of her beau as the violins ease into a melody. To a stranger, she appears the face of calm, but I can see the nervous shake of her hands as she parades around with Lawrence. Lawrence looks at my sister with a certain fondness that closely reminds me of the look I received from Russell that night by the fire. Florence laughs as Lawrence whispers something in her ear just before they change partners for a moment in the dance. Young ladies on the dance floor quickly notice the girl in the daisy dress, who slowly spins back into Lawrence's arms. There is no doubt in my mind that this potential marriage has turned into something equally beneficial for all people involved: Florence will gain a life-long companion who loves her, Mother's dreams of seeing her daughter in an advantageous union will be fulfilled, and I shall finally achieve the peace of not being compared to my sister every day of my life.

The strings quiver as the quartet's bows are lifted in the last note of the song. Instead of returning to the group filled with the mothers, Lawrence guides my sister away.

"Excuse me, please," I mumble as my eyes follow Florence and Lawrence through the crowd of people. I am soon lost from Mother's view, and to anyone who watches me it seems as though I am simply heading for the already crowded table of food. At the last moment, I spin to the left, weaving through the crowd to find my sister again. Searching widely for the sight of her daisy dress or blonde curls in the sea of grand ballgowns is infuriating. But soon, in the corner of my eye there is a flash of white going up the staircase, holding onto Lawrence's arm with a smile.

My shoes click softly on the floor as I race up the stairs, nearly crashing into a couple and slipping all the way back down. When I am halfway up the staircase, my sister rounds a corner, disappearing down the halls of the house. An older couple passes by me, grinning as I search for my sister and her beau. Yes, it is an invasion of privacy to want to listen to her confidential proposal, but I want to see my sister truly happy, and it is much more exciting to see her proposal firsthand rather than stay in the ballroom and listen to the ladies reminisce about the good old days of their engagement seasons.

Even though the evening is almost halfway done, couples still enter through the grand hall and down the stairs to the ballroom, which makes it all the more difficult to find my sister. When we first arrived, I was so enraptured by the heavenly glory of Mrs. Zerkel's house that I had not even noticed the two doors that are open to the warm nighttime air, leading out to the infamous terrace on which a couple is standing.

The young lady in the white daisy dress floats over to the terrace railing, which is as high as her hip and made from the same dark limestone as the floor. Her curls are coming undone and returning to their normal straightness due to the dancing she has just participated in. The familiar splashing sound of a fountain comes from the garden below, which contains a snaking pathway made of pebbles and many flowering plants and trees. Sounds of violins echo through the halls until finally escaping the building and leaking into the city. Stars twinkle above, and candlelit lanterns hang on either side of the doorway, facing the terrace and outside garden.

My back is pressed against the wall as I train my ears to focus on Lawrence and Florence's conversation. My eyes nervously smile at a passing couple, who direct odd expressions at me.

"Florence, I must speak to you of something," Lawrence whispers as his voice quivers in what I assume is a nerve-racking moment. A grin brims my lips as I laugh internally at the thought of Lawrence Jones, a young man who appears so intelligent and masculine, timid at the idea of proposing. But then again, if Pa was so timid all those years ago, then any man could be.

In a surprising twist of events, Florence speaks up, cutting off Lawrence's sentence. "If I may, Lawrence. Before you say anything, I must speak my heart…I love you. I was not certain of it until this very moment! My answer will be wholeheartedly yes, the moment you ask me. My mother would have a fit at my saying this, but I must unburden my feelings to you! I am sorry, have I said something wrong? You seem upset…Lawrence?"

Unable to contain my curiosity, I peek out from where I stand with my back to the wall. Both double doors open outward, revealing to me an obstructed view of my sister and her beau standing in the middle of the terrace. Florence is holding out her hand, her brow furrowed questioningly at Lawrence's back, which is turned to her. He runs his hands through his hair as if frustrated at my sister's shocking confession. Florence loves Lawrence! Truly and wholeheartedly loves him!

With a sigh, he turns back to her, a serious look painted on his face. "You seem like a nice young lady, but the only reason I courted you was so that I would not have to get married this year." His voice edges out the words that painfully strike my sister, who closes her mouth and brings a hand to her chest, offended by the outright refusal that neither she nor I had expected. My mouth falls open with a pop, but I immediately shrink back behind the wall, my eyes still set on Florence.

"I thought that you were…" Tears start brimming at her eyes as she speaks inaudible words. She stops talking and stares up at the nighttime sky as if asking God himself to turn back time and reverse the conversation. "You wasted my time carelessly, playing with my affections only to reveal that you never intended on asking me to marry you? I told you I loved you!" Her words seem to sink into Lawrence with little impact, as he remains stone-faced at the pain he has caused her. "How dare you! Our families were expecting and anxiously awaiting our engagement! What ever will I tell them now? I may as well be ruined; if you will not take me as your wife, then who will? Most of Brockschmidt has already heard of our courting. What ever will we tell everyone?" A few joyful partygoers stroll past with smiles plastered on their faces and memories planted in their minds of happy times at tonight's ball. They continue walking away, toward the front door through which we entered just a couple of short hours ago.

I listen to my sister's heartbreak and stare disappointedly at the display. Evelyn was right in saying she never thought Lawrence was the marrying type. He surely is not the gentleman that I expected if he does not care about my sister and would rather stall for time so he can go off on the traveling studies Mrs. Zerkel mentioned.

I wish more than anything to run out and comfort my sister, but something inside of me keeps my feet fixated to the spot by the doors. This is between the two of them, and even if I have the best of intentions, I might be hurting Florence even more by being witness to her heartbreak.

"I loved you," she proclaims once more in a whisper.

Without another word, Lawrence walks away, and as he rounds the corner to saunter back down the hallway to the ballroom below, I realize have nowhere to hide. So I remain standing against the wall by a portrait. His eyes show a flash of guilt as he halts, equally surprised to see me. My eye, which had been wide with shock, narrow into a glare as the sobs of my broken-hearted sister echo from outside. Lawrence glances down at the ground and saunters away.

Several moments pass by as my heart aches listening Florence's muffled cries that echo to me. I count down in my head until it is safe for me to step out onto the terrace. The glare is wiped off my face and replaced with an unknowing gaze.

"Florence? What ever are you doing out here? What has happened, sister?" my sympathetic voice asks as I rush over to where she sits curled up on the floor at the corner of the railing. In an attempt to conceal her tears, she wipes them away feverishly but fails because it is an unstoppable sadness that overwhelms her. She opens her mouth more than once without saying anything, but I am quite certain that the events of the past few minutes are replaying in her mind, giving her a more than excusable reason for her muteness. "I will fetch Mother, and we shall leave at once." I stand, brush off my skirt, and break into a run, my eyes set devilishly on the ballroom.

The crowd is thinning out as the table starts running low on provisions, and the dance floor is vacant due to the quartet's pause as they prepare their next piece. Mother's white collar and navy-blue dress stand out amongst the floral fabrics that surround her. She laughs in a ladylike manner as I rush across the floor, slipping twice but regaining my balance before finally sliding over to a spot near her. Mother turns around, noticing her youngest daughter's unapproved interruption to the 'important' conversation currently taking place between her and an unfamiliar lady around the age of thirty dressed in a bold orange dress that is fancy as Mrs. Jones's.

"Mother, I am sorry for the intrusion, but we must return to the hotel. Mother, we must leave!" I whisper in her ear as she whips her head around, trying to make sense of my urgent manner and at the same time trying to follow the conversation she is having. The orange-dressed lady has not seemed to notice my presence and just keeps on talking blindly about the decorations.

Mrs. Zerkel's face turns smug at the sight of Lawrence returning without his lady on his arm, and the meaning of this is clear to all. Several young ladies ranging in age and outfits start to crowd around him, striking up conversations as they stand near the scarce food table, which only has a few bowls of sliced fruit, some sandwiches, and small slices of cake and huckleberry pie.

Mother's full-hearted and hopeful dreams for her eldest daughter's marriage shatter in the moment when it is clear to everyone that Lawrence Jones has no intentions of proposing to or courting Florence any longer. Because he is really just biding his time until he can travel and leave my sister ruined without a care in the world for her feelings.

In that moment, several things become evident with one longing gaze from Mother's glassy eyes. Our time has been wasted coming here. We have risked our lives for the opportunity for Florence to find a husband, only to come up short-handed like a gambler who lost his chips after a bad card game. We have lost out on what was supposed to set us up for a few years. Now there are no powerful connections to keep our family's name on the city's social ladder and no life to look forward to between Florence and Lawrence. Mrs. Jones shall not become a part of our family or be a sort-of mother-in-law to me. And finally, we have lost everything we spent nearly a month working toward!

A simple "excuse me" is sufficient for the orange-dressed lady as we scurry off toward the staircase that goes up to the hallway where my sister remains, crying away the pain of being vulnerable.

I reach out, grasping Mother's arm, making her suddenly stop dashing through the thinning crowd of partygoers. "Florence is on the terrace down the hallway and to the left. I will be along shortly, but there is something I must do first." Preoccupied with worry for her oldest daughter and sensing my serious tone, Mother nods as I let go of her. I dash in the opposite direction, toward a certain honey-gingered lady who lingers near the same group of ladies from earlier. Mrs. Jones catches sight of me as I weave through people taking each other's hands for the last dance I am to witness this evening. She waves me over, bending down to meet me at eye level while beaming as she guesses what I am about to say, perhaps expecting it to be something cheerful like the news of a certain proposal, but my sober expression turns sour as the words process through my mind.

"I suppose I must give this back to you." In a swift movement I reach up, unclasp the necklace, and hold it out for the bewildered Mrs. Jones to take, which she does not.

"Whatever do you mean, Azalea? Where is…" I look down at my shoes as she stands up straight, searching for my sister and her son but only finding Lawrence standing with a bored stare whilst girls around him coo out their opinions on food, decorations, music, the weather, and other boring topics. Florence is nowhere to be seen. It becomes clear to Mrs. Jones: Lawrence no longer has any commitments or wedding in the near future.

My voice quivers as I continue. "There will be no wedding, after all. I am truly sorry that I'll never be part of your family. How joyous it would have been to have your family a part of ours, but we must return to Lorretta soon, and I am afraid our two clans will never intertwine again! You must take back the necklace, even if it is the most precious thing that has ever been in my possession. I cannot keep a gift such as this forever." Mrs. Jones stares down at me, disappointed at the thought that we will never be family and that everything that we all had expected would happen did not.

"Keep it, please. I insist on it, actually," she responds, outright refusing to take the string of pearls that sits in her hands. "It is a present that will be with you forever. And Azalea…you would have been a great sort-of daughter-in-law." Even if her last sentence is not meant to be hurtful, the realization still hits my heart at full speed: I am saying goodbye to another friend and kindred spirit with whom I have only been acquainted for a short period of time.

"Thank you for everything, Mrs. Jones," I whisper, disappearing into the crowd and hoping to someday see Mrs. Jones in heaven, if not again here on Earth.

My footsteps echo the lonely sadness of leaving the ball just as Cinderella had done when running back home before midnight. But in this version, there is not likely to be such a happy ever after, for at least Cinderella left with one glass slipper and the long-lasting hope of seeing her prince again.

Florence dries the last of her tears and soothes the heaving breaths that shake her body each time a sob parts her lips. Our footsteps are blanketed by the carpet in the hallway as the three of us huddle together, finding comfort in each other's presence.

The warm night air seems to be changed just like that, for even the twinkling stars above seem sad at our predicament. Mother looks wildly for our carriage. The driver stands with his back against a nearby tree, chewing tobacco and watching the three of us storm out of the house. In an instant he realizes that the party is over and that we wish to return to our hotel more than anything, so he spits out the tobacco and rushes to untie the horse from the hitching post.

Whatever interaction I missed between Mother and Florence when I was trying to give the strand back to Mrs. Jones has clearly made an impact because not a word is said, nor a question asked, as we board the carriage and travel back to the hotel. We each have too much on our minds to engage in any sort of discussion of what happened back at the ball.

Streetlights generate what little spark of flame they have left as the carriage is pulled by the trotting horse. My sense of time has left me; as the full moon peeks out from a passing cloud, there is not a hint of tiredness in my body after what has just happened. The only question I have is: what shall come next? We are bound to go home to Lorretta soon, if not in the next few days. But we never planned on returning without a ring on my sister's finger.

The hotel light glows from the windows as I step out of the stationary carriage and walk alongside my family, passing the doors that lead to the greenhouse and the portrait that once seemed so hopeful. As the key turns in the door, the lock clicks, and the door is pushed open to the darkness of our hotel room. Finding my way through the blackness of the night, I click on the lamp by the purple couch, adding light to the room.

Mother shatters the endless silence, saying the worst words imaginable, though they are meant to be comforting. "We will find another! Maybe a different city since everyone will hear of this by morning. We put all our eggs in one basket, and now we have nothing left. All the men are engaged or still courting! We may just have to wait until next year. Hopefully there is a man in Lorretta that would take you. I shall contact Mrs. Roast as soon as we get back home, for she will surely know of any engagement seasons going on within fifty miles! Charleston's engagement season has yet to begin if I recall correctly!" she remarks as if she has solved every problem. Florence's tear-stained cheeks and puckered lips tell me otherwise.

"Stop it, Mother! I am ruined! Nobody will take me when they believe that Lawrence himself won't! We are going home tomorrow. Until then, I do not wish to speak of anything that has happened or what may come of the future!" Florence yells, causing every muscle in my body to freeze up. I expect Mother to be angry at her favorite child for an outburst like that, but she is equally as surprised as me. Florence storms off, slamming the door to her room behind her as she goes.

With that we each retreat to our own rooms and thoughts. After clicking on my lamp, I stuff my bag messily with my clothes, an action that is sure to create quite the fuss when we unpack at home, but this has no effect on me as I continue shoving things into the bag. *Uncle Tom's Cabin*, which I have yet to read much into, sits at the bottom of the bag just waiting for its contents to be memorized. The ring necklace that Russell gifted me is placed with much care on top of the bundled-up pile, though it falls further into the bag with a clink, disappearing out of view. Next follows the pearl strand that gleams as an isolated tear goes down my cheek.

Slipping off my dress, I change into my nightgown, brush the waves out of my hair, and crawl into bed. I click off the lamp only to lie on my back and stare up at the dark ceiling with a sigh. Tossing from side to side, I cannot find sleep tonight no matter how hard I try. A sound comes from the hallway as a light is clicked off. With another sigh, I toss off the blanket and jump out of my bed, tiptoeing across the floor until I reach my door. The knob turns slowly in my hand, and the door creaks open to reveal light spilling out from under Florence's door across the hallway. Mother is most likely asleep, but I still creep silently across the floor, giving a small knock once I reach Florence's door.

"Come in," a voice croaks from within.

Just like the night before, the knob turns slowly, and I slip into the dimly lit room, closing the door behind me. Florence sits on the floor in her nightgown, fighting back tears as she folds her clothes. She carefully places them in the trunk to be taken back home. Her daisy dress is sprawled out on the bed. I join her, sitting on the cold floor while reaching into the lower drawers of her dresser and pulling out the clothes.

"What is wrong? You mustn't fret about Lawrence, for Mother will contact Mrs. Roast. She will surely find another season or young man for you, and everything will be okay! Things have a way of working out in the end," I say as I hand her one of her blouses to put in the trunk. She reluctantly takes it, placing it in the half-empty trunk. She turns back to me afterwards.

"That's the problem. Mrs. Roast may find me another season or young man, but that could take almost a year! The next season will most likely be in autumn or next spring, for surely we cannot travel anywhere in the winter months. How can I wait a year? How will we be able to wait a year?"

"I do not understand. Why does it matter so much to just wait another year? Florence, you are eighteen, for crying out loud! It's not like you will be an old maid in a year's time. Mother and Pa will understand. I am quite certain about that, for it is practically fact. Pa was saddened at the thought of seeing you leave so soon, so this will surely be a comfort in that perspective."

I reach over to tuck her messy curls over her shoulder, giving as much comfort as I can to my sister. My words do not seem to make much of an impact on her, but instead of responding, she sits in silence, which may be the better alternative for the both of us.

It is funny to think that one day in the not-so-far-off future, Florence will be married and will not think twice about the 'what ifs' with Lawrence Jones, for things would work out in the end. I can just faintly imagine my sister one day laughing about this very moment, when she thought her heart was shattered into pieces to never be put back together again.

This whole trip has changed our lives—for better or for worse. Yes, we have come all the way here only to leave without Florence finding a match, but it is only God's way of saying that He has something even better planned for her future. My sister and I have never been closer than we are now, and that would never have happened if we had not left Lorretta.

She clears her throat, standing up and stumbling over to her bed. "Yes, well, I am tired out, for today has been a long day, and tomorrow we must return home. Goodnight, sister." She stifles the last of her tears as she stands next to her bed.

A pang of hurt hits me as if I have been slapped across the face by her words. Have I not just comforted her in her hour of need? And now she has crept back into her shell, the one of the perfect daughter, leaving me behind. I tell myself not to overthink her two sentences too much as we part ways. I head back to my room, disappointed and wondering what I have done wrong.

~

I spend the rest of the night tossing and turning in my bed as questions fill my head but continue to go unanswered. Finally, when sleep takes over, sunlight has already started peeking in through the window. Mother soon rushes into my room to tell me that the breakfast cart has arrived and that we will be leaving on the eleven o'clock stagecoach this morning. I groan once she leaves, for today I am not in the mood for a solemn breakfast, even if my stomach provokes me to do otherwise.

Slipping on my Christmas dress, which I wore last night, I comb my hair and eventually decide against putting it in braids, instead leaving it down. The few waves that remain are brushed back to their normal straightness, taking away the last of the reminders of last night. My nightgown is stuffed into my bag, which is bursting at the seams due to my untidy packing. I pray Mother will not notice with her being preoccupied with my sister's welfare.

I look one last time at my bedroom as I stand in the door frame, carrying my bag out into the suite's hallway so that it can be packed for our journey home. The painted clouds above spin as I take one last twirl in the room, and the bed stands ever so comfortingly, even though I did not get one wink of sleep last night. The window shows the rooftops and the last sunrise I may ever see in Brockschmidt, for we will have no reason to come back now that every citizen shall know that Lawrence Jones did not propose to Florence. The mirror gazes back at me with affection, wishing me the best on my travels.

"Thank you," I whisper to the bedroom as the door closes behind me. I place my bag on top of Florence's packed trunk, next to Mother's bag that is surely packed to perfection as always.

They both sit one last time on the purple couch, slowly taking bites of the buckwheat cakes with honey on top. The breakfast cart stands steadfast, waiting for me to take a plate piled with pancakes, but my mind tells me otherwise. The red apples shine as they wait for a bite to be taken from their honey-crispness. I finally grab an apple as my stomach growls in hunger yet again.

Breakfast passes by in utter quietness—aside from the low crunching of my apple—and afterwards the hotel worker takes our bags downstairs to the stagecoach that waits for us. The books that Mother borrowed from the lady at the counter are given back, along with our hotel key, as we walk past the front desk.

I try to memorize every detail of the marble-stoned, velvet-covered staircase, gazing longingly at the portrait of the woman one last time. The French doors open widely to the greenhouse. I wish I could run outside and see it just one last time, but I have to refuse the temptation and walk on by.

It turns out that when the breakfast cart was delivered to our hotel room, Mother arranged for the coach to be stopped at the hotel so that we would not have to strain ourselves carrying the trunk and bags all the way to the station. A sad smile adorns my lips, gleaming a goodbye at the city that it had spent so much time being worn around. The driver offers his hand to each of us as we step into the coach, which looks exactly like the one we traveled in when we came to the city.

With a cluck from the driver and a snap from the whip, we are on our way back home after almost three weeks away. Oh, Pa shall be so excited to see us after such a long departure! Then again, we will have to tell him of our adventures, both good and bad. I still feel a little worried about the fact that there has been no response to my last letter, but it does not matter now, for we are finally going back home.

I take one last look out the window as we go past the fancy cafes, restaurants, and people on the streets. It is a sunny morning in Brockschmidt, and as we trot on by in the stagecoach, I resist the urge to wave goodbye to the strangers that we pass. The park flashes past us in the blink of an eye, holding the memory of my necklace and Florence's beau. With a jolt we are rolling over the train tracks where I last saw Evelyn and Percy, who have not departed my thoughts ever since they stepped aboard that train, vanishing from their lives here in the city but nevertheless leaving with the hope of finding new destinies with each other.

And soon the cobblestone streets transition back into dirt ones, the tall buildings thin out into smaller ones before disappearing as we leave the outskirts of the city, and the wagons going by become less frequent the further we travel.

The mountains in the distance, the sway of wind between the prairie grasses, and the cloudy blue skies above all remind me of home. Soon the rattle of the stagecoach turns into a lullaby that makes me drift off to sleep.

I am walking in a dark nothingness looking frantically for anything or anyone to save me. Finally, after what seems like hours of walking around and calling out for help, I collapse to the ground, curled up in a ball of loneliness.

"Azalea," a familiar voice above me whispers. Florence stands over me, holding out a hand that I so gladly take as she lifts me up into a standing position.

"Florence! Do not leave me again, please, I beg of you! I have missed you so much. Please, stay," I cry out as I hug my sister tightly in the room of pure darkness. A light comes from out of nowhere. We both look above, where a sky with fluffy white clouds is frozen in place. "No. Stay, please! Stay with me!"

Florence gives me a sad smile as our hug breaks apart. "I must go now. You know what is to come, and this may prepare you for it. Wake up now, Azalea. Azalea, wake up." My sister walks away as she speaks, leaving me alone once more and crying out her name repeatedly. "Wake up."

My eyelids open suddenly as I take in my surroundings little by little. Mother is no longer sitting next to me, Florence is in her place on the seat shaking my shoulder, and the stagecoach is no longer moving. My eyes adjust to the light of the world. The postal office is visible just outside the coach, and a few people walk past on their way to run errands or return home for the day.

Home. We are finally home! In a moment I dash out of the stage-coach, running to the back of it, where Mother stands as the driver unties our things. A smile is plastered on my face as I lift my bag, which seems two times heavier than it was when we left Brockschmidt. Florence climbs out of the coach, joining us at the back of it. Once the two bags and trunk are untied, the driver snaps his whip and is off to his next destination with two new passengers. Even though we are all disappointed to return home empty-handed, that disappointment is overshadowed by our joy to be back to this ever-so-familiar place we call home.

Mother and Florence each take one side of her trunk as I carry the two bags. The clear, sunny sky turns cloudy. As we walk down the dirt road, I hope that the rain holds off until we arrive back home. Not a word is spoken as we each struggle to carry the luggage with aching muscles and shallow breaths. Florence concerns me, for every couple of feet her arms give out, making us stop over and over again until finally I try to convince her to let me take the trunk.

"Florence, are you well? You seem tired, and the trunk is quite heavy to carry back to the house. Sister, let me take it with Mother so that we can both carry it along and you may take the bags."

Florence sits on top of the stationary trunk in the middle of the road. Thank goodness a wagon did not come by at that moment, for it would have rounded the corner where the trees to our right concealed us from sight. It would have had to be a miracle rather than quick thinking to save us from being struck in that case.

It is only another couple of hundred yards until we will reach the pathway up to the house, and Florence is already tired from carrying the trunk from town. Her face looks pale and solemn, which is quite unusual.

She takes in shaking breaths, holding a hand to her chest in an effort to regain her composure as she remains on the trunk with us watching. "No, Azalea, I am surely fine. Spending all that time in the city and not having to lift my weight or do chores at the crack of dawn has taken its toll on my strength. I must admit I did not get too much sleep last night either. I simply need to regain my strength before carrying my side of the trunk again. I will be improved in a few minutes is all."

I exchange a glance with Mother, who also seems worried about her daughter but refuses to say anything that might change my sister's mind about taking a rest. "Yes, well, how about we take turns carrying it? I can start, then once you have regained your strength and I am tired you may return to carrying it!" I offer with a careful tone.

It is a perfect solution to the given problem, and I mentally take note of how well it works as my sister gives a solemn nod, standing up from where she sat and bending over to grab the bags. I lift my side of the trunk at the same time as Mother lifts hers. If I'm being perfectly honest with myself, I have never been a very muscular girl, mainly because collecting the eggs each morning and doing the other basic chores are not very hard. Florence, however, has to walk back from the barn each morning with two pails filled to the brim with milk, taking time and much care to not let any spill over. Considering this information, it would only make sense why my arms immediately start tiring once the heavy trunk is lifted into the air. Every step taken is met with the huff of my breath, which I work hard to conceal, for I cannot let my sister go right back to carrying the trunk when she so palpably does not feel well.

With the house just in view, I channel everything inside of me to not collapse to the ground in exhaustion. True to her word, with each step Florence takes, she improves greatly from carrying something with much less weight to it. Her eyes do not seem to be shining as hopefully as they always do but instead are a dull glassy blue. Is she really that upset about returning to Lorretta without a match?

And so our eyes are graced with the sight of the mountains, our house, the field, and the barn as soon as we round the next corner. Birds swoop toward the ground, looking each way for food only to turn right back up into the air. It is always such a mystery to me how birds manage to fly, for it seems like magic that they can one day just spread out their feathered wings, just as my bluebird Vireo did even when I begged and pleaded for him to come back. It reminds me of how a caterpillar can somehow emerge from its cocoon as a butterfly, and despite living half of its life on legs it can spread the new wings and fly. Or how a spider may spin its web without any direction or example to go by but somehow still does the job effortlessly! Nature is so complex to the human mind that it seems as if we shall never truly find out the reasoning behind everything.

"Azalea, let us put the trunk down here," Mother huffs out, and I gladly lower it until it is placed carefully on the grassy ground. "Florence, can you please run up to knock on the door? Uncle Edward and your Pa will lift this inside with much more ease than we ever could!" Before my sister even reaches our front door, it swings open to the familiar face of Uncle Edward, who does not waste two seconds before starting a conversation as he greets each of us.

"Well, didn't I tell ya, Albert! I told that Pa of yours that I heard voices just outside and if I went on opening the door, somebody would be standing there! How nice to see y'all after so long. Skip to it and tell us all about your adventures in Brockschmidt! Oh, Margaret, leave that trunk so me and Albert can get it afterwards. Come in, come in." Uncle Edward is quite the character in my mind, for his endless talking seems to fill you up with energy but drain the life out of you at the same time. Nonetheless, the three of us walk inside our home, where Pa is sitting at the table with a newspaper in his hand. Mother, of course, does not hate Uncle Edward, but there is always something to be said in her mind about his demeanor, and that clearly shows on her face every time he comes for a visit.

"Pa! Oh, how glad I am to see you after what seemed like centuries of waiting!" I exclaim, pushing past Uncle Edward, who stands in the middle of the doorway. I run to Pa, wrapping my arms around his neck like I used to do when I was a child scared by lightning and needing to find comfort in my parent's arms.

Once all the greetings go around, we settle down at the table and discuss our adventures from the past three-ish weeks with greatly anticipated enthusiasm. "Oh, Pa, how frightful it was indeed, to be held at gunpoint by that man! Then, Russell St. Claire, a young man who was out riding on his beautiful Appaloosa horse looking for his lost cattle, shot the robber dead with one bullet as we were all lying tied up on the ground! One bullet! He untied us and helped us reach the stagecoach station."

Both Pa and Uncle Edward are left sitting on the edge of their chairs when I finish speaking. They usher me to continue. Mother sits in the rocking chair by the fireplace, closing her eyes as if reliving it all. "Well… you see this scar on the palm of my hand? That was from a piece of firewood when we had to camp out on the side of the road before we could walk to the station the next morning. Oh! And the soirée was quite extravagant indeed. There was this food called chocolate. It is so sweet, yet it had an almost bitter taste that was very addicting but not so much so that you would eat several at a time. That is where Florence met…Lawrence Jones, and I made a friend named Evelyn Puffin, who also invited Mother and I to come to her house that week, which we did. Evelyn's house was very homey—of course, not as homey as our house here in Lorretta, but very much near to it. You could have the biggest house in the world filled with precious and valuable things, but that all would make no difference to me if it does not feel like home. You see, in order for a house to feel like a home it has to have the presence of being loved. She also gifted me a book called *Uncle Tom's Cabin.* I have not read more than a few pages, but so far it seems rather interesting!" The words come out of my mouth in quick sentences as I hold out my palm for the scar to be admired for its uniqueness and use my hand gestures as I speak through our adventures. "We also went to a ladies' tea the next day in the park. Mrs. Jones, who we also met at the soirée, was there, as were Miss Hackenberry and Mrs. Epperson. Miss Hackenberry is a gossip if I ever heard one!"

"Azalea Stanton! I will not hear of you speaking that way of a stranger such as Miss Hackenberry!" Mother yells, causing all of our heads to snap to where she remains in the rocking chair.

I clear my throat, nodding at her words but not taking them into account. "Mrs. Jones said so herself that Miss Hackenberry is a gossip, so you cannot argue that is wrong unless you are claiming Mrs. Jones is wrong! Are you claiming that, Mother?" Mother's cheeks flush a quick red as she sits deeper into the rocking chair without saying a word, for my point has clearly been made. "As I was saying, Miss Hackenberry was talking up a storm about her opinions on the Puffins, which included my friend Evelyn. It is a rather long story, but apparently Evelyn and some next-door neighbor of hers ran away later that very same day we were at their house! What a shock it was to hear that my new friend had run away for good." I look down at my lap as if it is a shame that she is gone for good, when in actuality I was the one who had helped her run away. On our walk from the station, I fabricated the story that I would tell of how sad it was that Evelyn was gone and how heartbroken I was to hear it. In truth, the story was very believable because everyone in the room took a moment of silence to think of this Evelyn Puffin.

"Well, what happened next, Bluebird?"

I grin, happy that Pa is the one to encourage my talking. It is terribly exciting to converse of our harrowing tales in Brockschmidt. Florence listens to what I say but shows no interest in it whatsoever as she solemnly sits in her chair at the table with Pa, Uncle Edward, and me. "Mrs. Jones gifted me one of her pearl strings and also invited us to the fourth annual Brockschmidt ball, which was in a matter of almost two weeks! We went to a seamstress shop, where we bought Florence this stunningly angelic daisy fabric. Mother took us to an art gallery with ever so many paintings and sculptures that were very interesting and thought-provoking if you looked at them in the right way. The theme for the ball was flowers, so we also wore flowers in our hair, as did the other ladies attending, and we made the dress ourselves at the hotel room. It was an absolute miracle that the dress was finished in time, for I was terrified that it would not be. Mother let me help sew parts of the dress, but other than that I did not do too much work on it. Oh, and the ball was positively regal with all the expensive decorations, food, and dresses! There was this string quartet that played different songs all night long as couples danced to it. Apparently in Brockschmidt the ball is only held at the end of the engagement season, which means lots of people get engaged there!" I glance sheepishly over at Florence, terrified that I have said too much and made her embarrassed or mad, but to my surprise she is looking across the room and out the window that is next to Mother in the rocking chair. She hasn't heard a word I have just spoken, which is a relief and worry at the same time.

Pa catches onto Florence's daydream look of sadness and decides to speak up. "You girls must be tuckered out! How about you go on upstairs and get some much-needed rest whilst Edward and I handle the luggage? Florence?" Pa and Uncle Edward stand, ready to walk out the door to retrieve the trunk and bags, but await a response from my sister, who still stares stone-faced out the window.

Several moments pass by before she snaps back to attention. "What? Yes, Pa, I think it is time for rest…it was a long journey." With that she stands shakily and makes her way slowly up the staircase, causing alarmed glances to be exchanged between us all. She must really need the rest that Pa suggested!

⌇

"Just a minute, Pa, I must go and see my cows before I rest. It has been so long since I last saw Sense and Sensibility!" And with that, I skip out of the house and rush to the barn as a breeze blows through the grasses. The sun dips behind a few fluffy, white clouds, and the sunshine dashes as fast as it can along the ground as the shadows follow it, ultimately catching the light. A few moments later, the cloud passes, and the light once again returns to this spot of Earth as I swing open the barn door. For a moment it seems as if nothing in the world can ruin my happiness and that everything in life is perfect.

IN SICKNESS AND IN HEALTH

As THE DAYS GO BY, the newness of returning home dies down, and we fall back into our everyday rhythm. Uncle Edward left to return home the day after we came back. Pa thanked him for staying, and Mother continuously asked that he promise to come again with Aunt Nancy and Nora next time, for she already misses them terribly. Uncle Edward promised to visit soon, but they had already made plans to travel east for the next three months starting the second he returned home.

Each morning before dawn, I awake with a bundle of happiness to return to my chores, which had bored me before but now were dearly missed. The chickens cluck and call their hellos as I step into the pen with the wire basket on my arm. I reach my hands into the nests, pulling out the brown and white eggs before placing them into the basket carefully.

Several minutes go by, and there is still no sign of my sister coming to milk the cows, so I set the basket down on the straw-covered ground. I pick up the two tin pails, carry them over to the stall doors, and enter Sense's stall with a pail in one hand and the three-legged wooden stool in the other.

"Hi, girl! How are you doing today? Let us open this top door and get some air in this stuffy barn!" I stroll over to the back of the stall, unlatching the top of the door, which swings out into the outside world, letting the dark morning sky, the trees, the still prairie grasses, and the tweeting birds flying overhead be seen. Sense walks lazily over to the door, stretching to reach her head out and smell the fresh dew of the morning with her pink nose.

Both of my cows are rather small despite being nearly four years in age. They are the same chestnut brown, but Sensibility also has a few speckles of white along her stomach, and they both have cute pink noses matched with big round black eyes that stare into your soul, just begging for a treat from your hand.

A spray of milk comes from Sense's utter until the pail is almost all the way full. The whole process is repeated as I walk into Sensibility's stall, open the top of the door, and fill the pail to the top. Light flows into the room from the sunrise, and still my sister has not walked through the barn door. Unable to wait any longer for Florence to come do her chores, I climb the ladder to the hayloft and toss the hay to where it flutters down to the ground. The wood from the ladder prickles against my palms as I make my way back down. The soles of my shoes hit the ground with a thud.

The door creaks open, and the silhouette of a person stands in front of the bright morning sunlight. I squint my eyes against the light until the door closes slowly and my sister steps forward in utter dismay.

"Florence? Where in the world have you been?" I toss handfuls of hay into Sense and Sensibility's stalls, for which they happily moo a thank you and subsequently start eating.

Florence walks toward the cows' stalls slowly and leans her body weight against the stall door when she gets there. Her hands rub her temples as if there is a pounding internal throb.

"I'm dreadfully sorry. My head…and my muscles ache like they did when we had the flu when we were children, but this time it's much worse." My sister sways as she talks, closing her eyes because to her the room is spinning endlessly.

My concerned thoughts do nothing to calm the nerves growing inside of me. In the fall of 1889, the year before we moved to Lorretta, our whole family was struck with the flu. It started with me before eventually spreading to Mother and Florence, then to Pa. Even though it was many years ago I can still recall the memory as if it had happened yesterday.

It began with me awaking in the dead of night with a fever and chills. In confusion I got up from my bed and started walking blindly throughout the darkness of the house, calling out for Mother and Pa to help me. Mother ran to me, eyes ablaze with worry as she pressed her lips against my forehead and proclaimed I had a fever. My body shook from the cold night air around me as I was sat down next to the stove. Later on, Mother fell weak with a headache. The next day Florence's body ached to the point where she could not walk, and a few days after that Pa had a horrible a sore throat.

Our home in Colorado was closer to our neighbors than our Lorretta house, but there was still no town within twenty miles of where we lived, so a kind neighbor sent word for a doctor to come. Within a day the old man showed up at the door with his black leather medical bag, a dark brown suit with a bowtie, and a worn flat hat on his white-haired head. His brown eyes twinkled in sadness at the sight of us four battling the sickness. I had the worst symptoms, which included a fever matched with congestion that made my breathing come in and out in short wheezes.

"You must each take a small dose of strychnine and drink amounts of whiskey. If the child's fever progresses until tomorrow, give a dose of phenazone," the doctor said, holding up dark bottles. Florence lay beside me in the bed in the same state of illness.

We recovered in time, but the memory has forever haunted me since, causing an irrational fear of sickness to develop in my subconscious.

"Something is wrong. Azalea!" Florence exclaims as she sways before collapsing to the ground, covered in dirt and straw. My arms extend just in time to catch my sister as she falls forward. The chickens panic at the sudden shouts coming from my mouth and squawk loud calls that sound like screams.

My breath quickens, and my arms ache from Florence's weight. "Florence? Florence! Please wake up, sister, tell me what is wrong. No, no, no, this cannot be happening again. We cannot be sick again after facing death last time. Mother! Pa! Help me, Pa, help me!" I scream at the top of my lungs as my legs give out, sending us both to the floor.

My sister's head lies in my lap, her body limp and lifeless. Her eyes are peacefully closed as if she has been put under a spell of sleep. Tears begin flooding my eyes as if I am a child, but I cannot be bothered to hold back my emotions in a time such as this. "Pa! Mother!" I shriek one more time as my voice cracks. My hair sticks to my face as tears soak my cheeks, traveling down and then falling onto my brown dress. I use my apron to dry my face as the barn door is tossed open, slamming against the wall as it opens inward, and more light streams into the room.

"What happened? Azalea, what happened to Florence? Oh gosh, Albert, is she breathing? What happened, child?" Mother yells as she covers her mouth with her hands and turns away from the sight of my sister sprawled out on the ground against me. I smooth Florence's face with my hands as tears coat my voice no matter how many times I try responding to Mother's shouted questions. Pa kneels with his face creased in fearful worry as he touches two fingers under my sister's chin.

"Margaret, please calm yourself. Florence is breathing. Azalea, tell me what happened to her. Was she milking the cows? Did she get kicked?" Pa stares into my eyes, trying to get answers out of me, but it is almost no use, for I am hysterically looking around the room, sobbing uncontrollably. Pa reaches over my sister and takes my face in his hands, steadying my head so that I can only look at his face. Mother holds her right hand over her mouth, her left hand clutching her stomach in an effort to keep the nausea at bay.

"Oh, Pa…She was late to come"—My breathing becomes rapid as I struggle to speak through the salty tears that fall into my mouth—"do the chores. I milked the cows and was putting the hay into the stalls when she walked in. Her head was hurting. She said her body hurt worse than when we had the flu in Colorado, then yelled that something was terribly wrong. I caught her when she fell just now…Pa, what is wrong with her?" With that, he releases my head and stares down at Florence's sleeping face.

"I do not know," he whispers. Taking control of the situation, Pa lifts my sister into his arms, struggling to stand as he carries her limp body to the house. Mother and I run behind him, ready to catch either of them if they were to fall. Florence's head is bent awkwardly, and her arm hangs down. As we rush from the barn to the house, we spot a man riding by on his brown Morgan horse.

"Sir! Sir, please stop!" Pa exclaims as the man snaps his head in the direction of our predicament, immediately noticing Pa carrying Florence in his arms.

The man turns his horse off the road and quickly trots over to where we stand in front of our door. Mother and I exchange glances of panic conveying the same message: *What is wrong with Florence?*

"Mr. Stanton, is that you? What is wrong with your girl?" The man sits on his horse as he awaits an answer. If this stranger knows Pa's name, then he mustn't be a stranger at all. Who is this man?

"Yes, Mr. Bennett. My daughter has collapsed, and I need to ask a favor of you." Time ticks by slowly as the information is processed in Mr. Bennett's mind. In this time, I search his face before finally concluding that Mr. Bennett has a striking resemblance to Mrs. Roast. Last year Mother mentioned that Mrs. Lizzie Roast's younger brother had recently moved to town, and so we made cookies that Mother took into town to give to Mrs. Roast's brother.

"Of course!" he exclaims as his horse gives a loud whinny, tired of standing in the same spot for the past minute.

It isn't often that you would find Pa unnerved by a situation—because normally Pa is so level-headed and never loses his sense of calmness—but in this case he is completely undone. "I must ask you to ride into town and retrieve Doctor Carter Griffiths as soon as possible!" The urgency of the situation becomes unbearable as I bite my lip until it bleeds. Mr. Bennett gives a stern nod before slapping his horse and cantering off toward the dirt road, toward Lorretta.

A cold chill runs through my body as Pa sets Florence in her bed. To anybody else it would seem as though my sister is sleeping. But in reality, this is no fairytale that can be fixed through magic, although I dearly wish it could be.

The time ticks by slowly as we all sit in Florence's room. Mother took the vanity chair from my room and placed it next to my sister's bed. Pa constantly gets up from where he sits on my sister's wooden trunk—which has yet to be unpacked—pacing around the room before returning to his seat.

I, however, stay motionless on the floor of the room, tracing the grain of the wood floor with my fingertip. I cannot even imagine anything to do to occupy the time. It is as though my mind has been wiped clean and left utterly empty! The memories of our flu in Colorado are easily brought to my attention, an annoyance in many ways. I do not wish to worry myself to the point of making my subconscious think I am sick. Nor do I wish to remember the chills that shook my body every couple of moments and Florence being practically paralyzed because her legs hurt so bad that even moving them would cause excruciating agony!

My eyes flicker to Mother, who has a semi-permanent frown on her face, making it look as if she has aged five years in the past half hour. She strokes Florence's blonde locks of hair constantly.

Unable to contain my anxiety any longer, I resort to twiddling my fingers and picking at the dirt underneath my fingernails, in part because it has always annoyed my sister. She often scolds me for doing so, and for a moment I think she will awake from this odd sleep and sit straight up in bed to tell me to stop that infernal racket, but nothing of the sort happens.

After what seems like hours but is only forty-two minutes, an urgent pounding comes from the front door, echoing all the way up the stairs to where we sit in Florence's bedroom. Pa runs out of the room and down the hallway, his feet stomping down the stairs and across the stone floors until the front door is tossed open. Then the whole process repeats backward as Doctor Griffiths is led to us.

I have always prided myself in knowing all the sounds of this house, even though nobody else knows that fact. After living here for the past few years, every sound is permanently ingrained and committed to my memory to the point where I can distinctly tell when a pot is taken out of the cupboard, when the stove is lit, when footsteps come up or down the stairs, and who the footsteps belong to.

The only time that this supposed "superpower" has come in handy is in this very moment, when I conclude that Doctor Griffiths is very much indeed here. Pa enters the room with the doctor, who I have only really met on one occasion besides when we had passed by him in town. Doctor Griffiths has never shown so much a tiny smile in the few months I have known him, which is very uncommon in Lorretta. He is a twenty-something unmarried man from the east, who is fresh out of a medical apprenticeship, which is very remarkable for a young man in this day and age.

Doctor Griffiths is relatively new to our quaint little town, for he has just taken over the previously vacant post of town doctor. This man bends his neck awkwardly to make it through the door frame after Pa. His icy eyes focus on my sister lying in bed. He takes off his Stetson hat, placing it on the corner of the bed and giving us all a clear look at his slicked-back, orange-red hair.

"What seem to be the symptoms? Mr. Bennett proclaimed your girl was sick and rushed me out of the office at an inconvenient time for this." His voice is like the screech of wooden chair legs on stone floors, with each word followed with a voice crack. It is odd that someone with brilliant blue eyes such as his did them no justice with his monotoned voice and everlasting bored looks.

Pa opens his mouth to speak at once in this long-awaited moment, but Mother stands from her chair, holding up a hand to quiet him. "Doctor, my daughter Florence"—She gestures to the bed solemnly—"was out in the barn when she complained of a headache and body pains, then collapsed without waking up. There have been signs over the past few days, but I had assumed it was because of recent events."

He nods his head, looking strangely from Mother to me to Pa and back again without glancing at his patient once more. "You are, in fact, the Stanton family, is that correct?" his monotone vocal cords hum.

Even if it is more of a rhetorical question, Mother still sputters an answer, confused as to why he would need to know our name. "Well…yes. But I—"

"Yes, I have heard more than I wish to about your visit to Brockschmidt and the scandal involved. Well then, I shall perform a basic examination of the patient, and then I believe I know the answer to this sudden illness. Don't worry, it is easily cured." Our mouths all pop open in unison at his insensitivity, which does not surprise me too much, for I know he is somebody who is peculiarly quiet and has limited experience talking to people. "Scandal" was a bit extreme considering it was only a private rejection of marriage with no real proposal. We are all tossed out into the hallway as Doctor Griffiths performs the "basic examination," which was all but ten minutes long.

He steps out into the crowded hallway, which is only wide enough for one person with a little bit of room left over in case you need to carry something down the stairs. "The patient is awake, and I would like to ask your other daughter to come and explain what has happened."

"Me?" I exclaim, pointing to my chest in confusion. His response is nothing other than a nod before he re-enters the room with me following closely behind. The door is closed behind me, Mother and Pa's confused faces staring blankly back at me before they are shut off from view. Florence is lying on her back. As I walk over to her, she turns her head, giving me a small smile and reaching her hand out weakly. I so gladly take it in my mine. The doctor stands frown-faced with his head a mere foot away from the ceiling as he opens his mouth to grace us with his horrid voice.

"In my examination, I awoke the patient, then checked her breathing, which was clear, followed by a temperature check that was also perfectly normal. Considering both of these facts, I would like to hear firsthand what exactly happened." His manner is all very rigid and…informational, which makes me uncomfortable. I sit in the chair, shifting around before finally meeting his lazy eyes, which stare at me for an answer.

"I was in the barn collecting the chicken eggs and doing the other chores" —He rolls his eyes, awaiting to hear what happened to "the patient," but I continue speaking as if his rude manner has no effect on me, even though my voice quivers— "when my sister walked in slower than I have ever seen her before. She leaned against the stall, for she could not stand firmly on her own two feet, proclaiming that her head hurt and so did her legs like they did back when we had the flu many years ago. And she fell to the ground, but I caught her."

Doctor Griffiths nods his head, pacing and stroking his stubbly, non-existent beard. "I have come to the conclusion that you are pregnant, which proves my theory to begin with." He speaks directly to my bed-ridden sister, who immediately releases my hand in shock. My heart stops altogether at this so-called conclusion made by this idiotic doctor. He, however, has no emotion in his face at our staggering expressions. Thank goodness Mother is not in the room, for she would have a hysterical fit at this man's "diagnosis."

Florence struggles to sit up straight, but within a few moments she succeeds and directs her fury at the doctor. "Pregnant?" She laughs before turning deadly serious. "How dare you pose such a question against my virtue! I would never…how could you even…?"

"In my medical opinion, if you are not with child, then your symptoms are likely from exhaustion or lack of rest. Often enough, the change from country air to city air takes a brief toll on someone's health. You will improve and be okay in the days to come. My work here is done. Good day." And with that, Doctor Griffiths (if he even still deserves to be called a doctor after that ridiculous diagnosis of my sister being pregnant when she is as pure as the Virgin Mary herself) picks up his hat, places it firmly on his head, grasps his medical bag, then bends over once more to walk through the doorway and out of the house. Pa shows the man out of the house, paying him and wishing him well because neither of our parents know the state that their daughter is in.

Mother rushes into the room, leaning over me and extending her arms out to Florence to give her a hug that she weakly returns. "What did the doctor say? Will you be okay, darling? He seems to have left in a hurry without telling your Pa or me anything," she asks, glancing between me and my sister. "What ever are you gaping at?"

I realize my mouth is still open in shock at the offensive display that has just taken place with that horrid doctor. "Nothing. Doctor Griffiths said it was from exhaustion and something about the city air taking a temporary toll on Florence's health." I decide it would be better to spare Mother the details of what has just happened, for there is nothing to be done, and it would only make her mad.

"I shall be healed within the next day or so, Mother." Florence smiles as Mother tucks a piece of hair behind her ear.

"I am glad to hear that, darling! You gave us quite the scare this morning." Florence gives a giggle, as does Mother. "I must start breakfast, but if you need anything, just ask, and one of us will fetch it!"

With that, Mother walks out of the room with her head held high and the weight lifted from her shoulders. Even I feel lighter just hearing that Florence does not have the flu again and that we are all in the clear.

My heart has stopped beating so rapidly and I have unconsciously stopped picking at my fingernails. The footsteps remind me where I am, and that Florence most likely wants to rest rather than having someone watch over her all day long.

"I shall go help Mother with breakfast, but if you truly need anything or someone to distract you, just call my name!" I get up from the chair and start heading toward the door when Florence's voice stops me.

"Thank you, Azalea. I am sorry to worry you so much this morning. I should have just stayed inside the house rather than make a scene trying to pretend I was okay and do the chores," she lets out a deep breath, looking over at the trunk by the foot of the bed.

"Do not worry about all of that, dear sister, for you could not help falling unconscious! And you were trying to do your duty by helping with the chores, so do not worry about that either. The only thing that matters is that you get your rest. You heard the doctor say you will get better very soon, so there will be plenty of time to do chores later." Florence gives a small laugh that fills my spirits up and causes a smile to emerge from my lips. "Sleep now, sister. I shall be back up to check on you momentarily." My voice comes out in a whisper as I back away, closing the door behind me. Florence smiles weakly, shifts in the bed, then closes her eyes right as my fingertips leave the doorknob.

I make my way downstairs to where Mother is preparing our breakfast, which is very much delayed this morning, for good reason. It is not often that my sister doesn't feel well. Sometimes the occasional monthly pains cause her to move slower or to not be able to carry both milk pails at once, but besides that she always acts like everything is fine, even when it isn't. Is that what she's doing right now? Acting like everything is fine when it might not be?

No, there is absolutely no need to fret over something over which I have no control. The doctor said Florence is fine, needs rest, and will improve in a day or two, so she shall be fine.

The moment my shoes reach the last step on the short staircase, I become responsible for all my sister's daily chores and work. The list runs through my mind in a matter of seconds: light the fire in the wood-burning stove, sweep the kitchen, carry the milk pails inside and strain them, fill up the glass milk bottles and put them in the cold cupboard in the floorboards, then check to see if anything needs washing or mending.

Huffing out a sigh at the work laid before me in addition to my own chores, I shuffle over to the stove, grabbing the matchbox that sits on the counter near the water pump. Even though I've seen my sister light a match and throw it into the stove several times, I have never attempted it before. I glance over at Mother, who is putting her apron over her neck and tying the two pieces of fabric into a bow around her waist.

Unwilling to ask for help, I turn back to the cold stove and open the squeaky two-foot-wide iron door. The wood box sits in the corner behind the stove. I recall how Florence tosses in two pieces of wood and a crumbled paper and uses her finger to quickly flick the match against the sandpaper. A flame explodes from the red tip of the match, and then she throws it inside, closing the door to the stove.

Just as she does, I throw in the two wood logs, crumple the paper, and attempt to recreate the movement she does to light the match. But each time I flick the tip of it against the sandpaper rectangle on the side of the box, no flame sparks. After the fourth try, Mother notices my struggles and takes both the box and match out of my hand to demonstrate. With a flick of her wrist, she runs the match's red tip against the sandpaper, which is no bigger than my pinky finger, and starts the flame before tossing it inside the stove and closing the door with ease.

Even after I sweep the kitchen and carry the milk pails inside, break-fast is not yet ready, proclaiming the palpable fact that I cannot stop to rest yet. Mother places the plates on the table as I grimace, setting down the heavy pails. When I was walking the few yards from the barn to the house, I splashed the milk out of the tin pails and onto the skirt of my dress twice. With my apron now wet at the bottom corner, I untie it, lifting it over my head and hanging it across the back of my chair at the table.

"Azalea, I expected this milk to already be strained ten minutes ago! Come on, child, hop to it!" Mother exclaims the moment I sit down to catch my breath and relax. I groan, standing right back up and walking over to the buckets that sit by the front door waiting for me.

My mouth waters at the sight of the cornbread as Mother opens the oven door, grabbing the cast iron skillet out by the handle with the cloth oven mitts, then placing it down in the middle of the table with the extra oven mitt underneath it. Pa, who has just come from checking on Florence and delivering her breakfast, settles down in his chair at the table and takes a knife to the cornbread. The thin-cut strips of pork sizzle in the pan as I use a spatula to shift the meat around causing the liquid fat in the pan to sputter. Once the pork is fully cooked, I take the strips of bacon out and put them all on a plate on the table.

It feels like ages until breakfast is finally set out on the table for the three of us to sit down and enjoy. Freshly baked wheat bread, thin-cut strips of pork that Uncle Edward had given to us before he left along with a sack of potatoes, and cornbread made from great grandmama's recipe fill the house with a delectable scent.

With a nod of Mother's head, I am allowed to sit down, and we each begin cutting up the food and lifting it onto each of our plates. The cornbread, still hot from the oven, crumbles away with every bite I take. I lick the crumbs on my lips and take a slice of the wheat bread. I take advantage of the dish of butter and dull knife that can always be found on the table.

Swallowing my mouthful of food, I start up the morning's conversation. "Do you think the doctor was right about Florence? It seems like an odd diagnosis, especially since Mother and I were also in Brockschmidt breathing this same 'city air,' as he called it, but we are not sick! Pa, don't you find it odd?" Pa leans back in his chair as he chews the bacon in his mouth and gives my question serious consideration, while Mother rolls her eyes at the remark I have just made.

Unable to wait for her husband to respond, Mother bursts out with her opinion. "Azalea, Doctor Griffiths is trained in medicine. He spent many years learning the practice of treating sicknesses, so you mustn't expect to understand it. I have spent much time in cities before, so it cannot be too possible for me to become sick from the air."

"Didn't you see those factories in the city? Overcrowded and absolutely filthy. The pipes constantly spilling that smoke into the sky cannot be good for the air. Do you suppose it has some effect on everyone's health there? We stayed in Brockschmidt for nearly three weeks, but imagine living your life breathing that smoke through your lungs every single day! It is not natural! The girls working in those factories seem much too young for that kind of labor, but I do understand if they must work for the profit of their family if they desperately need it. How horrible a life like that must be!

"I shall never desire to live in a city in my whole existence but instead somewhere out west, as I have often mentioned before. Although, I am not fully sure of what I want to do as a career. Did we tell you, Pa, that we had a woman stagecoach driver? Yes, it is true! She even dressed like a man because I guess bandits might take advantage of her being a woman and think robbing her must be easier or something along those lines. As for Doctor Griffiths being trained in medicine, he was a doctor's apprentice wherever he came from back east. He looks no more than twenty-five years old, so how could he gain that much experience in such little time?"

Before Mother can open her mouth to answer, Pa politely interrupts. "Well, Bluebird, you do have a point. It is strange that you and your mother do not have any symptoms. But medicine is still progressing, and we still have much to learn about how our health works. Doctor Griffiths is a doctor, and there is no two ways about it. If he says Florence just needs rest, then he is right because it is not our place to question it." And with that, our conversation is brought to a close. Pa wipes his mouth with his napkin and leaves it on the table as he goes to the barn to pitch the hay. For a moment I am taken aback by Pa's tone, which is much harsher and more direct than usual. A glance over at Mother reveals that she must think the same thing considering her shocked expression.

Me and mother wash the dishes with a soapy cloth and cold water from the pump, wipe them dry with our aprons, then tuck them in the cabinets only to bring them out again within a few hours for the next meal. This endless cycle of cleaning, scrubbing, sweeping, and cooking goes on for two days.

On the third day, I awake before dawn to the sound of coughing echoing down the hallway. The candle that I left lit on its holder on my bedside table has long since gone out. With the exhaustion of doing both mine and my sister's chores, along with extra work, I have had no time to relax or read the book Evelyn gave me. Last night I finally found a moment after supper to sneak away and read my book but inevitably fell asleep, leaving the candle aflame. I whisper a quick thank you to God that it had not set my room aflame!

My bare feet touch the floorboards as I get out of bed. The coughing stops but is followed by wheezing breaths. I squint, trying to make out the shadows as I walk through the hallway to my sister's room. The orange light of a candle flame peeks out under her door. As quietly as possible, I open the door to find her sitting upright in bed.

"Are you okay, Florence? I heard you cough, and it sounded quite atrocious!"

She turns her head slowly to look at me with sad eyes that twinkle in the candlelight. "I don't know. Why am I not better by now? He said I would improve, but, Azalea, it seems to be getting even worse! I feel as though I cannot eat another bite of food without feeling sick, and this horrible rash started on my neck today. We came back from Brockschmidt six days ago…" She starts coughing again, but it suddenly ends with her grasping at her throat.

My eyes widen as I realize what is happening. I rush to grab the empty bowl that Mother used to hold water as she wet a rag and placed it on Florence's forehead earlier today. There are a few drops of water left in the bowl, and I toss them on the floor, soaking the floorboards without a second thought.

"Florence!" I yell, rushing to the side of her bed as she grasps at her throat with her mouth wide open and eyes full of fear. "Cough, dear sister! Please, please!" I scream, holding the bowl while using my other hand to hit her on the back until the undeniable sound of vomiting comes a few seconds later. She coughs into the bowl, then sits back, breathing in every breath she can as I release a sigh of relief. "Thank heavens!"

A door creaks open, followed by the flicker of a flame coming down the hallway. "What has happened? Dear child, what are you doing scream-ing at this hour of the morning?" Mother has her shawl wrapped around her shoulders, a candle holder in her left hand stretched out to see her daughters' weary faces. Her hair is a mess, and she is in a nightgown, as are Florence and I.

"Mother, Florence was choking on her vomit, but thank the Lord she did not suffocate! She has not progressed." Her eyes flicker to the solemn nod from my sister, who has returned to breathing normally.

"I see. Azalea, we must take turns watching your sister until we can send for the doctor, but who knows if he will even be at the office on a Sunday. We can only pray that he happens to be in town and not out hunting on that land of his. Azalea, you go rest, and I shall take first watch," Mother firmly instructs, taking the bowl away to be washed out. Her footsteps determinedly stomp away and down the stairs. I give my sister one last look of sympathy, then return to my bed, which is still warm from when I slept in it mere minutes ago. It seems as though I will never find sleep again, the wheezing breaths of my sister just within earshot causing my heart to beat rapidly at the uncertainty of what will come.

~

The moment the sun rises, Pa gets ready to walk into town and fetch the doctor, but a knock comes at the front door right as Pa is tying his shoelaces. Mother hastily opens the door to none other than Mr. Bennett standing there with his horse's reins in his hands. "Sorry to interrupt your morning, but I was just heading back into town and stopped by to ask how your daughter is doing. What did Doctor Griffiths say was the problem?"

"It is no intrusion! Please, do tie your horse up and come inside, Mr. Bennett!" Pa hollers as he stands up from where he was sitting at the table.

Mr. Bennet ties his horse to an old hitching post that stands at the side of the barn and hasn't been used for as long as we have lived here. Our breakfast was just a few slices of bread from yesterday's wheat loaf heated up and buttered. Mother sets a plate for him at the table, placing the stick of butter and slices of bread nearby. Once Mr. Bennett finishes eating, Pa finally answers his questions. I sit on the edge of the rocking chair, listening closely to the conversation, partly because I do not wish to work on the needlepoint that sits waiting on my lap.

"The doctor gave his professional opinion that our daughter's health was temporarily affected from being in the city," Pa says plainly.

"You seem unsure about that. Do you think it is something else?"

"Well, it just does not make sense why she hasn't gotten better when it has been nearly a week since they were in the city!"

"If you ask me, she seems to have gotten worse," I mumble. Every pair of eyes in the room turns to me, causing my cheeks to flush a bright red. I have already offered my opinion of Doctor Griffiths, but it appears as though nobody is on my side. What we truly desire is someone who can tell us what is wrong with Florence and how she can improve instead of making baseless accusations and then guessing it is caused by the city's air! "Doctor Griffiths is no better than a half-wit with a medical bag!" Once the words leave my mouth, I know a scolding will be coming shortly, but my anger at the doctor has taken over.

I can clearly recall the events leading up to the doctor's arrival in Lorretta. Mr. Griffiths agreed to abandon his post in the east and travel here to Wyoming to become Lorretta's new doctor. It was the talk of our town that this Mr. Griffiths was to become Doctor Griffiths in the coming days, but when he arrived it was quite disappointing to the single ladies, for from the moment he stepped out of that stagecoach with his black leather medical bag in his dominant right hand, a midnight black suit that was very baggy against his naturally skinny body, he was extremely tall to the point where he towered a whole head higher than anybody he passed by, his gait was uneven for his legs were half of my height, and orangish red hair that was slicked back under his flat-brimmed tan hat that had a straight sided crown and rounded corners matched with a real piece of straw placed next to the crown on the left side. Unbearable laughter had escaped my lips causing me to cover both my hands over my mouth when every smile fell flat off the ladies faces but were regained painfully with less enthusiasm when they went to shake hands with the man.

"Azalea—" Mother begins to yell, but I hold up a hand, which surprisingly quiets her in an instant, causing me to look twice at her frozen face.

"Please, Mother, you do not even know the half of his awful diagnosis given! He claimed at first that she was pregnant, saying his 'initial theory' was proven, then changed it to lack of sleep and the city air! We must get a different doctor, if possible, Pa! Florence could have suffocated this morning; we must not wait any longer to get her cured of whatever illness this is."

"My goodness!" Mother exclaims, pressing a hand to her forehead before sitting down blankly. I cover my mouth, shocked at the words I have just said, for never before have I spoken in such a way, especially on a Sunday! Pa appears absolutely beside himself, and poor Mr. Bennett looks between all of us with a new confoundment.

Moments of silence pass as Pa contemplates what is to come next now that this new information has come to light. For there would be no point in sending for a doctor that has so deeply offended our family name and been of no real assistance.

"Mr. Bennett, can I trust you to ride out to that settlement fifteen miles south of here and fetch their doctor? We will be lucky if he is even still there, but there may be a chance."

Mr. Bennett sits there just nodding his head with three pairs of eyes staring at him half-expecting this man to jump up, rush out to his horse, and gallop away in his Sunday best. Mr. Bennett is clean-shaven, well-rested, and dressed in a suit and matching bowtie sitting at our kitchen table while the rest of us have unruly hair and everyday clothes on. This must be the first Sunday in months or maybe even years that we are not all cleaned up wearing our Sunday best, which is quite an odd sight.

Mr. Bennett finally stands, shaking me out of my thoughts, and he hurriedly dashes out the door. Everyone in the room follows him, surprised at his manner.

In one movement he unties his horse's reins, swings his leg over the short pony, and shuffles in the saddle until he is properly on the horse. His Morgan horse, though far from being put out to pasture, is no filly in my books and is in dire need of a good brushing. With the click of his tongue and a kick, the tiny pony canters away, its hooves thudding on the soft dirt as it goes.

"I shall be back with the doctor before nightfall!" Mr. Bennett calls before he rounds the corner, taking off down the dirt road. He disappears amongst the trees, leaving us all standing outside of our front door questioning what is to come. Florence is sick with no real medical professional to give us answers except for a doctor that may or may not be fifteen miles away! There is nothing we can do until Mr. Bennett returns with the other doctor, and that shall take hours!

"It will be okay. Mr. Bennett will find the doctor in the settlement, and he will give us the answers we need," Pa says, rubbing my shoulder as I stare into his eyes, questioning if he truly believes the words that have just come from his mouth.

A breeze goes by, and the world seems to quiet itself as I speak. "What settlement, Pa? What if this doctor does not know what is wrong with her either?" Even at a whisper, my words speak volumes as if they have been shouted from the mountain tops.

Mother, who is still overcome with worry and shock, presses the palm of her hand to her chest as if in that one gesture her heart will stop beating rapidly and go back to her normal pulse. Her hair is up, twisted then wrapped in a bun at the back of her head with a few of her pins loosely keeping it together. Stray hairs stick out along the frame of her face. She wraps her shawl firmly around her shoulders as another cold morning's breeze sweeps by. Pa runs his hand through his short dark brown hair. Mother usually cuts it, but it has grown out a bit in the three-ish weeks we had been absent. The hint of a beard is at the lower half of his face.

"When your Uncle Edward was traveling down here to visit, he heard of a settlement established nearby and that there was an outbreak of sickness there. I heard in town that they sent for a traveling doctor, but nobody knows if he even got there since the settlement is in the middle of the woods. It's just twenty or so people from British Columbia traveling in search of land. We can only pray that this doctor will be there and can help Florence." Even though my question goes unanswered, I still nod my head because it is rather clear that none of us want to think of what could really be wrong with Florence.

⌒

The mood of the house is an empty soul-chilling feeling that is forever attached to the back of my mind no matter how often I try to shake it away. Pa stands up to read a few Bible verses, but even the inspiring story of David and Goliath does not lift our spirits. I pick up my book several times, attempting to focus on the words, but end up setting it right back down every time. Even helping Mother with the cooking does not occupy my unabated thoughts.

Half past five o'clock, a sudden knock comes at the door, jolting us out of our places where we each sit doing something to pass the time. Mother stands in her spot by the oven as she checks on a loaf of baking bread for the second time, but I jump up from the rocking chair, abandoning my hopeless needlepoint. Pa is the first to reach the front door, with me close behind him standing on the tips of my toes to look over his shoulder at the unfamiliar man standing at the door.

"Hello, Doctor…I assume Mr. Bennett has told you of my daughter?"

The doctor is dressed in a bright gray coat covered with buttons, a matching waistcoat, and black trousers. His hair is cut short and matched with a small, pointed beard on his chin. He looks no more than thirty years old.

"Doctor Vallance. Pleasure to make your acquaintance. Yes, Mr. Bennett told me all about what has transpired these past few days, including the misdiagnosis. Would you kindly lead me to the patient?" Doctor Vallance is led inside after Mr. Bennett waves a goodbye to Pa and rides off toward home. Pa and the doctor disappear behind Florence's closed door. It is fifteen minutes until they both step out into the hallway, where I wait to hear what is wrong with her.

"I have not yet determined what the sickness is, but there is a possibility of it being contagious." Doctor Vallance is professional yet unfeeling. He is only slightly better than Doctor Griffiths, which inflicts me to think that everybody involved in the medical profession must be unsympathetic, tedious, and unimaginative.

My blood turns cold. My heart seems to beat right out of my chest as each pulse shakes the word like an earthquake. "Contagious? What does that mean for us?" My voice is no louder than a mere whisper.

"You all must quarantine, myself included. Nobody can leave this property for the foreseeable future until I can confirm that no common symptoms have arisen between the four of us. To be honest, her symptoms are too common to properly identify. I must examine all of you to determine whether you have caught this illness." My whole body trembles at the words laid out before me.

I clear my throat and step forward. "I shall go first, then."

Doctor Vallance is then led to my room, where I am instructed to sit down on the chair at my vanity as he opens up his medical bag to pull out a notebook and a "stethoscope," as he calls it.

"Now, I would like to ask you a few questions if that is okay." I give no response except a silent nod as my heart beats uncontrollably. "First off: Have you experienced any symptoms similar to that of your sister, including fever, coughing, chills, nausea, et cetera?"

"No. May I ask a question, Doctor Vallance?" He scribbles in his notebook without looking up to meet my eyes. Even though I asked him directly, he does not give permission for my question. But nonetheless, I speak my mind, gaining confidence with every sentence that departs my lips. "Why must you examine each of us? Truly, it has been a week since Florence got sick, and one of us was bound to catch this sickness from her days ago! It seems as though this is a waste of time when you ought to be getting the details of how this sickness came to be with her. The story is that we were in Brockschmidt, and I suppose she started feeling unwell the night before we left, then when we got back, she was tired. A few days after, she complained of body aches and headache before collapsing to the ground and remaining unconscious for almost an hour! Then, she was misdiagnosed by that horrendous Doctor Griffiths, only to get even worse as time went on. Why do you not ask those questions instead? I do not feel a speck of illness, and nor does Mother or Pa. We all are perfectly healthy, and I do not need to waste precious time by responding to your usurp questions! Somebody needs to tell me what is wrong with my sister!" I declare out loud, finally stopping to take a breath and continue, but I am interrupted by the Doctor looking up at me with a peculiar gaze.

"Did you say you were in Brockschmidt?" This struck me, leaving me dumbfounded. Are all doctors half-wits? Out of everything I have just exclaimed, he truly only paid attention to our location?

"Yes…" He goes back to writing in his notebook, the small pencil in his left hand scratching against the page. I do not utter another word as he checks my breathing, feels the corners of my neck just under my chin and ears, and takes a look at my mouth and teeth in the sunlight from the window. This process is then repeated with Mother and Pa.

I sit in the rocking chair, patiently waiting for the three of them to return to the kitchen so that my parents and I can hear what Doctor Vallance has to say. The clock strikes six o'clock just as the three of them return downstairs. Mother and Pa sit at the table and offer the doctor a seat, but he refuses it and stands in the middle of the room for all of us to hear his words.

With a stone face he opens his mouth and begins the conversation. "Considering that none of you have caught this sickness, I have narrowed down what it may be. In light of this, the property is no longer under quarantine."

"Well, that is good news, isn't it! Whatever does she have? Is there a medicine for it?" Mother gladly exclaims, causing us all to glance at her then back at Doctor Vallance once her questions are spoken.

He simply remains frown-faced and goes on talking. "It is more complex than that. With the rash forming when it did, vomiting, body aches, fever, chills, and loss of appetite I can confirm by comparing this to other sicknesses that your daughter, Florence, has typhus." All of our hopeful looks turn to pale faces confused by what he has just said.

"Typhus outbreaks were recorded in Concord, Washington, and other large cities in the past few decades, causing a recurring pattern of symptoms and locations. Florence caught this in Brockschmidt, and since it is not contagious, none of you have gotten it. But there is no cure or treatment." He says this simply without emotion, as if it has been done hundreds of times.

The doctor's words echo in my mind as I peer at Mother and Pa for confirmation. More than anything, I wish I hadn't. Mother has become as white as a ghost, her hands covering her mouth as she shakes her head. Pa's mouth hangs wide open as he stares at the floor in disbelief. This image is sure to scar my mind for as long as I shall endure.

The silence is shattered with my whispered yells. "Doctors are supposed to heal people! Why can't you fix her?" Tears well up in my eyes as I stare at Doctor Vallance, who stands still with his hands tucked behind his back and eyes looking forward.

"There is nothing I can do. My estimate is a few days, maybe even less than that." And with that he declines Pa's payment, picks up his bag, buttons up his coat, and departs from our house, carrying every last shred of our hope with him.

A few days? How can my darling Florence be dying in *a few days?*

I storm to my room, slamming the door closed as sobs shake my small body and tears come streaming down my cheeks. The sunlight pours onto my face in all its orange glory as I rip the hair ribbons from the ends of my braids and let my hair fall freely. It wraps around me as if it can shelter my breaking heart from the inevitable truth.

"Azalea?" Mother yells through the closed door as I crumble onto the floor.

"Go away, Mother! I wish to be left alone!"

My eyes glance at the mirror from where I sit on the floor with my back against the door in case Mother ignores my pleas. I instantly regret what I said and hope she will come into my room and rescue me from my current state. But instead, she respects my wishes. The creak of stairs declares that she is going back down to the kitchen, leaving me utterly alone.

My green eyes return to the reflective glass. My cheeks are cherry red, and I watch as another pathetic tear travels down my face and drops to my shoulder. A headache starts as I hold back another sob for what I am about to lose. My palms wipe away any water from my eyes that is still waiting to be set free. With the folded-down collar of my dress, I wipe the snot from my nose.

Here I am sitting sad and broken when I am not the one dying! I smile at my reflection, even though it pains me to do so. I must be strong, a beacon in the night for Mother, a steadfast daughter for Pa, and a ray of sunshine for my sister. In this moment, I wish someone would tell me that it is okay to not be okay, that sometimes what you really need is to be broken in order to be repaired. But that someone is not here now, and I cannot leave my sister wondering what ales and infects her whilst leading her on and making her think that everything will get better.

I step out of my room, breathing in before entering Florence's bedroom. The curtains have been drawn to keep it dark, and winter blankets are piled over her. Her waves of coldness come expeditiously without warning. Her eyelids flutter open at the sound of creaking floorboards.

"Azalea! What has the doctor said? When…will I be better?" she whispers, holding back a cough. A single flicker of candlelit in the room shows me that her face has grown a pale white.

I open my mouth but am unable to find the words to say. How do you tell someone that they are…that they…?

She has to hear it from me, though. I must be the one to tell her. But how can I when there are no words to say? A lump rises in my throat, and my palms become sweaty as they sometimes do when I am nervous.

"You're…" Tears come again, threating to spill over, but are pushed back down. "He has diagnosed you with typhus. Florence, you are not going to get better." Her face changes from hopeful to grim, already guessing at what I have to say. "Because you are…dying." I choke on the word. My heart throbs with pain as it tears itself apart.

"I'm dying?" she asks as I burst out crying, clinging onto her hand from where I sit on the chair next to her bed. Every gust of air pulled through my lungs brings the reality of how her heart will not be beating forever like mine is now. I cover my face with my hands and place my elbows on my knees. I cannot bear to face her right now!

Once I regain my composure, I wipe away the tears again. "Dying?" she repeats in disbelief. "No. No! I can't be! Azalea, I can't be!" She cries into her shoulder as she bends her head downwards.

"I'm sorry. I am so…*sorry*," I whisper, looking up to the ceiling as if Jesus will come down from heaven to heal my sister in this very moment. "I cannot imagine a world without you. I shall be lost without you because, as it turns out, my greatest fear is being alone! After Nora leaving me…I am incapable of enduring it once more. Please do not leave me alone, Florence," I plead, as if it will make a difference. As if she could change it all, get better, live the life she wants. This is God's will, and the only thing on Earth more powerful than life is death.

"You will never be alone. And I will always be here…" A heart-wrenching pause came. "Tell me how life was supposed to be. I wish to see it."

I silently nod, sitting up straight in the chair to gaze at her beautiful face, which stares blankly across the room. "You would meet a nice guy from town or a city. Bring him home to meet Pa and Mother. He would ask for your hand in marriage with Pa's blessing. You'd be ecstatic planning the wedding! Then we'd spend weeks stitching your dress, partly because my horrible sewing made twice the work!" We both stifle a laugh.

"You never were a great seamstress." She laughs, breaking out into a fit of coughs. There is a long pause as our hearts accept the fact that the story I have just told will never happen. "May I have a few papers, your fountain pen, and envelopes?" Her hoarse voice pleads.

"Yes. Yes, of course." I run to my room, returning momentarily with the requested items. And with that, I abandon the room, leaving Florence to herself.

TILL DEATH DO US PART

How do you live every day, or continue living, when you know someone you love won't be here tomorrow? I do not know. Maybe I was foolish to think we would all live forever. I have cried every drop left inside of me. I bear nothing more in me except my hollow frame of a body. How shall I ever recover from losing her? Moments will turn into memories. Memories will be saddened by her missing presence. And memories? Memories shall hurt the most. Happiness, sadness, regret. They will just be a reminder of the moments we cannot get back. But they will also be a reminder of time well spent.

Mother begins spending tremendous amounts of time with Florence, but I suppose anyone would if their daughter could leave at any given moment. Pa does everything to distract himself. Each morning he does all the chores just to spend time away from the house and all its dreariness. Nonetheless, he too spent time with Florence. Even though the sunlight hurts her eyes, each morning she requests that the curtain be opened to the rising sun. And because she is too weak to walk outside, Pa has to carry her when she asks to view the sunrise from the field.

"It is beautiful, isn't it? Oh, how I wish I had joined you one of those days when you climbed up on the roof, even if it was dangerous," Florence admits as her fingertips graze the grass. We are both lying down with our backs to the dirt, eyes on the sky, tucked into the tall grasses like baby birds in a nest. The sky is exploding in an array of orange, pink, and yellow light as the sun peeks over the mountaintops. Clouds are ever so fluffy as they fly past us, morphing into different shapes. "That one looks like one of those fancy dresses they wear in the city. Look at that! There is even a parasol on that lady's shoulder!"

I smile, glad for this precious moment, then proclaim that one of the clouds resembles a rabbit. One day this may all be forgotten from my mind or burned into it forever. Oh, how I wish all the pain could be transferred to me, for it is too unfair for Florence to be taken away this soon!

"Azalea?"

"Yes, my darling Florence?"

"If I may ask, how ever did you find me so quickly after Lawrence refused me?"

I hesitate, unaware if telling the truth is the best option. But considering our predicament, I do just that. "Promise not to be furious at me? When Lawrence swept you away to the terrace, I followed, expecting him to get down on one knee and propose that very minute. But when he did not, I wanted to save you the embarrassment of me hearing it all, so I waited a few minutes before 'discovering' you."

In the most joyous of ways, Florence breaks out into a laugh and does not stop for several moments. "Oh, I could never be cross at you for that!"

I have never considered Florence to be a kindred spirit to me. We have fun times and are much closer now than when we were before the trip to Brockschmidt, but can it be called kindred? The phrase, "blood is thicker than water," would most likely be something used to describe our relationship, but that just does not seem right. Blood would represent my family, in this case Florence, and water would be friends like Nora had been to me. But blood contains water, does it not? We were merely sisters, strangers even, before truly becoming kindred spirits.

But over these past few months, I have felt closer to my sister than ever before, which is a blessing in itself. Our laughter quiets as we enjoy just being with each other in this simple time. "If only I could be with you forever. I guess I knew the truth before you even told me; I truly am dying. Please, do not be sad about it, sister, for I have finally come to terms with it myself." As she speaks, she pulls a crumpled envelope from deep within her dress pocket. "Here is a letter for you that I wrote with your fountain pen when I borrowed it from you. Please wait to read it until after…I can only hope that it gives you closure about my death. Do not worry; Pa and Mother both have letters, too." She hands the envelope that is most likely filled with her final words to me. My name is written on it in her fancy handwriting. "Mother helped use that wax seal of yours on the back."

"I do not wish to speak of when you are gone! How can I when the only life I could ever imagine is with you?" The letter lies against my chest like a weight that cannot be easily lifted. Florence wraps her fingers around mine as we continue looking up at the sky.

"Please, Azalea. I do not have long left. I can feel it deep within my soul. When the time is right for you, read the letter. I never was someone who could speak my mind as easily as you could or put my thoughts into such perfect words. But I believe this may just be the closest I can get to that. Promise me."

"I promise. Nobody could ever be as perfect as you Florence, that I am sure of! God will be lucky to gain an angel and subject as immaculate as you are."

That night I crawl into bed next to Florence as Pa reads us a Bible verse with Mother standing next to him. " 'He will swallow up death in victory; and the Lord God will wipe away tears from off all faces; and the rebuke of his people shall he take away from off all the earth: for the Lord hath spoken it.' " The heartfelt words shake me to my core as if God himself has sent them to me. Our parents kiss our foreheads goodnight as if we are both children. Mother blows out the candle, then closes the door, leaving us in the darkness of the evening.

"Do you remember our last night in Brockschmidt? The reason I pushed you away when you were only trying to comfort me was because I had to be married this year. Little did you know how much our family needed me to marry into a wealthy family. Azalea, I must make a request out of you…won't you please contact Lawrence Jones, wherever he is, and tell him that he is forgiven?"

"Florence, do you mean to tell me that Mother and Pa are broke? How can that be true? And why would you forgive Lawrence when he hurt you?" This newfound information swirls in my mind. That is why Mother wanted to go to Brockschmidt so bad and why Pa agreed when he'd put this off for so long!

The moonlight streams in from the window, leaving our corner of the room in complete darkness as both of us talk to each other whilst staring at the ceiling. "You may not understand now, but one day I promise you will. For me, please, will you do it?" My "yes" is satisfactory enough for her, and she lets the subject go. "One last thing. Please take care of Mother and Pa when I'm gone. They will be lost for some time, I imagine. I love you, Azalea."

My heart aches with pain, but I push the feeling away once more. "Of course I will. I love you, Florence, more than I could ever express."

Sleep overtakes both of us, and the last thing I hear is the sound of my sister's breathing and beating heart next to my ear.

‿

My eyes open to a bright room, and I squint, sitting up in bed. Birds tweet outside, and the sun came up long ago, making me wonder how late it is in the morning. Florence lies still next to me, and for a second it seems as if she is sleeping peacefully…until I notice that her chest is not rising and falling like it has always done.

"Florence? Florence, no! Please, no, come back! Come back to me. Sister, please! It is too soon for you to leave me. Pa! Mother! *Stay with me Florence.* They are coming." I hold my sister the same way I did when she collapsed in the barn. Pa and Mother dash up the stairs, barging into the room with their eyes soon witnessing Florence's body in my arms. "Mother, please make her wake up! Pa, what are you doing? No, she is just sleeping! Pa!" Mother sits next to the bed, weeping as she strokes Florence's face one last time. Pa walks over, kissing her on the forehead before picking her up in his arms. "No, she is just asleep! Florence, wake up." As Pa carries her away, I realize this is the last time I will ever see my sister. Her eyelids are closed, her hair ruffled like it always was when she first awoke in the morning.

"Azalea. Azalea!" Mother cries out, grabbing my face in her hands and forcing me to look into her eyes. "Florence is not asleep. She has joined our Lord and Savior in heaven." I shake my head as Mother wraps me in a hug.

"No. She cannot be gone just yet. She made me promise last night to take care of you both, but how can I do that when I myself am not okay? Florence…" I yell out into Mother's shoulder as I cover my face.

I don't know if it is better to pass away peacefully in one's sleep or in a different way. It was painless—something I tell myself as if I know for sure—but she will never see another sunrise on Earth again.

The black dress that was crumpled up in a ball at the bottom of my wardrobe had not been worn in many years, which is made evident by the skirt that stops several inches away from my ankles. But considering it is just us, it does not seem to matter.

There is a growing mist outside, for it seems like God himself is crying for what I have lost, but beyond the clouds is still the heavenly smile of sunshine. Sometimes it is hard to remember that the world does not revolve solely around you until something gives you a different perspective—like this day has done to me. For on the 10th of May 1894, in Lorretta, Wyoming, my darling Florence departed the world, her last words still echoing in my mind for all eternity: *I love you, Azalea.*

And even as Mother buttons up the back of my wrinkled black dress, it still doesn't seem real. My tired eyes glare out into the grayness of the morning just beyond my window. The door to Florence's room remains closed, as if it could preserve the memories even more if nothing of hers is touched. Every creak of a floorboard or noise from the kitchen is met with me looking over my shoulder, expecting my sister to be there sewing or cooking with Mother. Mother seems out of place, looking around as if seeing our home for the first time.

It has been quite a few years since we have all worn black, a fact that brings back faint but still painfully sharp memories of Grandma Flora's death.

There is no minister in Lorretta until the summertime, when Pastor Charles Winston will return from his home state of Nebraska like he does every year to preach to the people of our town for one month. It feels wrong to smile on a day such as today, but I cannot help but grin a little as I remember last summer when Pastor Winston called us all to the town one Sunday and preached his sermon as we sat on blankets on the grass. Florence actually paid attention whilst I attempted to make a flower crown.

When the rain ceases falling from the sky, the three of us walk out of the house toward the open field where Pa has buried Florence. Instead of a gravestone, there is a tiny sprout of a tree no taller than my hip growing on top of the mound of disrupted dirt. In no time at all, grass will grow over the dirt mound, and this tree will branch out with green leaves. Nobody will know that this is the final resting place of my beloved sister.

The small breeze sweeps by, making me shiver with dread as Pa recites a Bible passage. Without anything more to say, Pa and Mother leave, walking back to the house and leaving me be. Not wanting to go back to the dreary house, I remain at my sister's grave, for this is the one true place I where can escape to read what Florence wanted to say.

This morning I tucked Florence's letter in my dress pocket to read, thinking now would be the right time to hear her final words. 'Azalea' faces me, written in her handwriting, but I just cannot bring myself to break the wax seal on the back of the envelope. Instead, I sigh, tucking the letter back in my pocket and looking to the sky.

I haven't cried since it happened. When I had to tell her that she was…I couldn't stop crying, but now the tears will not come forth. I wish I could scream to make time go backwards and to have God take me instead, but it is no use. The empty ache in my heart only makes it worse, as if I will never find comfort again. I thought that comfort would come once I was alone, but there is nothing except the sob of my heart. I want to feel again! It is as if my mind and body are stuck in shock. My humanity has gone away from my soul! Pain, sadness, and ache are all inside of me but have no way to escape.

⌇

A week goes by, and life is still not the same. Her laughter is still ingrained in the wood of the walls, her room still closed off, reminding us that she is gone, and her absence is felt by all.

Mother wrote to Aunt Nancy when Florence first got sick, but considering they left home right when Uncle Edward returned, they will not hear the news for months.

Pa has been unusually quiet these past few days, speaking no more than a few words at a time. Mother remains in bed all day, staring at the wall for hours on end. I do my best to take care of them as I promised, but I sense myself slowly slipping away as well.

Water splashes from the pump onto a soapy plate, rinsing it clean before it is dried with my apron and placed back in the cupboard. An unsettling knock comes at the door, causing me to jump at its sudden loudness.

When I swing open the front door, none other than Lawrence Jones stands before me. He is wearing a crisp new suit, his hair combed back and a bag in his hand. His face is nowhere near as astounded as mine as our eyes grace one another. Thunder rumbles in the distance as the clouds threaten to bring a downpour.

"Lawrence Jones? What in the world are *you* doing here!" I say, disgusted at the sight of him. Then Florence's words come back to me. *Won't you please contact Lawrence Jones, wherever he is, and tell him that he is forgiven.* To be honest, I completely forgot that I made that promise until this very moment.

"Azalea." He nods stiffly. "Some time has gone by, and I have realized my wrongdoings, so I've come to speak with Florence. I wish to ask for her hand in marriage." He appears nervous as he admits this all to me before looking down at my small black dress with a questioning gaze.

My mouth falls completely open this time, causing me to nearly fall off my feet! Lawrence Jones, the young man from Brockschmidt who fragmented my poor sister's heart, wishes to make amends, perhaps realizing that he loves her after all, and marry her?

"Why ever are you dressed in black?"

"Lawrence…Florence became ill when we came back from the city. She had typhus and…Florence died last week. I'm sorry." The words that emerge from my mouth have been ripped from the depths of my heart, things I have put off admitting to even myself. It takes several moments for my words to register in his mind, but then his questioning gaze turns into full realization.

With his free hand, he reaches up, running his fingers through his tidy hair. "No, that cannot be! I came to marry her…how could she be…" I reach out to touch his shoulder but am refused, for my pitying looks cannot make things right. He straightens his suit, turning back to face me with a newfound personality, this time stone cold. "I am sorry to disturb you, Miss Stanton. My condolences for your loss." Lawrence walks away, going back toward the road refusing to look at me one last time. How can life be so unfair? If she had never gotten sick or if he had just proposed that night at the ball, then everything would be alright! But I fear I have broken his heart.

I slam the front door closed behind me, running into the field as the tears finally come. My lungs burn as I run away from it everything I have lost. The tall grass smacks my bare legs and rips at my long sleeves as I go. My shoes skid in the dirt as I suddenly stop just as another flash of lightning is followed by growling thunder. A shrieking scream comes from my mouth and soul until my voice cracks. Raindrops pour from the sky, leaving me drenched.

I am at the edge of the valley, where the ground slopes up to the mountains that surround us. The heartache has stopped, but the tears do not. Everything that I have kept bottled up this past week as I have tried to stay strong for my family has escaped. Because I am broken now. And she is really gone.

When you lose someone, it makes you wonder how their life was to them. Had she been happy here? No soul on Earth would ever hear from her lips where she wanted to go traveling or the memory that comforted her when she was sad.

I duck under a tree at the edge of the scattered woods, pulling out the letter that was still in my pocket. The branches catch the rain droplets before they reached me. I break the seal on the back of the envelope. It continues pouring rain as I unfold the wet page in my hands. I am careful not to rip it. It reads:

To my dearest Azalea,

I wish more than anything that I could be with you now. I wish that I could hug you. I apologize for everything. For not being there for you then and now. I want more than anything in the world to stay here in Lorretta and, as you described, meet a gentleman, have Pa's blessing, get married, and own a dress shop in town where I could make gowns like the ones we saw in Brockschmidt. It's everything I have ever dreamt of and desired!

I do not want to die. Even so, I want you to live a full life. Live for me! Do not let anyone hold you back from doing what you want. I know you too well, dear sister. Once I'm gone, please help Mother with things like I always did. I don't know what the future holds, but I will say this: be happy. Find your soulmate one day. I am sorry that you are reading this now when I won't be there for your future. I will be watching over you, though.

Thank you for the happiest moments of my life! Without your endless imagination and spirit, I would've never become the person that I am. Do not interpret my death as a bad thing, Azalea. God makes everything happen for a reason, even if we may not know what that is yet. I hope you never forget my touch or voice, but even if you do, I'm positive we will meet again in heaven one day. Goodbye for now, sister.

Love, Florence

I am overcome with emotion at her exquisite words. I look up to the sky just as the clouds part way for the sunshine. And so it changes from a gloomy and dark day to one that is luminous and peaceful, a day I would never abandon.

"Thank you, Florence. For everything. And I am sorry for not always being there for you, either." I shall just have to add this to the list of words I wish I said to my sister.

⌒

I awake at twilight with a stomach growling for food. Even though the late-May humidity lingers in the night air, I feel as though it is winter. My heart still feels heavy from the constant reminders around me, but no matter how much I have prayed that time will reverse itself, it hasn't.

The floorboards creak as my bare feet thud down the stairs. I squint, waiting for my eyes to adjust to the darkness of night. As I reach the last step, I see the light from a flame bouncing off the walls. Pa sits looking blankly at the vacant rocking chair by the empty fireplace. He is alone, for Mother is getting a full night's rest for the first time in over a week.

"Pa? What ever are you doing awake?" My eyes follow his gaze to the chair. With a sigh, I go over and sit across from him at the kitchen table.

"Pa," I say as he looks at me. "I know it hurts…and this place doesn't feel like home anymore now that it's haunted by her memory. But we must keep living! I want more out of life than this! There are mountains so high that they could reach heaven, oceans so vast they could carry messages in bottles to the other side of the world, people who speak and look all different ways! I want to embrace others' ways and ideas. See new things." As I speak, I slowly realize that there is one thing that night might ease our sorrows. "There is so much more than this town, this place. What if…we go west? The three of us can no longer stand to see everything that reminds us she is gone, so maybe we must create new memories."

Never before in my life have I seen Pa cry until this very moment. "You're right, Azalea. We cannot live like this any longer," he manages to choke out before covering his eyes with his hand.

"Oh, Pa," I say, rushing to hug him. "It will get better. I promise."

↬

Even though Mother was never keen on the idea of moving west, once Pa tells her of what I said, she is completely on board. With summer fast approaching, people are passing through Lorretta. Pa is able to sell the house, barn, and most everything else to a young man and his wife. They would soon start a family and raise their children in the house where we used to live.

It was painful to lose everything I have ever known, but it is what we need to do to live, and that is what Florence wanted. When Pa went into town to sell Sense and Sensibility, I gave them both tearful goodbyes before they were taken away by the new owner. And at the Postal Office were two letters addressed to me, one from Russell St. Claire and another from someone named Rose Walker.

That very second, I tore open the letter from Rose Walker, saving Russell St. Claire's words for later. The letter reads:

Dearest Azalea,

I have written to inform you that my husband and I have arrived safely in Colorado on the train. Thank you for the food you sent us! You are: Energetic, Vivacious, Efficient, Luminous, Youthful, and Neoteric.

Your niece, Rose.

My eyes widen at the sight of the last sentence, which is coded. Evelyn is safe with Percy in Colorado! The thought of them has crossed my mind more than a few times, but Evelyn—or Rose Walker—was only to write to me once it was safe to do so, and I have not worried about it with everything that has happened recently.

Upon my arrival back home to my room (completely empty except for the things that had been too heavy to carry in the brand-new wagon Pa had bought with the money he made from the sale of the house), I grab a piece of paper and my fountain pen, writing the letter that would be mailed off before we left tomorrow. I write to my "niece" Rose, saying that my sister fell ill and has sadly passed, so I will be mailing the next letter from my new address once I move. It is short, but I do not want to risk putting too much information in the letter in case it is read by anyone else. The wax seal is pressed onto the back of the envelope, which is addressed to Rose Walker, and waits to be mailed off.

Next, staring at me is Russell's letter. With a deep breath, I tear open the letter and begin reading the words written on the paper.

Dear Azalea,

I don't want to alarm you by saying this, but you need to hear it. I knew from that night by the fire, or maybe before, that it's you, Azalea. My biggest regret in life will be that I didn't propose to you that day at the stagecoach station. We might not see each other again, but I can't hold on to this anymore. Every night since, you have flooded my mind. Forgive my lack of words…I want you to know that you are the only one I ever could see as my wife.

-Russell

It would be an understatement to say that I am dumbfounded by the words staring back at me from the page. Russell St. Claire has just proposed to me through a letter! But what does that mean? I am only fourteen, and marriage is something that I am still not sure I even desire! And if I did marry him now, then what would that truly mean?

I pull out another paper and envelope, addressing it to Russell. I take a deep breath, and the words seem to flow from my mind to the fountain pen and onto the page.

Dear Russell,

I must admit there was something between us, and your words have truly had an effect on me, but I cannot marry you now or maybe ever. My sister has tragically passed away, and it has not only changed me but the course of my life. My family is moving west tomorrow, and I will likely not return to Wyoming in the future. I wish to remain the closest of friends, and I hope you feel the same! Please find love for my sake and yours. I will send you a letter once we have found the end of our journey west.

Your dearest friend, Azalea

My entire morning is spent next to Florence's grave, which now has a fresh bouquet of wildflowers on it. This is a goodbye to my home and to her, for we will likely never return to Lorretta.

"Thank you for everything, sister. Nobody shall ever forget you," I whisper just as Mother calls me to the wagon. I run to my parents with my hair flying freely in the wind and climb into the back of the covered wagon next to Florence's trunk, which still holds all of her things and some of the other supplies we have packed. "Goodbye, dear house, for I shall never see you again."

The valley that I have seen almost every day for the past four years slowly disappears as Pa drives the wagon forward, pulled by two new horses that I have yet to name. A single tear travels down my face as a hawk flies overhead.

There was once a girl christened the name Azalea, (after the flower). This girl was never what most would assume: a lady. Her imagination ran free, thinking up all kinds of adventures to embark on or stories to dream of.

But I am no longer this girl. I have endured heartbreak, guilt, sadness, regret, and joy in dark times. Although it pains me to think that I will never be the girl I used to be, I would not want to trade her for who I have become.

⌒

"A life with regrets is almost as unfulfilling as a life without regrets."

LANGUAGE OF FLOWERS

Elder .... Compassion

Ivy... Friendship

Almond Blossom...................... Hope for new beginnings

Hartsease................................... Think of me

Hyacinth (yellow) .... Jealousy

Hyacinth (purple) .... Sorrow

Daffodil .... Change of seasons and the triumph
of new hope over despair

Aconite .... Be cautious on the path ahead

Coreopsis................................... Love at first sight

Arbor Vitae .... Unchanging Friendship

Diosma .... Your simple elegance charms me

Maiden's Hair........................... Discretion

Sweet Pea .... Goodbye

Monkshood .... A deadly foe is near

Rosebud (white) .... Girlhood

Primrose.................................... I cannot live without you

Mourning Bride........................ Unfortunate attachment

Anemone .... Undying love

Michealmas Daisy..................... Farewell my beloved

HANNAH BREE CAMPBELL started her debut novel, Eunoia, at the age of fifteen. Her works have been featured in young writers' anthologies and recognized in national competitions. When she's not writing, Campbell can be found reading classic literature, traveling, or spending time outside in nature. Whether it's hiking in the rainforest or spontaneously meeting people while visiting new places, Campbell believes that life is full of adventures waiting to be experienced and written down so that they may last forever; for they are more than just words on a page, they are a part of who we are.